Moon Blooded
Breeding Clinic

C.M. Nascosta

MEDUAS
EDITORIALE

Meduas Editoriale

First edition published by Meduas Editoriale 2022

Cover: Chinthaka Pradeep

Interior: Dextrose

MEDUĀS
EDITORIALE

Author's Note

This book contains fertility issues galore!

TTC, infertility, breeding, etc.

Please protect yourselves, my loves!

This story takes place during the pandemic, and our MMC goes

through a LOT of the feelings

of isolation and uncertainty that many of us experienced in 2020 and

beyond,

but there are no specific mentions of illness or death.

Our non-human characters drew a luckier lot in their world than the

rest of us!

An Inauspicious Homecoming

"**S**evere thunderstorms and high winds outside of Denver may delay arrival times. The current temperature is sixty-two degrees."

The overhead lights buzzed with a low hum, which seemed to increase in volume the longer he sat beneath them. The disembodied voice from the monitor behind him was robotically stilted yet still unnervingly upbeat, giving a high-level overview of the weather in half a dozen major cities, and he supposed he ought to be grateful it wasn't raining on top of everything else. *Could be worse. You could be in Denver.*

Lowell Hemming was no stranger to airports. Quite the contrary — they were a part of his weekly existence, his time traveling in the air nearly equal to the time he spent in cars, particularly when he was shooting in a region where paved roads were a vague suggestion and automobiles were not commonplace. He'd slogged, barely awake, through customs at every major airport in the unification, Europe, and Asia; had hauled his gear through the single gates of small, rural tar-

1

macs, and had picked his way across muddy airfields in places where running water was a privilege enjoyed by very few.

Every birthday and holiday and wedding for which he'd come home, short visits between jobs that somehow had always managed to simultaneously seem interminable and like no time at all, each trip bookended with time spent in the Bridgeton airport. He was no stranger to helipads or landing strips, and he knew the Bridgeton airport better than any other aviation hubs he regularly traversed. He knew the fastest way to baggage claim, knew how to circumvent the food courts and where the cleanest bathrooms were. He knew the shortcuts between terminals and recognized the faces of employees who'd worked there for years, but the one thing he didn't know and had never expected to learn was how absolutely desolate the place felt when empty.

The food court, usually teeming with travelers and screaming children, was deserted and entirely at his disposal, his and his alone . . . if any of the chain restaurants were open, of course, but they weren't. The three bathrooms he liked the best in this airport were on less traveled corridors, frequented mainly by pilots and businessmen and other people who spent more time in the air than they did with their feet on solid ground, who knew the value in a quiet place to submerge their face in cool water and grab a quick shave before they were on to the next leg of their journey. Those bathrooms seemed too far out of reach now, those far-flung hallways even emptier and more echoing than the main thoroughfares, a creeping sense of doom bouncing off the marble floors with each footfall. He had never been in an airport as empty as the Bridgeton airport was just then, devoid of life and sound . . . except for him.

There had been no response from Grayson when he had sent the text that he was boarding his plane leaving Tokyo and then another as his plane was taxiing out of LAX. Gray hadn't responded until Lowell sent the third text, just before the seatbelt light dinged off on the connection arriving in Bridgeton, sudden anxiety kicking up his heart rate.

How is any of this my problem?

He hadn't known how to respond.

The only plus to the nearly empty plane and skeleton crew operating the airport was that his bags had been gate-checked, and he'd not been forced to leave the terminal to go down to baggage claim, where the chairs were few and the air always too cold as he waited. There'd been no further messages from his brother. He'd strapped his bags together and pulled them like a trolley, too keyed up to sit once he realized he was possibly stranded, a reality that seemed more and more likely as he did laps around the familiar corridors, until the silence and lack of people began to make him feel uneasy, sending him scurrying back to the main terminal to take up residence on one of the many banks of low seats that were at his singular disposal. *Are you a wolf or a mouse?*

He realized he'd already been there for an hour as the voice continued to cheerfully outline delayed arrival times. There had been no messages. No calls. Nothing from anyone that would have indicated he'd been thought of or remembered, or that Gray was en route. When his phone remained silent, no further communication from Grayson clarifying what the fuck he meant, Lowell swallowed down his frustration and sent a message to his brothers' group chat, his pulse thumping in his throat.

Is anyone picking me up?

I'm here. My plane already landed.

The six of them had an ongoing group text, occasionally full of banter and good-natured mocking, the occasional trip down memory lane, and threats of bodily harm for pranks enacted. The group text was most often used to communicate plans at home. Edicts passed on high from their father, brunch and dinner plans, baby and house sitting needs, full moon plans. Following along with the chimes of his phone, Lowell often felt like a spectator, looking in from the outside at the window of his brothers' shared lives. He knew that Gray and Jackson had a standing racquetball date every Sunday morning, except those weekends that fell over a full moon, and that Trapp and Liam studied pre-med work together every Wednesday night that Trapp wasn't scheduled at the firehouse. Jackson had convinced Owen to be a mentor for his Woodland Scouts' youth robotics club, and Liam responded to nearly every direct question with a gif or meme. Lowell didn't like admitting that he felt isolated or left out, and so he watched his brothers make plans and bicker, lurking silently as if it were a fandom group and he was an awkward teen with a secret stack of lovingly-made art, not quite ready to take the plunge on getting involved.

The first response to his query was from Jackson, whose house he would be traveling to for his stay in Cambric Creek.

Good thing you left when you did. I read they're starting to close borders

My first break in classes is at two thirty

The guest suite is all ready when you get here!

He stared at the phone uncomprehendingly, glancing in the upper left corner of the display to check the local time. 7:14 a.m. He had taken the redeye out of LAX, just as he normally did, for Grayson was an early riser and never minded being at the airport at six in the morning. Factoring in his layover, it had been nearly eighteen hours since he'd left Tokyo. The planes were nearly empty, with no in-flight dinner service, and the majority of the shops at the airport were closed. He wasn't sure what Jackson expected him to do for another seven hours, but he was certain, as the phone buzzed again, that the meager staff working at the airport would notice the presence of his emaciated corpse by then.

Kiddo has goldfish class today with mom, so I don't know if they'll be home when you make it over

Lowell had no idea what a goldfish class was, and at that moment, he decided he didn't care. Seven hours was still *seven fucking hours*, and apparently Jackson thought he was going to magically appear in the driveway, luggage in tow.

I read something this morning about species-specific travel staying open

This will be good for the non-human airlines

They need to figure this shit out before spring break

We already have our Cancun tickets

Lowell ignored the message. Liam was eighteen, still in high school, and was allowed to be completely self-absorbed, but that didn't mean

Lowell had to care about his youngest sibling's spring break plans, not just then.

Trapp was the next to respond.

I'm on my last 24 of house duty.

Why didn't you make plans before you left?

I didn't even know you were flying in today.

I would have had someone cover me

He let the phone fall back to the seat, dropping sideways against the bank of low, uncomfortable chairs, his head landing on his gear bag in the same divot in which it had rested across three continents. Involving the others was an exercise in futility, for none of them had ever once picked him up from the airport. Anytime he came home, he would simply text Grayson before the final leg of his journey, confident that there would be a car waiting when he arrived and a bed for him in his brother's house, a well-stocked refrigerator of sushi and organic vegetables, imported beer, and an excellent wine selection. Staying at Grayson's was like being a guest in a boutique hotel, right down to the filtered, fruit-infused water, only missing the warm cookies in the lobby. He'd never needed to ask before, and Gray had never thrown him out. Now he'd changed the unspoken agreement with no notice or conversation.

It wasn't as if he could just grab a cab, Lowell thought to himself for the hundredth time that hour. Service was temporarily suspended, as were the rideshare companies, and even if they weren't, he wasn't traveling with an average amount of luggage. When he went on shoots, his gear bag was the most essential thing in the world. Everything he needed was contained within, strapped around him as he set up on mountainsides or in caves or at the edge of a winding river in the heart of the rainforest . . . but that was hardly all he owned, for fuck's sake. Six rolling cases surrounded him, and that was *just* his camera gear. Two suitcases of luggage, a duffel, and a whispered prayer that everything he had already shipped home would make it back to Cambric Creek someday. He couldn't simply go outside and hail a cab, and Grayson knew it.

You're going to die here. Right here, in this airport. You've been in active war zones and hostile jungles, but this will be it. At gate 37B, right between an out-of-service restroom and a Mr. Toasty stand.

The phone buzzed against the vinyl of the seat next to him, the noise seeming over loud in the silent terminal. He fumbled for the handset, attempting to manifest the reality that one of his brothers was currently idling at the curb. *I'm outside. I'm outside.* He thought the words several times before swiping the screen open, slumping in disappointment as he read the most recent message, this time from his twin.

Sry I was in a meeting this morning & I'm walking into another one now

Only just seeing all this

I thought Gray was picking him up

Nearly another hour had passed, Lowell realized balefully. He could hear the droning whir of a floor cleaner several corridors away, evidence that he wasn't completely alone, which oddly didn't make him feel any better. When the phone buzzed again, he told himself he

7

wasn't going to look. It wouldn't be anything useful; it wouldn't be anything that would help his situation. He was going to ignore it, ignore them, and wait for Mr. Toasty to open, or else for death to embrace him at last.

He'd never been very good at ignoring things. It might have been someone from his office, someone from the publisher, someone calling with the first bit of good news he would have heard in several weeks. Or it might be Jackson texting to say he was leaving the university now, or Owen saying his meeting was canceled and he was on his way. His resolve to ignore things never seemed to last long, and this message would be no exception. Someday he might learn to control his impulses like a normal adult, he thought, but it was not this morning, not in this airport. After only a few moments, he was scrabbling for his phone once more, swiping open the screen and closing his eyes for a heartbeat, holding his breath.

Hold on, let me just tell the federal commission that I'm going to need to duck out of this hearing for an hour or two because my adult brother can't figure out how to travel twenty miles on his own.

It'll be fine.

I'm sure my client doesn't really need to win this case.

Lowell had to restrain himself from flinging the phone across the terminal. Grayson always had a way of making it sound as if he were the most important person in the world and the only one with a real job, which meant the rest of them were peasants with hobbies, by comparison. He didn't know what he'd done to earn his elder brother's ire already; didn't know for which invisible crime he was being punished, but some things hadn't changed since childhood — Grayson was punitive and harsh, and when he felt he'd been personally slighted, he was pro-level mean.

He wanted to respond to Owen's message that his twin was correct. *Grayson* was supposed to be picking him up. Grayson, who had an office relatively close to the airport, who Lowell was certain regularly took the time for two-hour martini lunches and illicit rendezvous with the wives of his partners, who had *always* picked him up from the airport on his previous visits home. Grayson, who had never communicated the plan had changed. The time was now 8:22 a.m., according to the television monitor behind him, and Grayson's snippy response to the text sent by his twin sealed the deal. He was going to die there.

Why isn't Jackson there?

Jackson's response to Gray's needling was immediate.

Because I'm at work, just like you, and no one ever communicated that I needed to come all the way into the city to be at the airport.

His brothers were talking about him as if he were a carton of milk they were meant to pick up or a particularly disgusting old toilet bound for the dump. Not their flesh and blood sibling who had boarded a plane on the other side of the world thinking there was a plan in place for when he arrived home after nearly a year since his last visit; not their displaced brother who had nowhere to go, his entire life put on pause. A chore, an obligation, one that, if they talked around long enough, might disappear.

The phone buzzed again, Trapp once more.

Maybe you should call dad

The phone vibrated with another response almost instantly, and Lowell squinted at the message from Liam.

Dad has a meeting this morning

I just left his office and he was right behind me

I have a history test this afternoon, but I can cut the rest of the day & get you

Panicked responses from Trapp and Jackson, nearly simultaneously:

N O

Absolutely not

He wanted to ask what Liam was doing at their father's downtown office an hour and a half after his classes started for the day but decided he didn't actually care, not when his own fate still rested in uncertainty. *Better yet, why the fuck didn't dad come to get me two hours ago?*

Lowell closed his eyes from his position in the divot of his gear bag, trying to pretend that there was a clear, wide-open blue sky above him, no walls or cars or concrete as far as the eye could see. It wasn't as if he could just stroll out of the airport, dragging his bags behind him. The terminal itself was surrounded by airstrips, further surrounded by parking garages and surface lots, highways that curled around the property, leading to arrivals and pickup, probably full of families who remembered their loved ones at the airport instead of abandoning them to a cruel death beside the Mr. Toasty stand, which still was not open.

When the phone buzzed again, he ignored it successfully. It wasn't as if it would make a difference. He was doomed to spend the rest of his brief existence roaming the halls of the empty airport, learning about the weather in places he would likely never get to visit again.

He hated this. He hated the uncertainty that had enveloped his life, hated being told that he *couldn't* do something, that he couldn't stay in his apartment, that his work visa was suddenly worthless. Every imprint at the publishing group that employed him was on hold, and all travel canceled as borders were closed because of the virus spreading through the human population, leaving him with nowhere he could go. All his work, a packed schedule that spanned months, was suddenly canceled. None of the friends he'd made across the world, who had so often stood in for the absent family he'd left behind, could take him in. He didn't like being told he couldn't do something, couldn't go somewhere, the road in front of him suddenly curtailed. Lowell Hemming did not like standing still, and now that was all he could do — wait and be patient, two things at which he had never excelled.

"The current temperature in Phoenix is 82° with clear skies. Your local time is 10:02 a.m."

He jolted when he realized how much time had passed since he'd dropped down onto his bag, getting lost in his head, as he often did. Time blindness, he once heard it called. Time usually meant very little to him, particularly when he changed time zones as often as he did, and even if he tended to let entire afternoons and evenings slip away from him when he was home, he told himself that didn't matter. He was meticulous about setting multiple alarms and alerts to always be on time for flights and shoots. He never slept through an alarm. On the contrary, whenever he had something looming on his calendar, anxiety kicked in and kept him buzzing in an anxious state of waiting, too keyed up to even think about being late.

He palmed his phone when it buzzed again, realizing he'd never even looked at the previous message. The Mr. Toasty stand was still not open, and his stomach twisted in hunger. *You're not going to need to worry about your bags because you're going to die of starvation first.*

The message he'd not looked at had been from Trapp.

I'm pulling away to swing by for you, be ready.

Lowell read and reread the message several times, realizing that it had been nearly 40 minutes ago, and the second message that had just come through was also from Trapp.

If you're not outside in two minutes, I'm leaving you

He sprung to his feet in one fluid movement, swinging his gear bag over his shoulder, scooping up his duffel, and grabbing the strap to his makeshift trolley of luggage. He knew this airport like the back of his hand, knew the fastest way to the arrival deck, and at that moment, his insider knowledge served him well. The outside of the terminal was just as eerily quiet as the interior, and even though the arrival gate was typically a congested mass of cars and trucks and busses, with travelers of every species pouring out of the doors and crossing through the lanes of traffic without heed, Trapp's truck was the only one idling at the curb.

"You'd better hope like fuck there wasn't a fire while I was gone."

"Thank you," Lowell blurted, slightly out of breath after racing to the exit doors from the main terminal and hauling his bags into the bed of the large truck while Trapp glowered in the rearview mirror. "Thank you for coming to get me. I hope this won't get you in trouble."

Trapp waved off the sentiment with a scoff, glancing into the rearview mirror before pulling away, leaving the terminal and the still-closed Mr. Toasty stand behind.

"The chief waved as I was pulling out, it's fine. Why the fuck didn't you let anyone know you needed to be picked up?! Like, yesterday before you left. None of us are mind readers, you know."

Lowell blew out an exasperated breath, pulling the seatbelt across his chest as his brother navigated out of the winding airport road and back onto the highway.

"I've never had to make it a group project to coordinate before. Gray always picks me up! I texted him before I even left Tokyo! He never responded, and then he acted like it had nothing to do with him this morning. He *always* picks me up. Why would I think this trip would be different? Why does he always have to be such a dick?"

Trapp's wide mouth pressed into a hard, flat line, weaving through the meager traffic on the highway until he made it to the far left lane, accelerating substantially. Lowell glanced surreptitiously into the side view mirror, hoping his camera gear wouldn't wind up bouncing out all over Bridgeton.

"Gray has a new job, did you know that? His office isn't on Swansea anymore. So why are you staying with Jackson?" Trapp demanded, dark eyebrows pulled together in a furrow. "You just got done saying Gray always picks you up. And you're right, he does. Because you always stay with him. So what made you decide to stay with Jackson this time?"

Lowell sputtered in outrage, realizing Trapp was turning this back on him. *Fucking typical.* He *refused* to take responsibility for this miscommunication. Jackson and Grayson had been ludicrously competitive over every little thing since childhood, and if they had not grown out of it, that wasn't his problem.

"Because Jackson offered! He called me like two weeks ago and offered up their guest suite!"

Trapp shrugged. "Then I guess you have your answer. You should've made arrangements with Jackson."

Lowell dropped his head back, closing his eyes. He was an adult, he reminded himself. He was an adult with his own life, far away from here, and he didn't need to feed into the sibling dynamic he'd grown up with. It was astounding, he thought, just how quickly he regressed into a frustrated 10-year-old the second he was with any of his family.

"Fine, whatever. This is all my fault because I didn't divine that Grayson was going to pick this random month to decide he has a singular feeling and that I hurt it somehow. How long am I going to be punished?"

Trapp shrugged again, grinning. "That's going to depend, but you're probably going to need to pick up some lip balm."

Lowell closed his eyes once more, sighing. Grayson was, by fucking far, his most challenging sibling, the prickliest and most mercurial, with capricious moods. It would've been far easier to simply write him off as his least favorite brother, if Gray wasn't also the only one who ever seemed to remember he existed.

He texted with his twin regularly, although phone conversations with Owen were rare. It was always a bit uncomfortable to tell strangers he was a twin. Popular culture insinuated he and Owen ought to have their own language, be able to sense when the other was hurt or sick, be each other's constant confidant and the recipient of every secret, and reality did not match up to the widely-held assumption. Lowell didn't tell Owen his every thought and innermost fear and wasn't told his twin's in turn. He suspected, as hard as it was to admit, that if they weren't brothers, they'd likely not even be friends.

Liam was eighteen and in a world of his own, and Trapp, while being the most agreeable, tended to have a somewhat out-of-sight, out-of-mind mentality. He could count on one hand the number of times Jackson had called him out of the blue in the past six months, and it had been a surprise when he had offered up his home to Lowell last week. *Should have fucking seen it coming.*

Grayson, on the other hand, called him regularly. He kept odd hours, and tended to be up at the same time Lowell was on the other side of the world, texted to check up on him, to ask if he needed money or if he was traveling anywhere dangerous, kept him relatively up-to-date on the comings and goings of the family at large, and acted as an arbitrator between Lowell and their parents. Gray was and always had been the most difficult, but he'd always been the one Lowell had turned to, even when he was a child. *And now you have to kiss his ass to get back in his good graces, just like you did when you were seven.* He wouldn't do it, he decided. He hadn't done anything *wrong*.

Grayson had never technically offered him a place to stay — he'd shown up on Gray's doorstep shortly after his brother's new house had been built, during a visit in which Lowell had decided that he would simply will himself out of existence if he had to stay under his parent's roof, and Gray hadn't said no.

It was true; he had never stayed with Jackson before, had never stayed with *any* of the rest of them before. Owen had halfheartedly offered the spare bedroom of the condo he shared with his girlfriend when they had spoken a few weeks prior, after it became evident that Lowell was going to have no choice about coming back to Cambric Creek, and while he appreciated the sentiment, the thought of being trapped in such a small space with two other adults for an indeterminate amount of time made him slightly nauseous.

Moving back into the home he'd grown up in was not an option. His mother claimed to understand his wanderlust, his need to always be on the move and feel the earth moving beneath his feet, but previous visits had shown him that it wouldn't take long for her to start making noise about how *nice* it was having him home, having all her boys within arm's reach, and did he know the paper in Bridgeton was always looking for photographers?

He'd grit his teeth, reminding her that he'd won international awards for his work photographing the civilian toll of the Rakshasa uprisings and for the results of him having gone to live with a closed community of selkies in upper Norway, but his point always fell on deaf ears.

His visit the previous Christmas had yielded a surprise dinner guest, one he hadn't realized until mid-way through the hot hors d'oeuvres was meant to be a potential date for him.

"She's a real estate agent right here in town, darling!" his mother had exclaimed, laying her hands on the beaming she-wolf's shoulders as Trapp snorted from across the table, his human girlfriend shooting Lowell an understanding, stricken look. Lowell knew his mother well enough to see through her strategy: a hand-picked mate from a respectable werewolf family who could find him a house right in the neighborhood.

He'd given the girl his most genial smile and had been as charming as he could the rest of the evening, booking a red-eye back to Tokyo two nights later, ending his visit three days early, calling his mother's bluff without a moment of compunction. Being the only Hemming in two generations to have left Cambric Creek carried a certain measure of guilt, but he was a pro at maneuvering his mother's traps at that point. She claimed to understand, but Lowell knew better. He loved his mother with his entire heart but being subjected to the non-stop barrage of insinuations that he needed to find a job in the unification, preferably one in their state and within walking distance of her street, would drive him crazy.

Jackson, on the other hand, had offered up his home. They'd put on an addition, he'd told Lowell, with his mother-in-law in mind. It wasn't much, a one bedroom, one bathroom suite, but it had its own entrance and a small kitchenette, providing him with a measure of freedom while he was there. Jackson's little boy was nearly school-aged, and the last time Lowell had been in town for any length of time, the kid had been little more than a toddler, and it would be nice getting to play fun uncle through more than the occasional video call. He was confident *he* would be the fun uncle. Grayson was undoubtedly the mean uncle, Trapp the impatient uncle. Owen was a twitch too uptight to be the fun one, and he was pretty sure the comedic nuances of internet memes would be lost on a four-year-old, leaving Liam out of the running. That left him, and he was eager to fill the part.

He wasn't going to apologize to Grayson when Jackson had offered, when Jackson had gone out of his way to call Lowell to do so. It didn't matter that he always stayed with Gray, that he had a key to his brother's home on the fob with all of the keys to his gear cases, clearly didn't matter what the previous arrangement had been when he'd been left to rot at the airport — Jackson had reached out first, and Grayson could die mad about it.

The Welcome to Cambric Creek sign loomed ahead, and his stomach tightened with nerves and memories and the shadow of his former self and life he'd cast off. It was only once they'd crossed over the first waterfall that the thought occurred to him, and once it entered his mind, he knew it was correct.

"Did-did Jackson only offer me a place to stay because he knew it would piss off Gray?"

Trapp smiled grimly.

"You've been gone for too long if you even need to ask, kiddo."

The radio on the dashboard crackled to life as they turned into the gated development where his brother lived, Trapp responding in a clipped voice that he would attend to the non-emergency call. Lowell struggled with his luggage, hoping none of the camera cases would roll into the street as he hauled himself up into the flatbed for the last of it.

"Thank you," he repeated mournfully from the curb as Trapp leaned out the open window. "I appreciate you leaving work so I didn't die of starvation."

Trapp rolled his eyes, sighing.

"Look, he won't be mad forever, okay? Get back on speaking terms. That's on you. He won't budge first, you should know that. He and I do dinner together at least once a week, you can tag along, okay? It'll be just like old times." Trapp smiled down wryly. "This pandemic isn't going to last forever either. You'll be leaving us all in your rearview again before you even get unpacked. Go get some food before you pass out, I'll talk to you later."

Lowell watched as Trapp pulled away; the truck's brake lights flaring to life at the corner, turning off the street and leaving him alone. Jackson's house looked as deserted as the airport, he realized, the weight of Grayson's key suddenly seeming like a ten-pound stone in his gear bag.

The front door was locked, as were the side and back doors, and he could find no decoy rock mixed into the garden. Nothing had been left for him, no plans made for him, and they were at something called goldfish class, he remembered. At least at the airport, he thought, corralling his luggage at the top of the driveway and strapping the cases together once more, the Mr. Toasty stand might be open by now.

* * *

Moriah

Moriah was familiar with the Azathé tea room.

She had been there once before with Drea, maybe a month or so after her divorce, two years earlier. A girls' day, one she sorely needed, her friend had claimed, showing up on her doorstep and ignoring the 4-day-old pajamas she'd worn, the rats' nest bun, and the plea to leave her to die alone with her stocked cupboard of peanut butter-stuffed pretzels and diet soda, the only thing she'd eaten in the previous forty-eight hours.

Drea had let her mope for exactly two weeks once the paperwork was finalized.

"Come on, let's go. Get off your ass and go brush your fucking teeth. We're not gonna sit home moping. Goddess knows he isn't."

They'd had their nails done at the salon on Main Street, where she'd commiserated with the harpy who owned the place, had spent too much money in the bookstore, winding up at the curious tea shop for lunch. The occultist decor and wide range of books available seemed an odd juxtaposition with the quaint menu. A little cat had shepherded them to their table, the lacquered top being a spirit board. Placing her fingers on the planchette had been a novelty that first visit, her order arriving on a little cart pushed by invisible hands, the hot tea and scones a perfect complement to the tiny finger sandwiches.

The shop didn't seem like an ideal venue for today's lunch, at least not to her, but it wasn't her choice to make, she thought, entering. The same little cat, black with silvery white points, meowed in greeting, the bell over the doorway clanging oddly as the cat hopped up from its tufted cushion, winding around her ankles before trotting away from the entrance, glancing back to ensure she was following, leading her to where their group was already seated. Their party of six crammed into the tight, twisting little dining room, seated around a cluster of three small tables that had been pulled together, the dainty seats of varying heights. She was certain if she leaned forward, she could rest her chin upon the table top, so low was her slipper chair, but as the only human at the table, she could suck it up.

Beyond Cambric Creek, the pandemic was raging, but her neighbors were thoroughly unconcerned. It was a human disease, not one affecting trolls or orcs or minotaurs, and their businesses were still open. They were not affected by the virus, and according to all of the current health reports, they were not significant carriers. She wouldn't be going to Bridgeton anytime soon, that was for certain, and she wore a mask whenever she was in public, as she did then, but working from home in a relatively insular community had enormous benefits, and she was relieved she still called the little town home.

The bric-a-brac around the shop had changed slightly since their last visit. Twisting spires of books were still everywhere one looked, and crammed in the midst of the library's worth of reading material were odd artifacts and ephemera. There was a skull with a candle half melted upon the crown of its head, a cluster of three crystal points on a bronze plate, and a cursed-looking locket with a large red gem, suspended over a velvet placard, all resting on the shelf just above her site line. The huge, two-handed sword against the far wall was new though, as was a long, black veil, moving like a waterfall down one of the towers of books, and a doll upon a high shelf, whose head turned to watch the progress of patrons as they came and went from the dining room.

Moriah shivered, looking away. The first visit had been a novelty — monkey paws and taxidermied vampire bats, old swords and clocks that didn't tell time, strange things, curious things all adding to the atmosphere of the unusual little shop, but the repeat visit made her curiously uneasy, like a portent hanging in the air.

The table she sat before, like the spirit board on the previous visit, had a glossy, lacquered surface, inlaid with the template for a three card tarot spread. Several of the other women in their group had never been to Azathe, the novelty of the table and all of the curiosities surrounding them making them ooh and aah. Moriah reached across her place setting to the tarot deck sitting just beyond her water glass in an open-topped box, trying not to feel the weight of the creepy doll's eyes on her back. Instructions rested beside each template in a curling gold script. *Shuffle your deck, cut from the center. Remove three cards & place in the spread. Once the cards are placed, do not disturb them. Return the deck to the box, face down.*

She unwrapped the tarot deck slowly, trying to tell if she was imagining slight vibration in her hands. Shuffle the deck. Cut the deck. Remove three cards. She followed directions, placing each card in one of the rectangular spaces, setting the rest of the deck aside, sitting back in her chair to examine her spread. At the sight of her first card, Moriah felt the hairs raise on the back of her neck. Her first card was inverted — a heart set on a stormy field, and in its center was an eye. The eye was green, like her own, fringed in lashes and overflowing with tears. She was able to feel the sorrow radiating through the waxed card stock, and could almost see the thump of that heart as it was pierced by three pointed swords. Despite being upside down, the eye seemed to stare directly through her, seeing the heaviness of her own heart, and judging her failures.

Her feeling of unease was not helped by the sepulcher figure in the second card. The death card stared back at her, right side up. The scythe carried by the skeletal figure glinted, and over its shoulder was a banner featuring a five-petaled flower. She didn't know anything about tarot or divination, but certainly nothing good could come from pulling the death card, she thought. The third card meant nothing to her, not really. A large golden chalice sat on a bright pink field, a pyramid of eight smaller chalices beneath it. The liquid overflowing from the large cup spilled over into the row beneath it and so on, water falling down from cup to cup in a bright cerulean deluge.

"Isn't this so exciting," squealed the neighbor beside her. "I had my fortune read by one of the witches at an event last year, but it was nothing like this! What are we supposed to do now?"

"I think we're just supposed to wait," Moriah murmured, unable to pull her eyes away from the eye on that pierced heart, staring balefully up at her.

All around their tables, the tarot cards were being scooped up by an invisible hand, one by one, and neatly flipped back into the deck. All around the table, it was the same — each of her neighbors squealing in delight as the cards around them were lifted and moved, as if a very direct wind carried them on a current. All around the table, until she was reached. For several long, echoing moments, nothing happened. Moriah stared at the eye and the eye stared back, no invisible wind lifting it from the template, no unseen hand snatching away the death card.

"Well. Quite the impactful spread we have here."

The voice seemed to be made of shadow and smoke. It whispered at the back of her neck, an invisible whorl around her ear, and from the way her neighbors on either side of her continued to chatter and laugh, she knew that none of them could hear it. In any other setting, she would have jumped to her feet. She would have screamed, been terrified . . . but the voice was at home in this strange place, and she could tell — why, she wasn't sure — that it meant her no harm.

"I fear you've suffered long, little one. But you see here, the three of swords inverted . . . a mitigation of the sorrow. Your suffering is not the end, nor will it have been in vain."

That didn't make sense to her, but that did not prevent tears from burning at the corner of her eyes, until she likely resembled the eye on the card. This disembodied voice, clever as it thought it was, didn't know the half of it.

"And what of the death card?"

"The most misunderstood card in the deck. Death is not the end, child. Death can be hard and harsh, but it can also be quick and merciful. Death feeds life, and we cannot begin again until we let go of those things that shackle us. Death may be an ending, but with that ending there is always a rebirth."

She nodded, not trusting her voice and hoping that none of the other women from the neighborhood seated around the tables would notice the tears about to overflow from her eyes.

"And this; this is a most auspicious sign. The nine of cups, a card of happiness and joy. Do you see how they spill into each other? Happiness brings happiness, joy brings more joy. These three cards represent stages in your life, sweet one. Your past, your present, and the future yet to come. Your past is the past and none can change that, but only you can control your present circumstances. Your cards have aligned to promise happiness in the days ahead, if only you allow that joy to find you."

When the cards flipped into the basket before her water glass, she sucked in a lungful of air, feeling as though she had just exited from a heavy shadow, one that had enveloped her fully, leaving her invisible to the rest of the table. The other women in their group had taken no notice, and Moriah breathed relief, dabbing her eyes as inconspicuously as she could and regaining her composure. Turning to her neighbor, she attempted to pay attention to the conversation already buzzing around her.

"Well, *I* heard from Kestra Kittredge that he lives right there *in* the house. Right there! Right next door to the old Slade place, can you believe it? I never thought I'd see the day when they were just out and about, walking around."

Several of the other women around the table clucked their tongues, heads shaking.

"Our babysitter's mother works part-time at City Hall, and she said that Ansleth made the suggestion to pass an ordinance."

"Past time, I say."

"Can you blame him? They need to do *some*thing!"

"He's looking at actually having to run a campaign next year, so it's not surprising to hear they're taking action on something."

Drea frowned. "Would they really do that? Pass ordinances restricting certain species from living here? That seems contrary to the town charter."

The group was composed of women of various species who lived in the same development, her neighbors, a lunch bunch idea born at a block party and solidified when they had all worked together on a fundraiser to install hanging floral baskets throughout the development to match the color scheme chosen by the residents. It was the most ludicrously suburban thing Moriah could possibly conceive, and she was low-key horrified that she had taken part in it. But, as Drea had pointed out at the time, it got her out of the house.

She watched as two of the other women sniffed, exchanging a fast look, clearly not in agreement with Drea's sentiment.

"In any case, it doesn't matter," the original speaker huffed. "Rixli's mother said Jack breezed in like he owned the place and shot that down immediately, no further conversation. You know, I really don't know who that man thinks he is. Bossing around the mayor! His son wants to run for office, that's fine, he can run and be elected on the strength of his positions. Things have changed in this town, and it's not going to be enough to simply be a part of the old guard. Jack's not *actually* in charge of anything, and he seems to forget that."

"Be that as it may," Drea pushed on, "if he's squashing ordinances restricting people from living here, more power to him. And if that's the platform his son is planning to run on, he has my vote. I'll be happy to have the old guard back, in that case."

"But if there is a threat to our children—"

"Didn't you just say this araneaen has been here for months? Have anyone's kids gone missing yet? If he's not bothering anyone, who cares? It's a slippery slope, is all I'm saying. Today you want to pass ordinances against araneaens, and then what? Outlawing mixed species marriage? Decreeing who can live where and with whom? That defeats the purpose of a mixed-species community."

The busybody with the connected babysitter sputtered.

"We could go in circles about local politics all day," interrupted the troll sitting at Drea's left, "but I think we have much more exciting things to celebrate today!"

It wasn't until a bottle of champagne was brought out that Moriah realized the afternoon wasn't going to be as simple and sunny as she had thought when she'd set out that day.

"Now, don't get mad at me," the troll gushed. "But I couldn't help bringing something to celebrate good news, and the owner here was good enough to indulge me."

Across the table, Moriah watched as Drea's cheeks reddened, her eyebrows drawing together first in confusion, then in mortification, her jaw working silently before her eyes flashed up. It was lightning fast, and if she'd not already been watching Drea's expression, she might have missed it. The look was aimed directly at her, to take her in, to gauge her reaction. It wasn't champagne, she realized. Sparkling grape juice. Non-alcoholic. An uncomfortable flip tightened her guts, her lungs unable to fully inflate as she watched her best friend squirm in her seat.

"Tuley, that's not necessary, I don't want to —"

"Oh, I know you don't. That doesn't mean I'm not going to! We just want to celebrate your happy news!"

Drea flushed as the bottle was passed around, glasses filled. The troll was her neighbor, Moriah remembered, Elijah and the woman's husband were friendly. Heat began to spread up her neck as the troll cleared her throat, swinging her long, frosty silver hair over her shoulder before raising her glass with a beaming smile.

"I'd like you all to join me in a toast. To Drea and Elijah and the little bundle of joy that will be joining their home later this year — Creek Rock Estates will be thrilled to welcome the newest member to our community!"

She managed to get through the toast. She managed to clink her glass amongst the cluster of other glasses raised, was able to choke down the overly sweet juice, sat there with a smile pasted on her face as the others of the table gushed in excitement. A baby. Her best friend was going to have a baby.

Moriah knew that she would be a despicable hag if she were anything but happy. How could she not be? After all, didn't she know, perhaps better than anyone, what Drea and her husband Elijah had gone through? Didn't she know the pain of trying and failing over and over again? Hadn't she heard people tell her for years that if it was meant to be, it would happen on its own? That everything happened for a reason? That this was all some larger plan? That all she had to do was dream and hope hard enough and she could manifest her reality, like she was some fucking fortune cookie and not a flesh and blood person who went through a tiny mourning every month that passed? She'd been told enough times that she was strong enough to withstand any curveball life threw her, otherwise, it wouldn't have been thrown?

She'd bitten her tongue and choked back her frustration for years, wanting to scream that sometimes the curveball hit you directly in the face, managing to restrain herself by the barest thread. She knew Drea had heard the same, so how could she be anything but happy for her friend? *Because misery loves company, and pretty soon she's going to be too busy with midnight feedings and changing diapers to hear you cry over not being able to afford IVF.*

She lasted through lunch, through more chatter and gossip until the split checks were brought out, and waited for one of the others to push back her chair first. *If you're not the first to leave, you can't be accused of running away.* The instant the old crone from around the corner stood, shaking out her shawl and draping it over her shoulders, Moriah sprung from her seat, saying her goodbyes with a false cheerfulness and an absolute finality, not allowing herself to be pulled into any further conversation before turning and hurrying to the front of the shop where she checked herself out at the automatic terminal, the little cat watching her every move.

The air outside was thick with an incoming storm, weighing on her lungs, forcing her to take shuddering gasps. She hated herself for being upset. She hated that tears were fast on the heels of happiness she felt for her friend, and the happiness *was* there, it was real. That was what she needed to focus on, she reminded herself. Put on a happy face and get in touch with the genuine joy she felt and survive. *Suck it up. You can cry when you get home. You can be as self-indulgent and selfish as you want when you get home.*

She was halfway across the parking lot when Drea's voice stopped her.

"Moriah! Please, don't leave like this. Please talk to me. I didn't want you to find out this way."

It had been a boon, finding Drea. Half human, half Sylvan, she was tall and lithe, with nut brown skin and long, honey-gold hair, the golden markings around her eyes catching the sunlight and sparkling like glitter. Drea would power walk around the block every day, arms and legs pumping in tandem and looking like something out of a retro workout video, and she and Moriah would stop to chat anytime she was passing in front of the house when Moriah was outside. They bumped into each other at the library, at the coffee shop, and finally, at the fertility clinic in Bridgeton, sealing their friendship.

It had been a horrible mistake, marrying a man whose biology was incompatible with her own. She knew that now. *I fear you've suffered long, little one.* She often wondered if she could go back and have a conversation with her younger self, she would've been able to convince her to run away from her own wedding day, to leave Sorben standing beside the lake with their family and friends wondering where she was . . . Or she could've also had a conversation with him beforehand, she would remind herself wryly. Not everything had to end in a runaway bride scenario. She had to remind herself sometimes that they had been happy once, she was sure of it, before things had broken, before she'd become consumed with the one thing it seemed she was destined to not have.

She wanted a baby of her own, more than she'd ever wanted anything else, and the fact that natural reproduction was rare in a marriage like hers had been an inconsequential detail in the beginning. One month turned into two, then four, then eight. The small spare room in their house which had been designated as the future nursery had remained their shared home office, a desk where a bassinet should have been; an ergonomic rolling chair in the spot where she would place a sturdy wooden model which rocked, her arms aching to hold a swaddled bundle instead of poised over a laptop. The struggle to conceive had eaten away at the fabric of her marriage, had burned through their savings, and her idealism along with it.

"I didn't know she was planning on doing this. *I* didn't even tell her, Elijah mentioned something to her husband, and . . . I didn't want anyone knowing, especially not like this. Please don't be upset."

"I'm not upset," she said quickly, spinning to face her friend, knowing the tears spilling over her eyelashes belied her words. "I'm not, really. I know that wasn't your doing in there. And I'm *happy* for you, Drea, I am."

She wasn't sure what she would have done if she hadn't had someone going through the same thing. She wasn't sure if she would have made it through the crushing disappointment and the innate feeling of failure, month after month. She wasn't sure what she would've done if she hadn't had a good friend to laugh and cry and scream with when her marriage fell apart, buckled under the weight of her singular fixation. It had been the one thing she and Drea had shared in the beginning, and it had opened the door to learning about all the other things they shared, but all along, that was the initial tie that bound them.

"I didn't want you to find out this way, I didn't want this to hurt you. Please don't be mad at me, please just —"

"I'm not! How could I be mad? I'm so, *so* happy for you. For you and Elijah both. You're going to be awesome parents." Her tears were threatening to choke her.

"Sweetie —"

"I'm so happy for you, Drea," she forced out, her tears flowing freely by then. "I'm happy for you, and I'm really sad for me, but one doesn't detract from the other. I'm able to feel both of those things."

Drea glanced back swiftly at the sound of voices, the rest of their party noisily exiting the tea shop. She gripped Mariah's hand, long fingers tightening around her wrist.

"Let's get together this week, okay? I need to tell you about this place. The only reason I didn't say anything sooner was because. . . Well, it's a little embarrassing. I didn't want to upset Elijah, and I didn't even know if it was going to work. But now that we know that it does, you need to try it. I'll give you all the details this week, okay?"

She had no idea what her friend was going on about, but at that moment, Moriah didn't really care. She just wanted to go home. She wanted to go home and cry out her frustration and her envy, and the shame she felt at both.

"This week then."

If there was one thing she was good at, it was holding herself together. She had always been the responsible one, the planner. She was the mom friend, the one who gave advice, who took notes, who packed extras. She didn't throw tantrums or fits when she didn't get her way, and had an excellent poker face. She employed it then, keeping her composure as she got into her car, weaving through town, traversing the short distance back to their housing development, keeping a serene smile on her face as she moved from her car to the front door, raising a hand at one of the neighbors across the street.

It wasn't until the door closed behind her that she broke. Shutting the world out, she crumpled, sliding to the floor with the world at her back, a world full of people who seemed to be able to pop out children with barely any effort. She *was* happy for her friend. That hadn't been a lie. She was happy for her friend and miserable with where her life was currently, the two opposing emotions each clawing at her throat, making her wheeze around her sobs. She didn't know what Drea had done, couldn't fathom what unapproved method of conception she had tried that had worked, and she wasn't sure if her heart could bear anymore disappointment.

She cried until she didn't have anything left in her to cry out, her quaking sobs quieting to shuddering breaths, dropping her head back against the door with a thud. The house — the house she loved, that she had decorated herself, that she was so proud of — was silent, and it was the silence that was so hard to bear. There was no laughter, no shouting, no nothing. The silence was what was going to kill her.

A mitigation of the sorrow. She didn't know what *mitigation* the invisible voice had been talking about, because her heart certainly hadn't felt any fucking mitigation.

It didn't matter what it was that Drea had done. It didn't matter, Moriah told herself, closing her eyes and breathing slowly. Her eyes were swollen and her throat stuck. It didn't matter, for the small room beside the master bedroom, the one she had painted a cool mint with dove grey and sunny yellow accents, was still her office, and the house was still silent. It didn't matter what it was, for she knew she would try it. She didn't like the feeling of desperation that accompanied her in her bed every night, but she knew of only one way to kick it out, before the silence choked her.

She would try anything if it would make this crushing silence go away.

* * *

Lowell

"Is there anything else I can get for you, Mr. Hemming?"

He'd been about to wish the woman a good day, but the sentiment stuck in his throat at her words, a clawing reminder that he was under a magnifying glass wherever he went.

"I'm all set," he peered at her name tag, "Daronda."

The troll blinked slowly, her lips quirking back into the smile they had briefly lost when his eyes raised back to hers.

"See? It's weird when people you don't know use your name. And besides, Mr. Hemming is my brother."

"Which one?" she deadpanned back, a bit more chutzpah than he was expecting at the grocery store, but appreciated nonetheless. After all, he was a troublemaker too.

He shrugged, giving her a genuine smile then, one she mirrored.

"Take your pick, probably all of them. Not me, though. I'm a child. And you can call me Lowell. Daronda. See? Still weird!"

The cashier's laughter followed him out the automatic sliding doors as he left the Food Gryphon, annoyed that he had to spend his dwindling savings on food at all.

It had been two months since he'd first flown home at the start of the humans' pandemic. He realized, after the first month and a half of being the third wheel in Jackson's home, eating cereal for nearly every meal and sitting glued in front of cable news, that some of the imprints that employed him might not survive being shuttered this way, and if they did, they'd likely not require his services in the same manner. It was anxiety-inducing to think he'd have less work when this was all over, particularly when he wasn't in the most lucrative profession to start. He'd still not been paid for his last two invoices, and he would burn through his meager savings at this rate, particularly if he was forced to find an apartment here.

Cambric Creek seemed utterly unfazed by the events happening in the larger world, and his siblings got up and went to work every day like nothing was wrong. He was the only one halted, the only one with his entire world thrown into flux, and he was crawling out of his skin.

Which brought him to his first bone of contention, he thought peevishly. The guest suite in his brother's home offered him privacy, insofar that it had a door that closed and he wasn't forced to sleep outside on the sidewalk, but the fact remained — he was never going to masturbate in peace again.

He had the realization nearly three weeks into his stay, the approaching full moon making his skin feel snug, as if it had shrunk in a too-hot shower. The shower being the only place he'd been able to jerk off since his arrival — not something he particularly enjoyed, nor did it fully take the edge off the tightness in his balls. He was used to having sex a few times a week, had friends and flings and hook-up partners in place for that very purpose, and failing that, he needed to be able to drain his balls dry well enough on his own to even be able to function.

His neighbor Nikkia had been one such fuck buddy, another ex-pat, but unlike his, her visa was permanent. She'd texted him two weeks into his Cambric Creek imprisonment, reminding him of all he was going to be missing.

I miss your big cock already

He had made Tokyo his main hub of residence three years prior, meeting the sparkling-eyed lagomorph the week he moved in. She lived several doors down on the same hallway, had insisted he come over for a welcome to the neighborhood drink, casually inviting him to stay for some welcome to the neighborhood sex, setting up the parameters of their friendship from the first day.

I think I'm going to start doing cam stuff.

You know all those humans are sitting home jerking off all day

This is the time to start!

He'd thought she'd been joking when she'd sent the text. He'd laughed, tapping out his response with a smile, in between kicking a ketterling ball for his nephew to chase.

You should

It's a prime market

They're all sitting at home with nothing to do.

He'd laughed again a week or two later at her next message.

I can't believe you left me to do this alone.

I'm going to be forced to start making videos with that asshole Daiyuu

and it's going to be all your fault.

Daiyuu was another neighbor, a towering, salamander-like lizard-man with a permanently dour expression. Lowell had grinned hugely, trying to imagine Daiyuu with Nikkia, finding the idea preposterous.

He's more likely to report you for noise violations and turn you in to the censorship police

He'd not laughed when she'd sent the video file a week later, Daiyuu's surly face contorted into an expression of extreme concentration, his hips hammering into the moaning lagomorph, two dark pink cocks filling her. He was furious, had practically combusted in jealousy, any vicarious enjoyment he might have procured from the video severely hampered by the sound of his nephew and sister-in-law just down the hall. He angrily masturbated to the video several times before deciding it wasn't healthy, and he mourned the luxury of having someone to fill the role of reliable fuck buddy.

It was an impossibility here. Everywhere he went, people knew who he was without knowing him at all. *One of those Hemming boys, one of Jack's handsome boys, Trapp's kid brother, you must be related to Grayson, is your brother Jackson going to run for office? I coach your kid brother's lacrosse team, you must be the one who lives overseas.* The weight of his name had chafed when he'd been in school, rasping at his skin from inside, and it had been a relief to flee it and this place.

There was no way to form a casual hook-up here, not without the entire neighborhood knowing by morning, completely impossible . . . and besides, he reminded himself — where would he take them if it was? The guest suite at his brother's house with the paper thin walls where he couldn't even jerk off enjoyably? Back to his parents' house? He was trapped with no recourse, and his balls ached from the punishment. He was dizzy from the backup, his balance affected by the extra blood permanently pooled in his neglected cock. It was bad enough not having a partner, but not even being able to rub one out in a satisfactory manner was killing him.

Lowell was convinced his little nephew had a built-in detection system to identify the moment he had his cock in hand, for he would barely get a few good strokes in before little fists were scrabbling at the door, rattling the knob. The problem with being the fun uncle, when fun uncle was a live-in diversion, he had determined, was that there was never a break. Little Jack was always there. He wanted to play the instant he came home from his Montessori school, had to be persuaded to eat lunch, practice his letters, and do anything that didn't involve being at Lowell's side. He would be tapping on the guest suite's door before he had his breakfast each morning, before Lowell even lifted his head from the pillow, still blurry-eyed with sleep, morning wood resting like a club against his belly.

The worst days were those when he actually rose first — when he had a chance to stretch and wake up fully on his own, check his phone messages, and let a hand wander down his body, easing his foreskin back to tap a finger against his already leaking slit, tugging his aching balls and caressing himself slowly . . . before the rattling door knob would nearly make him jump out of his skin. More than once, he'd had to open the door a crack, poking his nose out and telling the kid he needed to take a shower first, the door shielding the full mast erection he'd been stroking only moments before.

The other issue was the suite itself. It was commensurate in size to a hotel room, and Lowell was no stranger to hotel rooms. Hotel rooms were a welcome respite of silence and solitude when he was on a shoot, but beyond needing small pockets of time to himself to recharge, he *needed* to be around people. He desperately needed to engage and chatter, to get out of his own head and take energy from a crowd . . . but Jackson and Victoria seemed vaguely surprised every time they encountered him out of his room, surprised and slightly annoyed.

They'd both gone silent just that morning, their conversation over the kitchen island muting when Lowell came through the doorway, Jackson's eyes narrowing and Victoria's mouth flattening when he pulled open the refrigerator. He'd had the vague suspicion that he was about to be scolded . . . for eating their food? Leaving his room? Having the nerve to breathe their oxygen? He hadn't been entirely sure, and he'd never found out, for the blast of a car horn, long and loud from the front of the house, had saved him. Jackson had exhaled sharply, and Victoria shook her head in annoyance.

"Grayson's here," she'd announced flatly, "just in case you weren't sure."

"Such a fucking asshole," Jackson muttered, abandoning the glass of water he'd just poured. "Can you tell him I'll be out in five minutes and to calm the fuck down?"

Lowell had jumped when he'd realized the directive was aimed at him, spinning to shut the refrigerator, his quest for juice momentarily forgotten as he sprinted to the door. Despite Trapp's assurances that he would not be mad forever, Grayson seemed entirely willing to go the rest of his life without having another conversation with Lowell, which was abso*lute*ly Jackson's fault.

The month he'd come home, the full moon had occurred only a day or so before his flight when he was still in Tokyo. He'd spent the next few weeks trying to settle in, contacting the office daily, as well as a handful of his peers and other freelancers, reacquainting himself with his hometown after such a long absence. It was fun at first. He'd hung out with Owen, had attempted to sit at the table with Trapp and Liam as they reviewed a medical school textbook until his fidgeting and chatter had earned Trapp's stinkeye, and he'd gone off to console himself with attention from his mother.

Even though Cambric Creek boasted more businesses and nightlife every time he saw it again, the town seemed to be shrinking. His parents' house was the same. The big Tudor had felt like a castle when he was a child, with endless rooms, staircases, and places to hide. That first full moon he'd been home, however, it had felt like an impossible chore not to turn around and trip over one of his brothers, the rooms all seeming so much smaller than what he remembered. The invitation to join Trapp and Grayson for dinner had never come in those initial few weeks, and his first full moon home was also the earliest opportunity to be in a room with Grayson since his arrival.

"Trapp said you have a new job?" It wasn't the first overture he'd made since Gray and a petite, dark-haired woman had arrived, but it was the first time he'd managed to get his brother alone in the kitchen, trapping him.

"Yes."

"Oh. Well, that's-that's good? You like it so far?"

"No."

He'd swallowed hard. Grayson never made anything easy. He hadn't been able to fathom why his brother had left his own lucrative law firm, unless it was for something important. *Or something for dad.*

"New jobs are always like that, though, right? Once you settle in, things even out?"

Grayson kept his back to Lowell, examining the contents of their parents' refrigerator as if a movie had been playing inside, pausing for an interminable amount of time before responding.

"I'm nearly at that six-month point where things are allegedly supposed to be getting easier to swallow, but I'm not convinced it's going to happen."

"Wait, six months?! I've talked to you a million times in the last six months! Why didn't you ever say anything?"

Gray had never looked up from the cheese he'd located on the top shelf, unwrapping it and making several deft cuts into the wax without ever raising his head. Everything about his older brother was intimidating and meticulous — his size, his immaculate clothing and expensive-looking accessories, the icy cold exterior he presented when he wasn't being charming, right down to the perfectly coiffed woman he'd brought with him, another pretty accessory, hanging from his arm like a designer bag. He'd always felt like a rumpled pillowcase compared to Grayson, and the feeling had not abated, despite his satisfaction with his life away from Cambric Creek.

"Because you don't ask questions about anyone else, Lowell. I call you to make sure you're not dead, and you proceed to talk at me until you get bored. I send you money and I let our mother know that you're still alive, since you never remember to do her the courtesy of calling her once in a while. Anything else? Or are we done playing catch up?"

He'd sucked in a wounded breath as if Gray's overly harsh characterization of their phone conversations had been a physical blow, watching as his brother turned away from the cheese board to drop the wax into the garbage and wash his hands silently, striding out of the kitchen a moment later as if Lowell had vanished from the room. Grayson had left shortly after the tense encounter in the kitchen, his companion receiving a phone call necessitating their early departure, and Lowell had not had the opportunity since to either make peace or push back.

His second month home, the morning after the moon had found him groggy and sore, as it always did, dragging to his parents' house to find the atmosphere unusually somber. Grayson and Vanessa — the girl who'd been there the previous month, who evidently had a name, indicating she was more than just a temporary accessory; a shocking turn of events, he thought — wouldn't be joining them that month. Gray had a bad turn, had been in the midst of a cluster aura when the change happened and was still unwell.

Trapp had left brunch at one point to go and check on him, mumbling about the hospital, and their mother attempted to smile and make conversation with Victoria and Owen's coolly reserved girlfriend, although it had been clear she was fretting. Jackson hadn't known what to do with himself without their father as a captive audience, hovering in the doorways of rooms as if he wasn't quite sure if it was the one he wanted to enter. Their father had never come in from his position on the deck where he sat brooding, radiating fury over a situation involving a member of his family that had the audacity to be outside of his control, swirling the same glass of bourbon around for much of the day without ever taking a sip. Lowell escaped the oppressive atmosphere of the house, taking little Jack to the back of the property, kicking rocks into the creek, and searching for salamanders.

It annoyed him that Grayson still managed to engender sympathy from people, regardless of how much of a dick he was the vast majority of the time. His brother had suffered from severe migraines all his life, and several times a month throughout his entire childhood, Lowell would be practically threatened with life and limb by their father if he didn't find someplace to play quietly, far away from Jack's study, the room behind it being what they all referred to as Grayson's second bedroom, kept cold and dark and silent.

That had been almost two weeks ago. Two weeks more of Jackson and Victoria's waning hospitality, two weeks of feeling trapped like a bug under glass, the guest suite of his brother's home seeming to shrink as the days went by. The sound of his own voice was overloud in his head, desperate for company. He was bored, he was depressed, and he was not going to last if things continued on as they were, and no one, he realized, was going to get him out of this mess for him.

Being Jackson's best little brother had never really netted him anything valuable. Being Grayson's junior toadie, on the other hand, had provided access to cars and occasionally alcohol, his first sexual experience as a teen at an out-of-state party thrown by his brother, expensive camera equipment as Christmas presents, his first dabble with recreational drugs at another party, and the name and number of his very first agent, met at one of Grayson's annual Lupercalia celebrations, a night that had ended with his first threesome.

Grayson was hard and professional, had been the valedictorian of every school he'd ever attended and was an uptight overachiever in every arena, but he was a fan of over-the-top excess and nihilistic debauchery, and Lowell had benefited from all of the above over the years.

He'd had visa trouble his second year overseas, winding up in a temporary holding cell in a place where he barely spoke the local language, for a minor, *teensy* tiny transgression so inconsequential he refused to take responsibility for it, and rather than contact the Embassy as he was meant to, he called his brother. The entire thing had been fixed and washed away, and their parents had never needed to find out.

He had been taken in by Jackson's call, he accepted now; had forgotten how conniving both of his eldest brothers could be, particularly against each other, and had been too excited over the prospect of getting to know his young nephew. He loved spending time with little Jack, but he couldn't go on another day feeling like a naughty child who'd been sent to their room indefinitely, and the only way to course correct was to get back into Gray's extremely haughty good graces, a place he'd always comfortably lived.

The windows of Grayson's silver sports car were tinted, and Lowell was unable to see his expression as he came loping down the driveway in Jackson's stead, throwing open the passenger door and sliding in before Gray had a chance to run over his foot.

"Jackson said he'll be out in five minutes. You should've seen Victoria's face when you honked, that was great. Are you done being pissed off at me yet? I'm *sorry*, okay? I'm sorry I let Jackson trick me into coming here. I'm sorry I didn't ask about your new job. I'm sorry that I'm such a burdensome shit all the time. I'm fucking miserable if it makes you feel any better. I'm never going back to work, I'm not qualified to do *any*thing, and I'm going to wind up being the first Hemming to work at Blinxieburger. I'll probably have to be the mascot. I'm pretty sure I have the kind of clinical depression they put you in the hospital for, and Jackson seems to think I'm supposed to be happy being locked in my room all day and night. I don't have anyone to talk to, I haven't had sex in like four months, and I feel like I'm going to die. What more do I have to do? Tell me how much I have to kiss your ass to make you talk to me again. You wanna bend over and let me give you a rim job right here?"

Grayson's chiseled face had been screwed up in a scowl when Lowell began speaking, but by the time he was offering rim jobs, his huge shoulders were shaking in laughter.

"You're such a fucking punk, I can't stand you. She was mad?"

Lowell nodded enthusiastically.

"Oh yeah, they both were." He attempted to hide his laughter in his arm when Grayson leaned on the horn again, at the same time Jackson came out the front door. They were still children, and some things would never change. "Trapp said the two of you have dinner together often, and I'm inviting myself along, so let me know next time, okay? I'm not asking; I'm telling you. Do you have the day off or something? Did you have to go to the hospital last month? Why don't you like your job? Is that girl actually your girlfriend, or just your flavor of the month?"

Grayson huffed in exasperation.

"Lowell, get the fuck out of my car. I've been at my office since six. Jackson and I are pulling away to take care of something for dad, and then I'm going back to work, where I'll be until sometime this evening.

Not exactly a day off. The rest of your twenty questions are going to have to wait. The Pickled Pig, ten p.m. on Tuesday night, if you come in dressed like a fucking slob, you're not sitting with us. Have fun kicking rocks around town all day, kid."

Jackson glowered at him as he exited Grayson's passenger seat, tossing a smile back over his shoulder. It was stupid of him to have forgotten what the two of them were like, but it was a mistake he would not be making again. He had spent the majority of his childhood and teen years playing against his two eldest brothers and had forgotten the pros and cons of being aligned with either of them.

By the time he was back indoors, the house was empty, Victoria having slipped out the garage door before he'd entered the front door. He could hear the motor running, the door lowering, and the sound of her engine accelerating as she pulled away a moment later. *Good.* Locating the juice at last, he chugged half the carton, ensuring it was put back with less than a full glass remaining. He had the house at his disposal without their glares, at least for a short while, before she returned home with little Jack.

Staggering into the laundry room sideways, he dropped his overloaded basket on top of the dryer with a grunt. Jackson's home did not boast the same level of amenities as Gray's — there was no laundry service, no thrice-weekly turn-down service, and the housekeeper who came to Jackson's house twice a week seemed to have been instructed to leave the guest suite off her list. His fists bunched in frustration when he saw the full washer, a detergent pod and fabric softener bead already placed within. Loaded, but not on.

His sister-in-law had complained about his middle-of-the-night hours after the first few weeks. He couldn't help it, he'd argued with his brother — he was set to a completely different internal clock than the rest of them.

"Then reset it. We both have work in the morning, and Jack has to be up for school. I can't have you prowling around all over the house at night, keeping everyone awake. And what did you put in the dryer the other night, five pairs of workboots? Let's put laundry in the daytime activity column."

They didn't want him doing laundry at night, but he and Victoria had no qualms about keeping the clothes dryer full the other twenty hours a day. They didn't want him *prowling around* the house at night, an unflattering descriptor he didn't appreciate, but they didn't want him prowling around in the daytime either, it seemed. Lowell closed his eyes, sucking in a deep breath, holding it for as long as he was able, letting it out on a slow, controlled exhale, pretending he was back in that one temple in Hokkaido, the crisp smell of mint and lemongrass incense nearly tickling at his nose. Opening his eyes, he was disappointed to still find himself in Jackson's home.

This was fine, he reminded himself. It was fine. He appreciated Jackson giving him a place to stay, deciding to pretend the offer had been made from a place of altruism and not solely based on the desire to make Grayson angry and gain a live-in babysitter in one fell swoop.

It was fine. His mother was always happy to see him, Lowell reminded himself, and he could employ the time-honored tradition of doing laundry at his parents' house. *Someone might even make me a sandwich and let me sit in the room with them.*

Or an even better idea — pack his stuff up right now, put the key to Grayson's house to use, and soak in the cool, dark atmosphere of his choice of oversized bedrooms. He could have his laundry done by Grayson's service, avail himself of something delicious from the always-stocked refrigerator, and masturbate until he was unconscious. *You might wake up actually able to think.* It was a no-brainer, he decided.

He turned to pack, pausing to spin the washer's dial to the hottest settings, hoping they wouldn't notice before they punched the start button, too confident in the knowledge that they'd already loaded it up to check.

* * *

Moriah

"Okay, so tell me again how this worked. You sign up and get the shots, and it realigns your cycle. And then at the full moon, you go back to the clinic and you just . . . Do it? With a random stranger? On like, a gurney?"

"*No!*" Drea squealed, hiding her face in her hands as she shook with laughter. "Sweet Mother, why do you have to make it sound like that! I already told you, it's not a stranger! *You* are the one choosing them. You can take the time to interview them after your selection process, before your first cycle!"

"First heat, you mean, right?"

Drea blew out an aggrieved breath.

"It's like you're going out of your way to make everything sound as salacious as possible."

Moriah grinned cheekily. She wasn't sure how she was meant to be responding to her friend's disclosures. Drea had left the fertility clinic in Bridgeton, too much money wasted, she had said, and Moriah nodded her agreement. She and Sorben had run through a good chunk of their savings on the ineffective treatments, a contributing factor in their marriage's demise, one for which she assumed the sole blame. It was impossible to say no. It was impossible to look hope in the eye and say 'not today.' Not when the people at the clinic were so encouraging, so optimistic that the next round would be the one that worked, seeing a dollar sign over her head every time she came back, month after month, unable to go in and quit.

Drea and Elijah had the same issue, but Drea had found out about this other clinic. A fraction of the cost, she had told Moriah. Unprecedented success rates. All she had to do was sign up, get a monthly shot, and have sex with a werewolf.

"Elijah was just okay with it?"

At that, Drea sipped her lemonade thoughtfully.

"No, he wasn't. Not at first. I mean, can you imagine? Who would be? You have to tell your husband that in order for you both to achieve the one thing you want together, you have to bring in the help of a different man who can get the job done where your husband can't. I can't imagine how demoralizing it was for him after the first conversation. He was upset. He didn't want to think about it, didn't even want to consider it. I didn't push. We're either in this together, or we're not in it at all."

She paused, sipping her drink again. The Black Sheep Beanery was bustling as it always was, and she waited until a noisy group of teenaged trolls and goblins passed their table before she resumed speaking.

"He said yes about two weeks later. Just out of the blue. 'Yes, let's do it. If it's going to work, let's do it.' He just needed time to come to terms with it. We're never going to conceive on our own; we both knew it. We toured the facility together, and I think the sterility of everything really solidified his decision. We made sure to interview our donor together. He seemed like a good, stand-up guy. I'm not going to pretend it wasn't awkward as hell the first session and only marginally better the second month. But then the third month took. And now here we are."

Her eyes were glossy, and her hand dropped to her midsection. Drea's husband, Elijah, was a soft-spoken batperson with kind eyes and a hesitant smile. Moriah tried to imagine him spending those two weeks coming to terms with things and conceded that she was in a more enviable position than her friend, at least in that regard. She had no one else who needed to come to terms with anything, only herself.

"And all you had to do was fuck a strange werewolf to make it happen."

Drea exclaimed in outrage again, hitting Moriah with her napkin as the latter laughed.

"You are the *worst*. I mean, yes. You're absolutely right; that's exactly what happens. It's not on a fucking *gurney*, though, you hag. It's... well, there are actually a few options. It's all right there in the examination room, but it's the size of one of those big hospital suites, you know, like in a private hospital if you're in extended care? There was an examination table with stirrups, a little armless couch thing, and-and a bed.

55

Everything is monitored, so you're never in danger, and like I said, it all happens in the clinic."

She had trailed off, and Moriah leaned over the table expectantly.

"And?! You honestly think I'm going to be okay with 'it all happens right there in the clinic' without any details? You said you wanted to tell me all about this place, so tell!"

She watched as her friend covered her face with her hands, the gold markings around her eyes catching the light streaming in from the coffee shop windows.

"Well, the first time we used the examination table. I think I felt more comfortable telling myself it was a procedure, you know? I had my legs in the stirrups as if I was there for a pelvic exam, and he stood between my legs and . . . Did his thing."

Moriah held up her hand and shook her head in stupefaction.

"If you think you're going to gloss over the details and hand wave me through, you're going to be sorely disappointed." Drea moaned, hiding her face in her hands again. "Suck it up, sunshine. I have cried my little tears and have had my little moment, and now I want to hear all the gory details."

"Well, we started on the examination table the second month, but we moved to the bed." She looked as if she wanted to drop through the floor, and Moriah had no doubt that if she laid the back of her hand on Drea's cheek, it would be burning hot. "He-he said he wanted to be able to get in deeper." She dropped her head to the table in mortification as Moriah leaned in, full of wonder.

"Like, hands and knees? *Doggy-style?*"

"I can't stand you. I don't know why we're friends."

"Well, am I wrong?!"

"Then the third month," she went on, ignoring Moriah, "we just . . . used the bed the whole time. Didn't bother with the examination table."

"And did he?"

Drea's brow wrinkled, not understanding the question, the gold marking shifting like flower petals.

"Did he get in deeper?"

Drea leveled her a malevolent look, but Moriah didn't care. She tried to imagine herself at such a facility, meeting with a strange man for something so intimate with doctors and nurses bustling around, her mind only able to conjure up the examination rooms at the fertility clinic with which she was already familiar. It was hardly an environment that would inspire lustful feelings, she thought.

Drea huffed in annoyance, glancing swiftly around before leaning over the table conspiratorially.

"Oh yeah, he got in deep. *Real* deep. Like, 'I'm pretty sure it was bumping into my tonsils' deep. The whole point of aligning your cycle to the moon is they get triggered by the smell of the heat, and the closer to the moon, the more their anatomy . . . changes."

Moriah sputtered.

"What the fuck is that supposed to mean? What do you mean *changes*? Are they actually *changed* when you meet for your procedure? Like, are they already wolfmen? Do I have to fuck a strange wolfman?!"

She thought her friend was going to leave. Either that or crawl beneath the table.

"No! I swear to the Mother, I am going to kick you under the table so hard . . . stop making people look at us! No, they don't change like that, not-not yet. It's the lead-up to the moon; the clinic is super particular about the timing so that no one gets hurt. But they have . . . you know, *knots* by then, and that's the point. They can go over and over again because the smell keeps them hard, and the whole point of knotting is to increase the possibility of insemination. You're basically corked up like a wine bottle."

"Wow. That sounds *so* messy."

They both dissolved into laughter at that point, but Moriah was amazed at what her friend had done.

"So now what? You're going to raise a werewolf baby then? Do you have to take classes or something?"

Drea shook her head, getting serious again.

"No, it's not like that at all. Once it takes successfully, you stay partially under the clinic's care the entire time. Like, you could still see your own OB and go to the hospital of your choice for delivery, but you'll still go to the clinic every month. They start administering in-utero suppressants at the start of the second trimester."

She must've seen the concern on Moriah's face because she quickly went on, waving her hand as if to brush away any objections Moriah may have had.

"And it's totally safe; they monitor everything every step of the way. The clinic is run by doctors, actual doctors, not like, quacks with one year of medical school. The doctor who runs the clinic, he's legit. I looked him up before we started anything, and he's been in private practice for decades; he's worked at major hospitals. He's been pioneering this process for years, so it all feels very on the up and up. And they are *busy*. Like, I thought the first time I went into the clinic, it would be this empty, depressing place, but the waiting room was full. There are a lot of women using this place, and when you consider how expensive interspecies adoption is, it's not hard to see why."

Moriah sat back, trying to absorb everything Drea had said. It gave her pause. She would be lying to her friend and herself if she were to claim that it didn't. A clinic she had never heard of, with a waiting room full of women all there to be railed by their sperm donors. It seemed preposterous. Not having to see the other person, not having to contemplate the reality of sperm donation was part of its charm, she had always thought . . . but here was her friend, happily expecting, her hand still resting over her belly, the fruit of her labors with this unnamed werewolf.

She was not averse to the idea; on the contrary. She'd always had a higher sex drive than her ex-husband and regularly made use of toys on the nights he wasn't in the mood. And if she was being honest, the almost two-year dry spell since the end of her marriage was beginning to wear her down. She didn't know how to date anymore, never really had, to be honest.

She and her ex-husband had a bit of an opposites attract relationship right from the start. He was a CPA, already five years into his professional career, and she had been finishing a fine arts degree with a specialty in interior design. Sorben was serious and stern, hard edges where she was soft, gray and practical where she embraced color and whimsy. She had been his first human relationship, and although she had dated plenty of nonhumans over the years at that point, she'd never been in a serious relationship with one. His family was friendly, if not a bit perplexed by her, and she thought it was fair to say her family was the same towards him. A human and a lizardperson were an odd match in her hometown, but once she'd moved to Cambric Creek with Sorben after university, it had seemed like anything was possible for her future.

They'd met when she had interned with the firm hired to redo the offices at the company where he worked. She had been given the opportunity to create the design boards, to collect fabric swatches and colors, creating presentation boards for the client. It wasn't his company, and he wasn't the one in charge, but he had been there the day she'd presented, a riot of butterflies moving through her as she pasted on a sunny smile, taking them through a 3D model on her laptop before showing her meticulously put together boards with colors and fabrics, an interplay of textures to give their waiting area a serene, comfortable vibe.

They'd not chosen her design. They'd gone with the bland, staid board put together by one of the senior designers, grays and blues with no pop of brightness, the same sort of hazy, indistinct pattern on the Scotchguarded chairs that one might find in any dentist or real estate office across the unification.

The experience had deflated her, buoyed only when she received an odd text, leading to an even more puzzling conversation with the stilted, awkward man on the phone. He'd picked up her name from the information left by her firm, had picked and dug until the name yielded a number, and wanted to know if she would like to have drinks with him sometime. Opposites attracted, she'd told herself, and she had enjoyed breaking his stern countenance, learning his smile was filled with more teeth than she could count. He loved the softness of her skin, and the first time she'd gone to bed with him, the sight of his two cocks, dark pink and slippery, had been overwhelmingly exciting.

She knew there were plenty of humans out there who would encounter a reptilian species and assume having two cocks would simply be too much, but she had loved taking a turn on one and then the other, and that was usually the way it went for them, particularly when Sorben had trouble keeping up with her.

"You would've been better off marrying a mothman," she remembered him grumbling at her one evening, gripping her hips and pulling her to the end of the bed. "He could fuck you all night long."

It was a nice plus, him having two members that needed satisfying. They got hard at the same time, but they wouldn't finish at the same time, not unless she persuaded him to penetrate her with both simultaneously. She loved it, but he never lasted long that way, and once he was done, she had learned to her disappointment, he was done for the night. It seemed like a waste, in the beginning, having a husband with two cocks and not taking advantage of the DP possibility as often as she could, but she was hornier than him, wanted to have sex for longer than him, and so being able to take a ride on one and then the other was an excellent way to stretch her pleasure. Different biologies, different reproductive processes, different sex drives, and different personalities. A heap of red flags foretelling an end she should have seen coming.

The thought of a partner who could go multiple rounds was thrilling. She knew from bitter experience that every month that passed was crushing, but the method of trying again would at least be a small consolation prize, a way to take the edge off for the month. And then, when you're raising a baby alone, you'll be too tired to ever have sex again. She'd never been with a werewolf or a wolf shifter before, and she was going to need to read up on this *knotting* business, she considered . . . but so far, it didn't sound like there were too many downsides, other than the mortifying awkwardness of it all. *This will catch two birds*, she thought. *Get laid and pregnant.*

Dating had been easy when she'd been in school, the proximity of her classmates fostering relationships and hookups readily, and Sorben had sought *her* out. She never had to date as a fully-formed adult, and the thought of signing up for a dating app now — thirty-four, divorced, with no idea what she was doing — terrified her. She wasn't sure if she was ready for a relationship, and in any case, she wasn't looking for one, not for this. She wanted a baby, not a partner. She didn't want to find a boyfriend, but she wouldn't say no to some mind-blowing sex. *And this place can give you both.*

"Do you have any questions?" Drea asked hesitantly, and Moriah barked out a laugh.

"I am sure I will have a million questions, but right now, I can't move past the have sex with a stranger aspect of it."

Drea glanced around again to make sure no one was there listening in.

"It was really good sex. I'd be lying if I said it wasn't. I would never cheat, and I don't need to do it ever again, but, you know. If it walks like a duck and quacks like a duck, call it what it is. Like I said, it's awkward in the beginning, but once you get used to the clinical setting, it's hard not to enjoy yourself. Plus, you know what they taught us at the place in Bridgeton, in those conception classes? If you come after he does, it sucks it up higher into your cervix? Well . . . he got that memo. He didn't stop touching me the whole time we were tied; that's what it's called, by the way, being tied. Anyway . . . yeah. It was good. Not at all a bad or scary experience, and I'm really happy with the donor partner we selected. It's all about the interview and ensuring you're comfortable with him."

Moriah found herself dropping back against the pillows on her bed when she came home that afternoon, repeatedly thinking through her friend's words. She would need to interview a stranger, would need to have *sex* with that stranger, and would do so in a hospital setting! It all seemed too outlandish to be real.

That didn't stop her from palming her phone, biting her lip as she tapped in a search for *werewolf knots*, cheeks heating at the cache of videos that popped up instantly. She clicked on one featuring a muscular man with well-defined glutes, hammering into a petite woman with blonde hair, his enormous scrotum slapping into her obscenely as the camera panned around. She got her first good look at the bulge at the base of his shaft. With every thrust into the young woman, the bulge — his knot – pressed to her opening, threatening to breach her. When he did so at last, the young woman moaned, her back arching from the bed, and Moriah was almost surprised to find that sometime throughout the video, her hand had slipped beneath the waistband shorts, her fingers circling insistently. The man dropped against the girl, his cock still firmly lodged within her, and Moriah decided she needed to see more.

You don't want to go into this unprepared, right? That would be embarrassing! It was going to take, she decided, settling back to get comfortable, after kicking off her shorts and scrolling on to the following video, a *lot* of research.

* * *

Lowell

"You should find some volunteer work," his mother advised several weeks after his move from Jackson's guest suite to Grayson's pool house.

He grumbled something he hoped sounded like an answer, hauling the last of his equipment cases he'd left at his parents' house down the flatbed of the enormous truck.

"Volunteer work will center your chi," his mother went on, surveying the collection of rolling cases littering the walkway of Grayson's front yard. "You're too restless; it's not good for you. You should come to the meditation studio with me sometime. And I don't understand why you'd rather sleep next to barrels of chlorine than just come home. I have a room all ready for you."

"Because I want to swim every day," he rationalized, ignoring both her frown and the fact that there was a pool at his parent's house as well. It wasn't as big as Grayson's, though, nor did it possess the tiered decks and spa-like opulence, and if he was going to waste away from loneliness, boredom, and depression, he at least wanted to be surrounded by his brother's extravagant taste. "And this is the guest cabana, not the storage room. It's a decent size guest house, too! That's not just a 'whoops, my car is blocked in' option. Wow, how wild *are* Grayson's parties that he needs to give people a place to crash? They must be doing some hardcore partying to necessitate this whole set-up."

It took several beats for the implication of his words to sink in before his mother stiffened, marching off back to the house where Grayson — who was meant to be taking a day off but was actually working from home, a fact which Lowell could discern from the occasional heated shouting coming from the house — was visible in the kitchen window, her younger son's guilt trip forgotten for the moment. Lowell stifled his laughter when Grayson appeared at the glass doors several minutes later, scowling toward the pool house. *Better him than me.*

Victoria had arrived home with little Jack before he had left, and Lowell was glad she at least got to see her mother-in-law's vehicle in the driveway. *Maybe she'll tell Jackson I'm just moving home.* It might be a few days, perhaps even a week before Jackson found out the truth, and by then, Lowell was confident he and Gray would have already moved on to some new contest that didn't mean anything to anyone else in the entire world other than the two of them, that they would still manage to make everyone else's problem.

His sister-in-law had seemed relieved, although she had tried to feign disappointment. She wasn't as good an actor as Jackson, and she would need to work on that before they entered the political sphere, he opined, reminding himself that he had been an intruder in her home, a disrupter of her routine, and that Jackson had probably not even asked her first before calling him. She covered it well enough, exclaiming how much little Jack would miss him, and that part, at least, was true.

Lowell was going to miss his nephew. It was the *only* thing about Jackson's house he was going to miss, but it was a significant thing. He often felt left out and isolated amongst the family, but he hadn't realized what else he had been missing out on.

He'd been home for a holiday shortly after little Jack's birth, when he was a black-eyed, squalling newborn, too terrifying to hold. He saw his nephew again when he was slightly older, able to sit up in a high chair at the edge of the table, covered in food from his hairline to his chin, giggling and babbling at everyone, not at all interesting. Lowell wasn't sure how he had gone from saying no words one of the last times he saw him, when the kiddo was only one or two, to now being able to say *all* the words, including those he wasn't supposed to. Everyone in the family seemed to have endless patience for his nephew — even their father, who had only ever had a rumor of patience for Lowell, but was somehow his grandson's best friend — and everyone was endlessly amused by the things he did and said. Despite the long absence and being a virtual stranger, Lowell had done the same.

He had always liked children. Unsurprising, when he still considered himself to be practically a child. There had been a nearly embarrassing moment earlier that same year when a shady-seeming character had trailed after him as he navigated his way back to his temporary lodging during a shoot. The man tailed him as he rounded corners and doubled back, and the hair on the back of his neck had prickled, his wolf shifting uneasily in his bones. The country was known for being a hub of trafficking, and he had wondered, for a brief instant, before he remembered that he was, in fact, both a werewolf and a grown-ass man, if he was about to be kidnapped. The week had ended with his thirty-second birthday, celebrated with a handful of his friends, copious amounts of alcohol, and a threesome — a sobering reminder that he was far, far away from being a desirable target.

He wasn't sure if it was a personality defect or not and didn't really want to examine it that closely, but whatever it was that made him feel like he was actually three five-year-olds in a trench coat made him entirely approachable to actual children, and his little nephew had been no exception. He had lost track of the time he spent photographing the rambunctious pre-schooler — at play, at rest, eating, bathing, sleeping, it didn't matter: the youngest Hemming seemed to be a flurry of motion at all times, flailing arms and fluttering eyelashes and non-stop energy, and Lowell attempted to capture all of it, his mood buoyed by his nephew's wide-eyed exploration of the world, understanding the boy's frustration at having to sit and eat his vegetables when the evenings were so warm, wanting to liberate him from the shackles of an early bedtime.

"That's fine, Lowell," Victoria would sigh. "As long as you're the one responsible for getting him up tomorrow for school."

Thus far, his nephew had been the only bright spot of his forced visit home.

"You and your dad need to visit me every week, and we'll swim in the pool. Okay, buddy?"

He hadn't been prepared for the strange tightness in his chest as he crouched to say goodbye to his nephew, unprepared for the moment when little Jack had wrapped tight arms around Lowell's neck, planting a wet kiss on his cheek, certain the last time he'd been home for any length of time the kiddo had still had a gummy baby's smile. *He's not even going to remember you the next time you're in town.*

If Grayson had been surprised to see him, that day he'd left Jackson's house for good, he'd not let on. He'd not said anything at all, really. Lowell had been in the living room, sitting cross-legged on one of the chairs, his laptop balancing on his knee and his pulse jumping in his throat when he heard the car door slam. The sky had been dark for several hours, and he had begun to wonder if his brother was coming home at all. Gray had come in through the attached garage into the kitchen, tie loosened, jacket slung over his arm, and radiating weariness, slowing slightly when he spotted Lowell but not stopping until he had reached the refrigerator. He'd paused, disappearing inside and reappearing with two bottles, before crossing the room to drop heavily into the other chair.

"You'd better not fuck up, because Trapp doesn't want you. Just putting that out there. You're going to wind up sleeping on Owen's couch."

Lowell had grinned, taking a long sip from the bottle he'd been handed, shaking his head.

"I'll move to Bridgeton, take my chances with the humans first. It's not like they can get me sick. I could probably clean up doing pizza delivery right now."

Gray had laughed, a deep rumble that was familiar and oddly comforting.

"I guess that's better than the Blinxieburger mascot, right? Although I'm not sure 'the kind of clinical depression they put you in the hospital for' is the kind of thing you should share in your interview. Do we need to admit you to a clinic or what?"

"I don't think I'm that far gone quite yet. It's just that, you know, existential dread of being trapped in a place where I'll never be anything more than someone better's little brother and a general feeling of internal worthlessness. Normal stuff. Plus, I have no friends here, no one to talk to all day, and I haven't had sex since I left my apartment."

"Well, there's the problem, kid. You need to get laid. The alarm sets automatically. I'm going to bed."

That had been several weeks ago. His mother was right — he hadn't intended to call the guest cabana his temporary home, far from it, but he was set in his decision. It had happened a week or two after his arrival, right before the weekend, not that weekends were any different than Mondays or Tuesdays, not for him. Grayson stayed at his apartment in the city several days a week, quashing Lowell's tentative overtures that perhaps he could simply move in there.

"That's a shared cohabitation that is not big enough to add a Lowell tornado. No dice, kid."

He hadn't elaborated and Lowell had been too busy huffing in outrage over being called a tornado to question Gray's words, but he had a moment of dawning clarity late one Friday night, returning from an evening run. He had just let himself in through the kitchen door, still slightly out of breath, stopping short at the sight of a barely dressed woman, bumping the refrigerator door shut with her hip, twenty paces ahead.

Her ass was a perfect heart, emphasized by her lace boy shorts, the matching lace bralette not leaving much to the imagination above the waist. Her dark hair was pulled up in a high ponytail as she crossed the long room, dropping to the sofa and stretching herself out against the supine form of his equally undressed brother.

Lowell realized he was still standing in the shadow of the doorway, still hidden in the darkness of the hallway leading to the utility and laundry rooms, that he still might be able to slip out unseen. He couldn't tell if it was the same woman he had met at his parents' house, for he had been too busy sulking that Grayson wasn't speaking to him and playing with little Jack to pay her much mind. It seemed an impossibility, for Grayson went through women the way most people changed their underwear, but as he watched, his brother's giant hand landed on the dark-haired woman's hip. She flipped through channels with the remote in front of the projection screen she had lowered from the ceiling, seeming entirely comfortable in the space and with

Grayson beneath her, in a way that spoke volumes. As comfortable and unselfconscious as if she practically lived there.

A shared cohabitation.

He didn't know why the thought of playing the third wheel to Grayson and his apparent girlfriend made his stomach twist in a way it never had with Jackson and Victoria. Perhaps because Gray had always been reliably single, a reliable womanizer, a reliable partier. He didn't want to stand awkwardly before them in this little domestic tableau, a reminder of how utterly alone in the world he was; didn't care to learn what sort of perfect princess this woman must be to have tamed his immoral rake of a brother, and Lowell decided he didn't really want to find out.

He stepped backward out of the doorway, slipping out of the house. He would have to move back in with his parents, the most humiliating prospect he could imagine. He wasn't going there tonight, though. He would make do in the guest house by the pool. He didn't know at the time if the cabana was heated or not, but he decided one night of being miserably cold would be worth not needing to walk through that room, past Grayson and whoever she was.

The guest cabana was heated. Heated and had wifi. It wasn't as luxurious as his bedroom in the house, but it had *a* bed, a perfectly serviceable bathroom, and a refrigerator. He would still need to go into the house, but it wasn't as if Grayson was kicking him out. It was far enough away that he may as well have been on a different block, giving him all the privacy he wanted. It would do, Lowell decided. He'd crept into the house the following morning with a laundry basket, grocery shopping from Grayson's refrigerator as if he were stocking up for the winter, generously deciding to put back one of the imported beers for his brother. *Ms. Perfect Ass can fend for herself.*

The months were passing him in a blur. He barely knew what to do with himself without work providing him a schedule. Without flights to catch and shoots to coordinate, he felt adrift, unsure of what to do with his time and thus squandering it in afternoons that turned to evening in a few minutes and days that seemed to run indistinguishably into each other. He still didn't have anyone to talk to, didn't know how to make friends in his hometown, particularly with the Hemming name hanging on him like a sash everywhere he went, and for the first time since he had left Cambric Creek for University, Lowell regretted not keeping in touch with any of his friends from high school and from the neighborhood. But now he was still bored, still lonely, still so horny he thought he might perish from the ache of unfulfillment. The days of the week ceased to have meaning, every day felt like it might have been a Thursday, and before he noticed, another whole month had passed, another month of twenty-four-hour news coverage and cereal and no answer from his office, the full moon was nearing again.

The only time he didn't feel as if he were adrift in an empty sea was during the change. His wolf was able to *run*. Ran without care, without worrying about his career or his future, didn't think twice about the fact that he had no friends here, no love interest, nothing but a phone that didn't ring, an itch under his skin he couldn't scratch alone, and days that slid into each other with an alarming speed. His wolf was free in a way he could never be.

The previous month, he had strapped one of the kayaks to the hood of the car he'd been given to drive, and had driven as far into the woods as he could go. Past Shadowbend, where his three eldest brothers had been left cabins, past the last ranger station, which signified the end of the Applethorpe Wood, into the Black Hills beyond, until the road had run out, and he was forced to stop. He would kayak until his arms were like noodles, and prepare himself for the change. Unlike his pampered brothers, he didn't need a fancy cabin. He had pitched a tent and slept on the bare ground more times than he could count, in conditions far harsher than the Applethorpe Wood. He liked going this deep into the forest. He knew there would be a chance of other werewolves there as well, but he was less likely to run into anyone he might know.

He woke groggy and sore in the morning, with a gash on his forehead and a pleasant ache in his groin, the pleasurable emptiness of balls drained dry. There was dried blood crusting down his temple and more on his pillow, but his cock was soft and satisfied. He had no idea who he'd been with or what happened, and it was a dangerous situation that made him tighten in panic.

Dangerous for himself, dangerous for whoever this unknown partner had been, and most importantly, it was not the sort of risky behavior he undertook when he was living overseas. This was a new development, and he didn't like what it said about his current state of mind. He felt trapped in a box, and maybe his mother was right. He wasn't sure about volunteer work, but he needed to do *something* before his recklessness increased and he wound up getting himself killed.

He swam laps in Grayson's pool like he was training for the Olympics, trying to outswim the creeping ennui that seemed to shadow each day. He couldn't account for the hollow feeling that had taken up residence in his chest since he'd been home, the way he was beginning to second guess every choice he'd made in the last decade. *A feeling of hopelessness is to be expected right now, particularly with no end to the disruption of our normal lives in sight,* that was what the mental health experts on cable news said every day, but that was for *humans,* nevermind the fact that his life was being impacted because of them. He was unused to feeling uncertain, just as he was unused to staying in one place for long, and the feeling was unsettling.

The only time it abated were those brief hours beneath the shining full moon, running through the forest with the wind whistling in his ears, free for the moment.

His mother was right. Volunteer work wasn't a terrible idea, he supposed.

He'd been still chewing over the idea a few mornings later when he saw the flyer. The silhouette of a happy family, the mother cradling an infant to her chest and smiling beatifically beneath the intriguing text.

Are you a healthy werewolf aged 25-40?

We need you! Help families achieve their dreams

Call us for information today

Lowell read and reread the flyer several times, not gleaning any better idea of what service it advertised on the fifth reading than he had on the first, before snapping a photo with his phone.

He was unprepared for the conversation which resulted.

"What we offer is a revolutionary new way for families to achieve their goal of natural childbirth, particularly those interspecies couples unable to have a child together due to reproductive incompatibility."

The doctor to whom his call had been transferred — once he'd answered a brief survey of questions confirming that he was, in fact, a healthy werewolf within the desired age bracket — had an impassioned manner of speaking, and Lowell leaned forward on his elbows, eyebrows drawn as he wondered if this actually constituted as "volunteer" work.

"Our donors are not just contributing genetic material. They are providing the opportunity for these families to end months of frustration and money wasted. Interspecies adoption is cost-prohibitive for most families, as you may know, and the viability of in vitro fertilization is extremely low for mixed-species couples . . . in contrast, we are not another dead end. Due to the uniqueness of our service, our success rate is unparalleled."

Contributing genetic material.

"It's sperm donation," Lowell cut in, attempting to find the straightest path forward, as he always did. "Why do you specifically need werewolves?"

"Ah, that is where you're wrong. The service we provide is far more than merely donating sperm in a specimen cup. The success rate depends on actual copulatory practices, and the unique physiology of the lupine male provides the most effective method to ensure successful insemination."

"On actual..." His cock twitched as he considered the meaning behind the doctor's words. "Actual *intercourse*?"

Being trapped in a succession of his brother's homes had been challenging in more ways than one, and if he didn't have sex soon, Lowell was sure he would perish from terminal horniness. Grayson's pool-side cabana afforded privacy, but being a Hemming in Cambric Creek was a handicap in and of itself. He couldn't simply walk into one of the numerous bars and restaurants and pubs without people knowing who he was merely by knowing one of his brothers. Eyes followed his family wherever they went in Cambric Creek, waiting for the misstep that would add to the daily gossip mill, and the scrutiny had been a significant factor in his leaving. He was never going to be as upright and perfect as Jackson, or as smart and successful and conniving as Grayson, or as handsome and beloved as Trapp, and being lost in the middle of the shuffle meant always being compared to one of them. No one expected *him* to be mayor or a judge or sit on the commissioner's board, and somehow the *lack* of expectation cut almost as deeply as the presumption that he would live up to his name.

He would love to simply go out and get laid as his brother suggested, but it wasn't that easy, at least not for him.

"That's correct. You see, a lunar estrus cycle is triggered in each patient . . ."

The doctor's words fell away as Lowell mentally slotted the final piece of the puzzle together. Lunar estrus was just a fancy term for a heat, and if the *copulation* would be taking place at the full moon . . . *the unique physiology of the lupine male.*

"I'd be *knotting* someone?!"

His cock twitched again, thickening at the thought. The danger of the turn, the reproductive ramifications, outing oneself as a werewolf — there was much that could go wrong in such a scenario, and it was an act rarely indulged in.

It was a lecture they'd all received from their father once puberty hit, and from the notes compared with his brothers, Jack's speech remained the same from son to son: you do *not* knot your partners. The risk of injury was present, the risk of an unwanted pregnancy substantial, and life as a werewolf outside of Cambric Creek's well-sheltered borders was not always a picnic. It had been mortifying, and he clearly remembered holding his breath, trying to disappear into the cushions of the sofa as his father paced agitatedly before him and Owen, but the lecture had stuck. He'd had more partners than he could count who'd been disappointed he'd not knotted them, not understanding that the *unique physiology* was something that came with the turn. *And these people are willing to pay for it!*

On the other end of the line, the doctor cleared his throat.

"We don't like to use that term, but yes, essentially. The breeding instinct triggered by the smell of a receptive female, coupled with the reproductive advantage of the bulbous glandis is quite sufficient to—"

Lowell shifted, his erection practically scraping the table's underside. *The breeding instinct.* Completely animalistic, mindless rutting, over and over into a woman in heat who would be writhing and begging for his cock, for his knot, tightening around him as he filled her repeatedly, again and again until he was spent and she was full of his seed.

"The process is completely safe. Everything happens in our clinic, and the safety of both the donor and recipient is our utmost concern. If you are worried about being unduly othered, let me put your fears to rest — the clinic founders and all its doctors are of the lupine persuasion, and we take the privacy of our donors very seriously. You will be in good hands with us."

He thought of Jackson's little boy, running and playing at all hours of the day — catching fireflies and frogs in the creek, chasing his ball, asking to be pushed on the swings, never slowing. He'd told himself that he'd taken endless photos of the boy to make portraits for mother and grandmother alike, but there was a nagging remorse that he'd missed so much of his nephew's life. He didn't want to exist on the forgotten edge of another family member's life; he wanted to *be* someone to his nephew.

"Helping" another family experience the joy of those toothy smiles and sticky hands and ice cream-smeared chins sounded wonderfully altruistic if one ignored the reality of the expectations. The donor werewolves were compensated, and he could donate those funds to the clinic or another charity. He may have been from a highly sought-after bloodline, but he had no plans to tie himself down to a mortgage and family in Cambric Creek, not anytime soon, despite his mother's wishes . . . . but he could give that gift to another family.

The clinic was in Starling Heights, a decent enough distance from Cambric Creek to ensure he'd not likely run into anyone who would know him. Devotion to family, loyalty to pack, service to community, that's what his parents were always going on about. There seemed no better service to the community than to help a family achieve their desire for a child . . . and the fact that he would actually get to enjoy the process was all the better.

"I'll do it," he blurted, knuckles tightening on the table. He was going stir crazy, the open road normally before him abruptly curtailed, and he *needed* something to break up the monotony of his new non-routine. He could help a family, could do something worthwhile with his time for as long as he was stuck here. *And it won't be so terrible for you either,* he thought, an end to the hometown dry spell. "Where do I sign?"

* * *

Moriah

She had visited the clinic too late in the month.

It had been her own fault, Moriah reminded herself. Too late in the month, and it was no one's fault but her own. She'd been told the clinic's protocol and the strict adherence to the lunar calendar she needed to adopt. She'd waffled thinking about it, had agonized over the ethics of artificially suppressing a baby's nature, had hesitated over how comfortable she'd be with the insemination process, and her indecision had cost her precious days.

Her return to the clinic had come with both a warm welcome and a good-natured tongue click from the same doctor, reminding her of the importance of adhering to the lunar calendar going forward.

"The good news is we can get you set up this month, the first exam out of the way and in the system, and start you on your first shot. We won't be able to match you with a donor at this point, but you have an extra few weeks to choose someone. We'll just look at that as our silver lining. How does that sound?"

The doctor was lovely, unfailingly kind, and she found the initial pelvic examination not quite as coldly invasive as she had grown accustomed to at the fertility clinic in Bridgeton.

"Cervix is an ideal length and texture, no problematic angling that I can feel. We don't seem to have anything impeding us from proceeding."

She'd given blood, had a Pap smear, and was sent home with the glossy catalog of donors once she had signed a privacy contract and paid her first deposit. The collection of donors was simultaneously not as thick as she'd been expecting and completely overwhelming, page after page of headshots with accompanying statistics. She'd started reading each caption, applying the information to the faces above, but after a few pages, she realized it would take her several months to get through the whole thing, and she began flipping.

Some of the wolves captured in the pages had attempted to look as sexy and seductive as possible. They had practiced broody expressions, and while they may have been attractive, the artifice of their photos put her off. After all, this wasn't a dating site. *If I wanted someone to give me Blue Steel, I could go to Gildersnood and Ives on any Friday night.*

In addition to the posers, there were several pages worth of men with harsh, stern expressions, unsmiling and humorless. Sorben had been severe, and although her sunny optimism had softened his edges in the beginning, when it became clear they would not conceive on their own and she fell into depression, his soberness had provided her little comfort. She supposed the icy aura the stern, unsmiling men projected might have been attractive to some women, but the idea of undertaking this with such a partner made her guts twist with anxiety as she lingered over their photos, quickly flipping the pages away.

It was then that she saw him. She turned the page away from one of the unsmiling, stern wolves staring up from the catalog, and her eyes landed on the center of the next page, meeting the eyes of a handsome, dark-haired man with a brilliant smile. He was the first photo she'd come across where his smile seemed genuine. Many of the other wolves in the pages were smiling, but it was the forced smile of a posed photograph, resembling high school yearbooks and professional headshots.

This man, by contrast, looked as though he had been laughing only a breath before the photograph was snapped, his smile big and unconscious, eyes crinkled with the force of it. He was different from the dozens and dozens of other pictures she'd looked at by then. He seemed to radiate a happy sort of energy that was palpable even through the flat, glossy booklet in her hand.

He sparkled, she decided, grinning back, in spite of herself. Handsome, well-educated, and athletic, with no known health concerns. He came from a big family, had been tested for illness and reproductive issues, passed all with flying colors, and made a living as a photojournalist.

He's probably seen the whole world, she thought giddily, genuine excitement overtaking her nerves for the first time since Drea had made her disclosures about the clinic. His eyes held a mischievous gleam, and she could tell without needing to hear it that he had an excellent laugh.

They really ought to show full-body shots. I wonder if they have a feedback section. They're giving weight and height, would adding dick length really kill them?

He was two years younger than her, not that it made a difference, she reminded herself hastily. It wasn't as if they were going to be dating; besides, two years was negligible. *That doesn't make you a cougar.* He was handsome, and more than that, he looked friendly. *Now you need to interview him*, she thought, remembering Drea's advice. *Lowell.*

The only thing that gave her any pause was the italicized notation that he was a twin. She desperately wanted a baby but didn't want to have two to raise on her own. *But twins don't run in your family, so it'll probably be fine, right?* She would pick a backup to be safe; that was the responsible thing to do. She continued to page through the catalog until she found a second face that appealed to her, although not nearly as much as the sparkling man called Lowell had.

It had been a relatively straightforward process from there. She'd logged into the clinic's online portal, typing in the number that corresponded with his picture into the required field, receiving a slightly more detailed statistical sheet that included a breakdown of all the blood tests he'd already completed, as well as the results of a semen sample he'd provided. Moriah attempted to parse the medical jargon, happy with the clean bill of health he'd been given, unable to stop herself from going to the kitchen and fetching a measuring cup once she had done the metric conversion on her phone to see exactly what his semen output had looked like. *Not bad,* she thought, swirling around the measuring cup of water with a grin. *A lot more than a human dribble, but nothing like a centaur's fire hose.*

She'd already done her homework and knew that werewolves were not the same as humans, as she had previously thought. She lived her entire life assuming they were normal humans with a monthly affliction, not realizing they were, in fact, a completely different species, possessing a different genetic makeup. She had examined the side-by-side double helix of an average human man and an average werewolf man, reading about the different genomes and nucleotides and other words she didn't quite understand until she was dizzy, deciding to simply accept that her assumptions had been incorrect.

From there, her search history had become a little less academic. It was no secret that multi-species pornography was a booming industry, and it hadn't taken long to find videos featuring werewolves. Their cocks were bigger than humans'; that was the first thing she noticed. Larger penis and fatter, heavier balls, and then, of course, there was the knot. Almost all of the videos featuring werewolves featured a knot, because wasn't that the whole point, she thought with a queasy laugh. The size and color seemed to depend on the wolf, but they all shared the same shape — a plump protrusion at the base of the shaft on both sides, the thickness varying slightly between men. The women in the videos seemed to take the thick bulbs with ease, and she wondered if she would eventually reach that level of expertise. *You're getting so far ahead of yourself . . .*

She had twisted in nerves all day and night, wondering how she ought to go about contacting him. Once the clinic called to confirm that he had been notified of her choosing, Moriah decided it was time to stop waffling.

Hi there, this is Moriah. I'm the one who picked you. From the clinic, I mean.

They already let me know that you've been notified.

I was hoping we could set up a time for an interview to make sure we are a good fit together. I look forward to hearing back from you!

As soon as the text was sent, she dropped her phone, burying her face in her hands. You probably sounded too stilted and professional. *Maybe you should have just called him. Perhaps this is all a big mistake, and you should just forget it. Move to Paris or Amsterdam or Rome, do some traveling like you've always wanted. See the world and just forget about this.*

When her phone buzzed across the table, she almost screamed.

I was so excited to receive the call!

Absolutely, just tell me when and where.

I hope you think I'm a good fit!

She squealed at his use of exclamation points, able to feel his bright smile and energy radiating through the phone. She wasn't sure where Drea and Elijah had met their donor wolf, but there was strength in numbers, and she didn't feel comfortable meeting him alone right off the bat. *It would be wise to pick a public place, she decided. But so many businesses are closed.* If it weren't for the news, it would be almost easy to forget the pandemic in Cambric Creek. The grocery store was still open; restaurants and pubs were operating normally. She and Dr. Ulric had discussed the current state of things when she'd been in the office, and he'd shaken his head mournfully.

"Absolutely dreadful things going on in the world right now. But you can rest assured that your donor wolf will not be a carrier of this virus. All you need to be concerned with is keeping yourself healthy."

I might need to make a few calls to see what businesses are still open, she tapped out, biting her lip. Starling Heights was also mixed-species, although there was a much larger human population. She felt okay going out and about amongst her neighbors here in town, but she wanted to avoid mingling with her own kind as much as possible.

If you don't mind traveling a bit, there's a town nearby without a substantial population of humans where we could meet?

Her cheeks flushed as she sent the text, not wanting to admit that "the town nearby" was where she called home. *Let him think you're from Starling Heights. That's for the best.*

I think I know the place? It's right before Bridgeton, right?

She sagged in relief.

Yes, I think that's the one!

Let me call and make sure their businesses are still open.

Then I can let you know where?

Would next Tuesday work for you, or is that still too close to the full moon?

She held her breath, exhaling in noisy relief at his immediate response.

Tuesday is perfect

Just shoot me an address when you decide on a place!

I'm really looking forward to meeting you.

She wasn't proud of the way she squealed into a pillow once she set the phone down, nor of the happy dance she did around her living room, but there was no one there to see, she rationalized. The Black Sheep Beanery would be too noisy, too crowded, the entire town moving through its doors several times a day. There was another coffee shop, though, near the industrial Parkway, sandwiched between a gym and a laundromat that would serve her purposes admirably for this meeting. *There might even be a little lunch café over there that would work.* It was a bit off the beaten path, not anywhere close to the downtown's hustle and bustle, where they could take their time talking. This is going to be great. Everything is going to start looking up. *You're letting joy find you,* she thought decisively, once again allowing hope to take up residence in her chest.

By the week's end, she was sure joy had taken a wrong turn. What had found her instead was a twisting, cramping agony that she was sure would be the end of her. Her pulse was racing, sweat beaded on her forehead, and she hunched around a pillow on her sofa, breathing shallowly. Her hips canted on their own accord, seeking a relief that was not present. She needed to be filled; she knew in her bones. It was the only thing that would stop this aching burn, to be fucked and filled until she forgot her name and her heartbeat finally evened out.

Moriah swallowed, shifting on the sofa miserably. The ticking of the clock on the mantle seemed to echo through the house. Each hollow click brought her closer to the full moon, closer to her fate, and the sound reverberated through her chest until she was unable to distinguish it from the beating of her heart. Drea hadn't mentioned anything about this part. She hadn't said that going into heat was tantamount to torture and that Moriah could expect to feel as if she were being fully alive every moment she was not stuffed full of a fat werewolf knot.

She never experienced this because she understood how to make an appointment at the right time of the month, you fucking idiot. When the phone buzzed beside her, jarring the monotonous syncopation of the clock, she nearly jumped out of her skin. Lowell's name flashed on the screen, and her heartbeat outraced the ticking of the timepiece.

Hi, just wanted to check in and make sure nothing has changed

I hope you're holding up okay

See you Tuesday?

He's so nice, she thought, pushing the pillow between her knees. He was friendlier than Kinley, the other face she'd chosen from the catalog at the clinic. She'd reached out to him as well, feeling obligated once he'd been notified that she'd potentially selected him, although his responses didn't send a riot of butterflies moving through her.

I'm okay. Getting through it.

Thanks for checking in

The overwhelming silence of the house seemed to press her into the sofa, flattening her with its oppressiveness, but there was nothing to be done. She had to stay indoors. Despite the tardiness of her consultation, the injections had triggered her period right on time. The temperature chart that she filled out diligently showed that she was, in fact, ovulating, the heat burning through her. It wouldn't do to catch the nose of a werewolf she hadn't vetted from a glossy catalog, after all.

Thumbing open her pictures, she scrolled to the photos she'd snapped of her two donor choices and set Lowell's contact info to show his bright smile before she could change her mind. He was potentially going to be the father of her child, after all.

She'd already decided that she would tell her parents that she had conceived via artificial insemination. She knew they wouldn't care, would be over the moon and wouldn't ask questions, wouldn't need to know she'd gone two towns over to be literally bred like a bitch in heat. No one would need to know the process, she thought, staring at his picture. *He seems nice, nice and friendly and laid back. It's going to be okay.* It was a pep talk she gave herself often. She'd read her fill on the way he would smell her heat, how a werewolf on the cusp of the change could breed repeatedly, of the way she'd be stoppered by his knot until he softened, and the process would start all over again. *It's going to be fine.*

Staring at the phone, she tried to reconcile the fact that the smiling man in the photograph would be fucking her senseless in one month, harder still to understand how much she *wanted* it, that she was twisting on her sofa, thinking about being filled and stretched, over and over again until he was a snarling beast, all trace of the smiling man gone. It was going to be a very long month.

Have a good change?

Lol, is that right? Happy full moon?

I can't wait to meet you next week.

* * *

Lowell

"Okay, first of all, let's get something clear. I never want to see your balls on my phone screen first thing in the morning ever again. *Ever* again. Don't send me pictures of your scrotum unprompted, understand? For that matter, let's expand that to include your entire lower anatomy, since I know you're a fucking stickler for semantics. I don't want to see your asshole. I don't want to see your chewed open frenulum. You want to let your girlfriend treat you like a Milkbone? That's between you and her; I don't care what goes on in your bedroom. But here's the important part — I'm not your doctor. So before you even think about asking me if that looks infected, why don't you consider that the question you really ought to be asking is why the woman who allegedly loves you bit your scrotum so hard that we would be able to identify her through dental records from your ball sack."

Grayson's deep laughter reverberated through the truck's speaker, and Lowell mumbled to himself that this was one call Trapp could have used the handset for.

"Okay, but *does* it look infected?"

"I mean, it doesn't look great, Gray. Most bites to the balls don't."

"I'm supposed to be able to eat breakfast after this?" Lowell piped up, earning Trapp's wide grin.

"I don't see any discharge——"

"If you say the word 'puss,' I'm jumping out into traffic," Lowell interrupted, scowling as Trapp continued, paying him no mind.

"——But I don't like how red it looks."

"So you're saying I need to see the doctor."

"I'm saying you absolutely, one hundred percent ought to see a doctor, both of you together. For couple's counseling. But you might want to see if that needs debridement, and you should probably get a two-course antibiotic."

"I don't like the way that sounds."

"Yeah, well, you're going to like the way it feels even less. Next time get her one of those rubber balls you stuff with peanut butter if she wants to bite something so badly. Or don't and let her keep trying to pop your balls like they're water balloons; it's your life. But stop sending me the proof. You're making me an accessory."

"Is she a wolf or a rabid dog?" Lowell muttered under his breath, not loud enough for Grayson to pick up, earning Trapp's silent laughter.

His self-imposed banishment to the pool house had turned out to not be as dramatic as he'd led his mother to believe. Grayson still spent the majority of his week in Bridgeton. His girlfriend only showed up at the house on weekends, sometimes not even then. He had alluded to the fact that they lived together in the city only that one time, but he rarely talked about himself and his private life to anyone but Trapp, and had never mentioned that fact again.

The only time Lowell mentally made the house off limits was when Vanessa was in residence, which usually meant the week leading up to the full moon and the day after, and when the heat of summer set in, not even his guest cabana was safe. She liked to lay out beside the pool, and he had only needed to catch her topless twice before he decided to simply take himself out of the equation during the full moons altogether, loading up the kayak and driving to the lake. He didn't need to be inadvertently aroused by his brother's girlfriend, didn't need to catch them having sex next to his cabana's little window, and didn't want to be made to feel like he was in the way.

He'd sat on the kitchen counter stuffing his face with takeout noodles a few weeks earlier, on one of the rare weeknights Grayson was home, having just flown in from several days in the capitol. He listened, from his position atop the counter to his brother's phone conversation. It was work-related, and most of the legal jargon went over his head, but Lowell could tell it was Vanessa on the other end of the line from his brother's tone of voice, slightly gentler and less strident than he usually was.

"So, is she actually your girlfriend, or what? Never thought I'd see the day where you settle down with only one. Does she taste like candy or something?"

Gray had grinned in response, pulling a fork from the drawer and the takeout container from Lowell's hand, helping himself. Lowell had scowled, removing the second white takeout container from the bag on the counter beside him, glad he'd been prepared.

"She's smart, she's ambitious. She's mouthy as fuck. Gorgeous tits. Puts up with me, somehow. And yes, she does taste like candy, now that you mention it. What's not to love?"

"Trapp said she's kind of crazy," Lowell pointed out in between a mouthful of noodles.

What Trapp had actually said when Lowell had questioned him about Vanessa's monthly presence at Grayson's home, including joining them for brunch at their parents' house after every moon, was that she was crazy, but her crazy complemented Grayson's crazy, and that they were very good together. Lowell remained unconvinced. He didn't like sharing the limited attention he received with anyone, least of all some stranger, particularly one who had displaced him from the main house and sat whispering with his father each month, an indulgence usually only granted to his eldest sons.

Gray had only laughed, turning away with Lowell's noodles.

"If they're not a little crazy, what's the fucking point in living?"

The point is not needing stitches on your scrotum, he thought, mentally revisiting the conversation. Lowell closed his eyes, resting his forehead against the passenger window of Trapp's truck as he and Gray continued their conversation. It was too fucking early to be awake, too early to hear about his brother's violent sex life with his supervillain girlfriend, too early to do anything but bundle up in a cocoon of blankets and go back to sleep. *You should just get out at the next intersection and walk home. It's not like they really want you there.*

They were going to meet Jack and Liam for breakfast, a standing date the youngest Hemming son had with their father twice a week from the sounds of it, skipping his morning study hall every Monday and Wednesday, a luxury that had not been afforded to Lowell at any point in his life. Trapp joined them on Wednesdays, and he had been invited to come as well.

He had been at the Pickled Pig with Grayson and Trapp when the former had instructed Trapp to bring Lowell to breakfast, the first time he was learning of the standing affair, even though he had been home for what felt like six years at that point.

"Can you please bring him the fuck with you next week? I realize it's just for an hour or two, but it'll be two hours less of him creating mischief in every fucking room of my house."

"I can't believe you've been getting breakfast together all this time, and no one ever invited me," he had fumed after two rounds of drinks, feeling incredibly sorry for himself. He had been home for *months*. Months that felt like years and only a handful of weeks depending on the hour of the day with nothing to break up the monotony, and just across town, his brothers were yukking it up with their father twice a week over bacon and eggs.

Trapp had merely rolled his eyes.

"Lowell, I have asked you to come with us so many fucking times, I can't even count. I asked you the first week you were home, but you had to call your office every day to see if there were any updates, even though they had just kicked you out of the fucking country forty-eight hours earlier. I asked you a few weeks later when you were staying with Jackson, and you couldn't be assed to get out of bed that early. I just texted you, like, two or three weeks ago, as a matter of fact, to let you know I would pick you up on the way, and you never responded."

"Yeah, because I was asleep! Who has breakfast at seven o'clock in the morning?!"

"Grownups with jobs," Grayson had answered succinctly, and Lowell had just groaned. He'd walked into that one and knew better than to let Grayson trap him any further.

"Yeah, you know what? That's fine. Get me out of the house for a few hours. It's not like I have anything left to see there. Did you know he has a sensory deprivation tank and a marble steam room in his bathroom? Who the fuck spends that much money on *humidity*? Did you actually have a custom drawer made for all your sex toys? Did you tell the carpenter what he was building? Or did you pretend it was for socks that need their own long compartments and a convenient charging dock? Can you imagine what he went home and told his wife?"

Grayson had only shrugged, tipping back his drink with a smug smile.

"I hope he told his wife that his clients fuck so much they need a way to keep electronic reinforcements at the ready twenty-four hours a day.

Real men can get on their knees and take a strap. I don't want to wait for shit to charge when she's in a toy kind of mood, and that was the best money I've ever spent."

Lowell snorted. "Real men can take the real thing. No fancy dresser drawer required, and I'm not running up anyone's electric bill."

They had all laughed, Trapp almost falling out of the leather banquette, as Grayson shook his head, shoulders shaking.

"That knowledge does not surprise me one bit. But it makes it even more pathetic that you've been here for how many fucking months and still can't get laid."

He knew if he didn't make a point of being up and ready when Trapp pulled into the driveway at too fucking early o'clock a few days later, he would not be invited again. Lowell had set his numerous alarms, dragging himself out of bed at an utterly unacceptable hour, sitting bleary-eyed in the passenger seat of his brother's truck, forehead bouncing against the passenger side window as he tried to sneak a few more minutes of sleep.

"Why does Liam get to hang out in Dad's office whenever he feels like it? What do they even *talk* about?"

"Oh, Liam and Jack are great pals. They can't get enough of each other. Dad's gonna sob like a baby when he leaves next year, and mom will need to be the stoic one."

Lowell snorted.

"*Our* father? Jack' if you call me Jackson, I might eat your face off' Hemming? That one? Jack 'there's a rumor I have a bunch of kids at home but I haven't seen any of them in two weeks, I hope they haven't killed each other' Hemming? Him?"

Trapp, as good-natured as ever, only laughed.

"That's the one. You *do* remember the fact that he was with two different Fortune 500 companies when we were kids, right? It's different now that he's retired. Semi-retired. Whatever."

"What does he even do all day?"

"Grayson is convinced he doesn't do anything. Catching up on two decades of sleep and shopping for property down south that mom won't let him buy and playing online poker. Or at least, that's what he was doing. Now he's causing trouble at City Hall like he's being paid to do so, but that's only in the last year or two. Rhonda is so good at giving people the runaround, who even knows what he does all day? His clients aren't complaining, so it's not like we'll find out."

Their father had retired from the world of corporate finance the minute he turned forty, occupying an office at the center of Main Street in a building the family had owned since before the town had been incorporated. It had been his part-time office for years, where he ran *family business*, as it was referred to, but after his retirement, it became a second home. He allegedly did private financial investing for a select, privileged few — Sulya Slade, the Deliquesce heiress, and a few other members of the Cambric Creek elite.

Lowell had always consoled himself with the fact that he might not be his father's favorite, but at least Owen wasn't either. That dubious honor rested on the bickering shoulders of one of his older brothers, at least, he had always assumed. Jackson, who was so respectful and respectable, who had fully embraced his role as *the* Jackson Hemming of the future, a community pillar. Or Grayson, smart and calculating and ambitious, so much like their father . . . It had nearly been a relief, not needing to worry about entering the rat race for Jack's limited attention. He was Gray's and, by extension, Trapp's favorite little brother, which was more than good enough.

The knowledge that it may, in fact, be *Liam* who was Jack's favorite, Liam the baby who had everything handed to him, five elder brothers who had already gotten in any and every sort of trouble there was to be found, who had paved the way for him to coast to adulthood . . . Lowell knew he wasn't supposed to care about such things, particularly as he had his own life, independent of the family name and the shackles of expectations that weighed it down in Cambric Creek. Still, he couldn't help feeling miffed, as he had somehow been passed over for a promotion.

If you act like a petulant baby, you're just reinforcing the assumption that's what you are. He needed to school his face and tamp back his annoyance to get through breakfast. *Who knows, you might even enjoy yourself.* Gray was right. He needed to get out of the house, needed to do *some*thing that would take his mind off the fact that his phone had not rung in weeks — no call from work, no news from his office, and most frustratingly, nothing from the clinic.

An entire month had passed since he'd driven to the clinic, undergoing a battery of tests to determine his ability to participate in the donor program. Bloodwork, a physical, urinating in one cup and ejaculating into another, providing a detailed family medical history. Having his photo taken had reminded him of grade school picture day with its generic, gradient background, and then he'd been sent home, having done all he could do at that point.

"We'll be contacting you if you're selected," the doctor in charge of the program had told him, "please refrain from all recreational drugs and follow our guidelines on alcohol consumption until then."

He wasn't sure why he thought his phone would be ringing the very next day. Perhaps he *was* a typical Hemming after all — arrogant and over-privileged, expecting the world to cater to him — he pondered from his favorite sulking location, in the middle of the pool, laying atop the cover with his legs over the inflated cushion in the center. Grayson would have been wroth to find him there, so Lowell made sure he was back on solid ground well before the time his brother might come home, ensuring the cover was undamaged and tightly secured.

His mother had not come from the same world of open doors and easy privilege, and had ensured each of her sons knew the value of work and independence, at least, that was what she told people, but there was no denying their family name carried considerable weight. The Hemmings had been one of Cambric Creek's first families, wealthy and in positions of power continuously. Business owners, presidents of the werewolf labor union, head of the hospital board. His grandfather had been mayor, like his father before him, and a great-great uncle before that. Lowell's father had broken the tradition, the first Jackson

Hemming in half a dozen generations to not pull the town's strings in an official capacity, but his eldest brother was on track to set things to rights, having been elected to the city council the moment he'd expressed the vaguest interest in the job, and was now running to unseat the mayor who'd taken their grandfather's place.

Lowell had always prided himself on being different, on having outrun the privilege of his name and forging his own path to success, but as he stared dumbfounded at the silent phone in those first weeks, he was forced to accept that he simply *expected* doors to open for him, at the very least when he was here, at home.

When Trapp's phone rang again, the electronic melody overtaking the car radio, Lowell assumed it would be Grayson again. *Probably found another hole in his dick.*

Instead, their father's voice cut through the music.

"Sorry boys, I'm going to need to cancel this morning. Something came up that needs my immediate attention. I'm heading over to the big house now."

Trapp frowned, directing his pickup into the municipal lot across the street from their father's office.

"Do you need me to go with you? Or is Jackson meeting you?"

Lowell listened to the rest of the conversation with half an ear, waving off Trapp's overture about bringing him home to Grayson's once the errand was complete. The historic Hemming family home, the house his father had grown up in, had been given to a foundation his father bankrolled and was now a halfway house for werewolves escaping packs, populated chiefly by young women running away from the same sort of circumstances his own mother had fled. Lowell had only ever been in the big house a handful of times, and he was glad that his father had never made them live there. Too big, too echoing, and extremely haunted if his elder brothers were to be believed.

"Go ahead, I know you want to get over there and help him, and I'm going to get a coffee since I'm up this freaking early now."

The Black Sheep Beanery, just down the block, was already bustling as he stepped through the doors. As he stood in line, he wondered if Owen had ever been invited to join Liam and Trapp for breakfast with their father, if Jackson had ever sat with them before his early class. He was confident that Grayson would never voluntarily leave work for something so trivial, but he didn't like the idea that everyone else was spending this quality time together without him.

Homesickness had always been the deciding factor in his previous visits, his throat sticking as he searched for flights, wanting to crawl into a ball of loneliness as he booked the arrangements. He missed his mother. He missed his twin, missed having someone there with whom he'd been on the same level since the time of their birth. He missed Trapp's easy-going smile and Grayson's non-stop ball-busting; he missed cooking that was familiar and streets he'd walked down a million times before, the smell of his father's study, and the security that came with being part of a large, tight-knit family.

He would be fidgety on the plane, anxiety tightening his lungs as they touched down in Bridgeton, unsure if he was simply that excited to see everyone or already regretting his decision. His homesickness would last approximately twenty-four hours after his arrival, his mother's overbearingness and desire for him to move home grating on his nerves by the end of the first shared meal, the battle for his father's attention, in which he'd never been a contender, still going strong, and the claustrophobia of being surrounded by his brothers inescapable. He felt lost in the sea of his giant family, lost and unseen.

But ......he didn't like the idea of them all having fun together without him.

He had just begun to plot mischief against the lot of them; payment for forgetting about him as always, a comeuppance they would deserve, when his phone rang, the buzzing of it across the small tabletop startling him from his malicious reverie. His first thought was that it would be his office, someone from the publisher calling with some news. *We have a job for you. You can fly back. Good news, restrictions have been lifted.*

It was a local exchange, dashing his hopes. He had no idea who would be calling him from an unknown local number, not when the only people he talked to were family, and all of their numbers were saved.

"He-hello?"

"Good morning. I'm looking for Lowell Hemming?"

"This-this is . . . um, what is this concerning?"

"Ah, perfect. Mr. Hemming, this is Dr. Randolph, calling from Moon Blooded —"

"The clinic!" His annoyance with his family was instantly replaced with nerves and excitement. This was it, the call he'd forgotten he was waiting for. *You've been chosen. You've been chosen. You've been chosen . . .*

"Correct. I'm calling to inform you that you have been selected by one of our patients as a potential donor."

His balls contracted in excitement. The moon was only a few days away, and soon they would be emptying into the willing, enthusiastic body of his unknown partner. Lowell pumped a fist in the air in triumph, uncaring who may have been watching his one-sided reaction to the conversation. The end of his hometown dry spell was in sight.

"— Unfortunately, she contacted us too late in the month for this moon's viability. We will be in touch before next month's moon to set up your intake procedure, and I see here that you have checked off on your donor survey that you release your personal information to the patient. She may be contacting you in the interim for an interview to determine if you will remain the donor of her choice. In the future, if you wish for your contact information to not be shared, you must update your preferences on the clinic's portal under your login credentials. If you have any questions in the meantime, don't hesitate to reach out. That's all for now, have a safe turn this moon!"

He closed his eyes in disappointment at the doctor's words. His balls deflated. Lowell thought he felt one of them crawl up inside his body, probably looking for a place to cry, and he empathized greatly with the desire.

An interview. *You fucking suck at interviews.* It was up to the girl now, whoever she was. He wondered if she would call him, if they would have a video call or just phone conversation, if she would find him charming enough on the phone, wishing he had a deeper voice like Grayson's or possessed Trapp's good-natured humor. He didn't have his twin's calm, soft-spokeness or Jackson's ability to doublespeak his way out of anything. He could make himself sound good on paper, but on the phone, she would be able to tell that he was a high-strung, needy mess. The only thing standing between him and what he wanted was . . . him.

Leaving the coffee shop, his feet took him on a familiar route, one he had walked hundreds of thousands of times since childhood. He'd always been in a rush, according to his mother. He leapt before he looked, and had always looked for a faster route forward, even if it meant he forged it alone. Sandi liked to reminisce that Lowell had stood before he'd crawled, walking before Owen, despite being the smaller twin, the *runt of the litter* as Trapp had called him when they were children.

There were no social groups he could join or professional associations currently meeting. The human's pandemic had put everything on hold. He couldn't meet anyone in Cambric Creek, and he understood why Trapp, arguably the most attractive person in town, had taken up with a human, brand-new to the area. Jackson had met Victoria in grad school, far away from here, and Owen's girlfriend was from Bridgeton, met through their mutual friend group. Grayson and Vanessa met in the city and shared a profession; even his father had left Cambric Creek to find his mate. It didn't matter how often Grayson told him he needed to go out and get laid — it wasn't that simple, not for them. Not for any of them.

When his phone went off again, he had just turned off an alley on the side of the building that housed the small local newspaper.

Hi there, this is Moriah. I'm the one who picked you. From the clinic, I mean.

The thunderous sound of his own heartbeat was all he could hear as he staggered out of the alley, cutting around the side of another building and crossing the street against traffic until he could find a bench. He used too many exclamation points, he thought, reading over the messages he'd already sent, his brain in too much of a rush and flooded with too much excitement to think about looking them over before hitting send. *You probably sound like a little kid.* He hoped his enthusiasm wasn't a turn off for her, hoping he wasn't being too agreeable with her plan for them to meet a day or two after the full moon. When she suggested Cambric Creek, he accepted without hesitation. *You can wear a disguise if you have to.*

When he packed his borrowed car with the kayak the day later, eager to give Grayson and Vanessa their space, he had sent her another message, wishing her well, hoping her first heat wasn't too intolerable. He hoped she would find him interesting and attractive and not as annoying and in the way as his family seemed to. He hoped she would pick him. Hope was all he felt, and it had been so long since he had hoped for anything that he didn't know quite how to process the emotion.

It was going to be, he thought with a sigh, a *very* long month.

* * *

Moriah

The first time she'd met Sorben for drinks after he'd tracked down her number, Moriah remembered crossing the room with a flutter of nerves in her belly, resting on a large dollop of confusion. She still wasn't sure how she got there, why she'd said yes, and had been crafting her exit excuse as she smiled across the table. It wasn't until maybe their third date that she had begun to see the appeal, the slightly softer center beneath his hard-scaled outer shell.

The werewolf approaching her now possessed no such hardness. He had an unselfconscious, confident air, loping along on long legs. Dark eyes and wide mouth, a square jaw and sharp cheekbones . . . He was even more handsome in person than his photograph had led her to believe. Moriah straightened in her chair, tugging the edge of her dress as she took him in from across the dining room.

Thick, dark hair, just like his photo, slightly overlong and curling against the collar of his shirt, which stretched across his broad shoulders. Decent height and a lean, muscular build, he certainly fit the description of tall, dark and handsome. *Which is all good, but that's not why you picked him,* she reminded herself. He slowed as his eyes scanned the room, and when they landed on her, his smile split. *That's the reason. Right there.* When he raised a hand in greeting across the cafe, his eyes crinkling with the force of his smile, a breathless giddiness overtook her nerves, and Moriah beamed, squeezing her thighs together. *He's fucking gorgeous. If this were a blind date, you'd be thrilled.*

"Moriah? I'm Lowell. It's great to meet you!"

The next moment seemed to be a carefully choreographed ballet of awkwardness as she stood to greet him. She stuck her hand out as he placed his own over his chest, giving her a small half-bow, freezing as her hand extended. Moriah felt outside of her body, watching in slow motion as his hand left the center of his chest, stretching to meet hers . . . just as she withdrew the gesture, slapping her hand over her breast, mirroring his greeting. She watched as his hand hung in the empty air, meeting nothing, and felt fire burn up her cheeks.

You should run. Maybe there's a hole outside you can fall into. Time seemed to grind to a halt, suspended in space alongside his abandoned hand, the ticking of an invisible clock rattling her insides until the mortifying moment was broken by his snort of laughter, long arms engulfing her in a hug before she could embarrass herself any further. He was warm, *so* warm, and her shoulders shook in laughter as she pressed her cheek to his broad chest, breathing him in, pushing away the nausea-inducing thoughts of the last five days.

She'd spent the better part of the week braiding herself into knots of anxiety, second-guessing all of her plans. She had wanted to travel before she'd met Sorben, had aspirations to see the world and live abroad, wanted to start her own interiors business and be her own boss, wanted to experience all that life could possibly offer . . . and it had all been eclipsed by her desire to have a child. Dreams of a cozy little flat she'd envisioned in some picturesque European town where she would run her design business had been traded for daydreams of a sweet-smelling bundle pressed to her breast, a rocking chair in a mint green-painted nursery in place of the well-appointed fantasy flat.

Maybe the divorce was her chance to do everything she'd put on hold, she told herself, to see the world beyond the town she was from and the town she now called home. The end of her marriage could mean the beginning of her new life. *Maybe you're making a terrible mistake.*

All of her anxieties fell away as she inhaled deeply, pressing herself to this stranger's warmth. He smelled like crisp, fresh spearmint — and as she rose slightly on her tiptoes to press a kiss to his cheek, surreptitiously sniffing his neck as she lowered — there was something spicy and wild, a hint of the beast beneath, she thought, flushing once more. *Lowell.* The only new life she wanted was the tiny one she would create with this unfamiliar, fresh-smelling man, and the nearness of her dreams made tears prick at her eyes unexpectedly. *This is it; this is what you wanted.*

"I'm sorry," he laughed once they parted, his dark chocolate eyes sparkling down at her. "I've spent so long training myself *out* of a western handshake. I'm terrible at interviews and I've been a nervous wreck all morning, so I was bound to screw something up."

"You don't need to be nervous, I promise I don't bite! And I'm not good at interviews either," she agreed. "I'm not good at talking about myself. I'm good at *doing*. Just let me do my thing and rate me on that. Portfolio presentation in school was always the worst. I've done the work, and you have eyes in your head. Why do I have to stand in front of a room and squirm and talk about each piece?"

Lowell was laughing, his head tipped back slightly.

"Exactly! The worst was when they would ask about the motivation for each piece. My motivation was to pass the class, sir. My motivation for this one was also to pass the class. And finally, my motivation for this last piece was, you may have already guessed, to pass this class. Just mark that you hate it and let me go home to die in peace."

The small goblin waiting on tables sighed heavily as she eyed the table where they sat, laughing raucously. It was already more laughter than she and Sorben had shared in their first several dates, an auspicious sign, she thought.

"You're an artist then?"

She shrugged self-deprecatingly at his question.

"I mean . . . sort of? Interior design."

"So . . . yes," he grinned back hugely. "I sat next to design students in the same color theory and art history classes. I don't remember any of them only 'sort of' graduating . . . I, on the other hand, almost "sort of graduated". We had this 'first last night' tradition at my school, and we partied a little too thoroughly the night before graduation, and I almost slept through the ceremony."

"We had the same party! If I wasn't already engaged, I probably would have missed my ceremony as well. You're a photographer, right? And you don't do handshakes. So I'm assuming that means you're a glamorous globetrotter? Wait, I-I'm getting ahead of myself."

The goblin had arrived, clearing her throat impatiently, and Moriah thought to herself that it was no mystery why this cafe and coffee shop beside it were always empty.

"Um, can I just have the yogurt and fruit plate with a strawberry lemonade?"

Across the table, Lowell was flipping through the pages as if it were the first time he'd ever seen a menu, and she had to bite down her laughter at his perplexed look. *I think he had it upside down there for a minute!*

"There are too many options, I'll just have the same."

She swallowed a giggle as the goblin rolled her eyes, leaving them alone once more. Moriah took a deep breath, steadying the out-of-control butterflies thrumming in her chest. *He's so cute. He looks so young, he has such a baby face! Maybe he thinks you're too old.* She shook away the thought. He was only two years younger than her, regardless of his appearance. She'd never been self-conscious that way, and she wasn't about to start now.

"Thank you," she breathed out, gripping the table for support. "Thank you for meeting me today, and-and thank you for doing this.

You have no idea how much I appreciate your participation in this program. As soon as I saw your picture, I felt really good about you, you and and this, and I'm so glad you're here. So thank you."

"Thank you for picking me," he said earnestly. "I was so excited when the clinic called me. I feel like I won the lottery!"

She laughed at his enthusiasm, and he grinned hugely.

"Seriously, I never get picked for anything; I never win anything. Especially being back home right now, I'm sort of stuck in place. Finding out about the clinic was happenstance, but I was thrilled when they said you had picked me. I'm so glad to be able to help you."

She thought she was going to burst with happiness.

"Okay, so . . . tell me a little about yourself. The most dreaded question, I know."

He sat up a little straighter, clearing his throat.

"Okay, I can do this. Don't choke, Lowell. Let's see . . . yes, to answer your earlier question, I'm a photojournalist. I have a fine arts degree from MAIA, that's the Mid-Atlantic—"

"Institute of Art, I know. Wow, that's a really good school."

"Don't be too impressed, I almost flunked out twice. Two of my brothers went to Ivys, top of their class, summa cum laude, the whole nine yards. I failed Theory and Application. So you know, it's a sliding scale of accomplishments in my family."

The goblin arrived with their order, interrupting them again. Across the table, Moriah watched him suck in a breath as if his lungs had been deprived. See? He's as nervous as you. That's the most precious thing in the world.

"Um, I've been overseas for the last eight years," he went on after a moment. "I've been based in Tokyo for the last three years or so, I think? Three or four, time has lost all meaning since I've been back home. This appointment is the only reason I know what day of the week it is. And I say 'based in Tokyo' because that's where my apartment is, but I'm not there that much. When I was working, I would be on shoots sometimes four or five times a month. Now, though?" He chucked weakly. "Not so much."

"Oh no, because of the pandemic! I didn't even think of that affecting work like yours. Is that why you're back in the Unification?"

He nodded grimly. "My travel visa is work-based, so it's not worth anything right now. So I am back home for the foreseeable future."

She thought he seemed distinctly unhappy about that, but even his unhappiness was cute. Moriah had the impression that if he weren't trying to impress her, he would have folded his arms like a child, possibly even stamp his foot.

There was a petulant edge to his voice as he described vacating his apartment and flying back to the states, telling her about his eighteen-hour flight that had culminated in being stranded at the airport; how he had almost died of starvation in front of a closed Mr. Toasty stand, and that no one in his family had come to pick him up for hours.

"Oh noooo! See, you could have called me. I would have been there with a little 'welcome home' sign and cupcakes."

His nostrils flared as he breathed in sharply, leaning in with wide eyes, and she had the most preposterous image of doing precisely that for him in the future. *Easy girl, calm down. He's just your sperm donor.*

"And how are you doing with being back?"

"Oh, not well." His eyebrows arched, and his voice took on the guise of someone explaining an accident with too much cheer and enthusiasm, and she couldn't help her laughter. "Not well at *all*, Moriah. I *need* people. I need to be social, and this whole 'stay at home every day' business is killing me. I'm not good at holding still."

She'd already noticed that. His fingers tapped on the side of his water glass as though it were the fretboard of a guitar, and he was ripping through his big solo. His knee had not stopped bouncing beneath the table, his fingertips leaving the side of his glass at one point to stir his ice so aggressively that the cubes gave up, kissing their futile existence goodbye and disappearing in the maelstrom within the glass. He seemed to be a flurry of movement and energy at all times, even when he was ostensibly holding still . . . but his eyes were expressive and bright, his smile wide and toothy, the exact opposite of her ex-husband in nearly every way. Sorben could sit like a stone, unblinking, barely breathing, often leaving her feeling like she was in the room alone.

"What about you? You're the human. Are-are you okay with being out today? I'm sorry, I didn't even think about —"

"I'm good," she assured him, offering him a sunny smile, which he tentatively returned. "I work from home, so it wasn't much of an adjustment. It's difficult to get stuff in right now, that's been the biggest challenge at work, but I'm already used to staying home every day. I'm afraid to be out around humans right now, so it's a good thing I don't need to be. I *do* know what you mean, though. I miss talking to people. And I didn't realize how much time I actually spent talking with my neighbors and people at the grocery store, just little things. It's hard being cooped up all day with nothing but my own thoughts. Sometimes they're not the happiest place to be."

"Yes, exactly!" He exclaimed in agreement again. "My head is full of jealousy and horniness and existential depression, and it is the *last* place I want to be. Being home is . . . hard, I can't even convincingly lie about it. It's mostly horrible. I'm the middle child of six, and all of my family still lives in the area. Growing up, it was already too easy to feel lost in the crowd, and now that I don't even have any friends or distractions here? It's miserable. If I have to spend much more time with just myself for company, I'm going to wind up walking into traffic."

They were going to be asked to leave, she thought, wheezing in laughter again, earning the goblin's stare once more. Despite the server's stern glare, Moriah was glad she'd chosen this place. The restaurants and coffee shops near the industrial park did a brisk enough lunch business, but none were top-tier, and most of the Cambric Creek executive elites ordered in from their favorite shops on Main Street or huddled into the Black Sheep on their lunch breaks. The little café was sparsely populated, perfect for their little rendezvous.

"I have specific spots I like to sit in during the day," she offered after a moment, controlling her laughter as the goblin came by with their drinks. "Like, in the morning, I'll sit at the desk I have near my back door, overlooking the yard. It gets lots of light, so I have some hanging plants and a few prism crystals, so it's really nice. I pretend I'm living out my European cottage core fantasies. Then, by mid-morning, when I really need to buckle down and get to work, I move to my main workspace. It's a repurposed architect's desk, and everything around it is all wood with black metal hinges and brackets with gold accents. Feels very old world, like old Eastern European villages; that's how I have it decorated. During my break for lunch, I move to my little breakfast nook. I have a little wrought iron table and chairs, and it's all painted pastel pink and buttercream, and I like to pretend I'm at a cute little French sidewalk café. Then after lunch, I'm usually sad because I'm not actually in a little French sidewalk café, and I remember I haven't left my house in three days, I'm wearing the ratty old sweater from undergrad I should have thrown away a decade ago, and I haven't had a reason to wash my hair in a week. So then I go sulk in my basket chair by the bay window."

Lowell was laughing again, nodding as if he understood completely.

"Oh, I have several dedicated moping areas. I'm staying with my brother right now; he works really long hours, so I usually have the house to myself. I'll go from bedroom to bedroom and pretend I'm in a hotel some days, just to break up the monotony. I have a lot of incense from some of the temples I've visited, and I'll burn some and try to meditate and pretend I'm still there and not eating my sixty-third bowl of cereal for the week in someone else's house. I like to lay on top of the pool cover in the afternoon. He just closed it up for the season, so now I can't pretend I'm training for the Olympics anymore, but at least it's like a waterbed."

"Were you going to qualify for the team?" she asked cheekily, enjoying that she wasn't the only one who submersed herself in fantasies of being somewhere else every day.

"Oh, I was already there. Medaled in two events, but then I choked on my backstroke. *Everyone* fucks in the Olympic Village, so that's a nice perk. It was definitely not just me alone on a flamingo-shaped pool floatie. Overall, I made a respectable showing; I'm optimistic I'll make the team again."

Tears were streaming down her cheeks as he went on, one of the two satyresses at a table across the room turning to look at them before bending her head to her companion to whisper.

"I also like to lie on the roof of the garage and contemplate the futility of getting out of bed every day. Sometimes I'll contort myself into really horrific positions, just in case one of those mapping drones is flying around, so it looks like my brother keeps corpses on the roof."

The satyresses both turned to stare then, heads coming together to whisper again, as Moriah imagined him stretched out like a long, lean, sexy crime scene photo on his brother's roof. *He can come lie naked on my roof, and we can really give the drone something to see.*

"Oh! Then one day, I went exploring and found a sensory deprivation tank in his bathroom, and it was the *worst* trip. Like, it's bad enough not having anyone to talk to all day and being trapped in my own head

119

when I'm outside, out in the world. That was like a nightmare, though. I actually *had* nightmares for, like, a whole week after. I couldn't tell if I was the voice in my head or if I only *existed* in the voice in my head, like my whole life has just been a big illusion and I'm someone else's daydream. Zero out of ten experience, do *not* recommend."

"I love the fact that *exploring* somehow led to your brother's bathroom. That feels like a fancy word for snooping," she giggled, her face beginning to ache from the force of her smile.

"So, what sort of interior design do you do exactly?"

She forgot that she was meant to be interviewing him as she talked about some of the projects she worked on and her ambition to start her own company.

"I've always wanted to travel, but there was never an opportunity. I went from high school to university, and I met my husband while I was still in school. We got married shortly after I graduated. He had a good job, but there was always something bigger to save for, you know? Our first house. Paying down our student loans. And then the baby stuff came up, and . . . Well, that was the end of that. But I have all these inspiration boards that I make based on different places I want to see someday. I would love to start my own design firm based on that idea, that you can create a whole world within one finite space."

She flushed again when she glanced up to meet his eye, the soft expression on his face making her stomach flip-flop.

"So six siblings, that's a whole lot. I'm an only child, so I cannot relate."

"Yeah. It's a lot. We have weird age gaps too, so it's like these built-in hierarchies. My eldest brothers are barely a year apart, then there's only like two or three years between Gray and Trapp. Then six years before my brother and I were born, and more than a decade between us and the youngest. The baby is closer with the older ones than with me, because they were already in university when he was born. By the time he was school-aged, they were already a few years into their professional careers and moving back closer to home. I moved out of the country when he was in middle school. Being an only child still sorta sucks, though," he said thoughtfully, earning her outraged laughter. "I'm serious! I wouldn't want to be an only child, especially with my parents. No way. My mother already loves us way too hard. If I were the only one, I would've never been able to move away or do anything that didn't involve her holding my hand. She would be here with us right now, giving you the third degree."

Moriah laughed. "Hey! I'm probably going to have an only child, don't curse me that way. Maybe your mom is just extra worried about you because you live so far away."

"It's because of how she was raised, and objectively, I know that. It doesn't make it any easier, though," he murmured. She raised an eyebrow, waiting for him to continue. "She grew up in a wolfpack, you probably don't know what that is, but it's. . . it's a hard life. Everything you have belongs to the pack. Your house, your jobs. Your kids, really. You're raising them in the way of the pack, so someone else is always calling the shots. She left when she met my dad and was basically starting her life from scratch at twenty years old. So I appreciate why she is the way she is, and I can forgive her for being a little overbearing sometimes. She loves us so hard because we were the first things that were truly hers. So I get it, but sometimes it's just too much. For me, at least. My older brothers are all mama's boys. But I would *not* want to be an only child."

Her insides felt like a pool of melted butter. *You can't resist a guy who loves his mother.*

"I get what you mean. Yeah, I guess you're right. I spent a lot of time around adults growing up. I don't come from a big family at all, so there weren't a lot of kids to play with. I've always been the mom friend, ready with everything, because that's how my mom always was. I can't even imagine having five brothers or sisters. I don't even have five cousins!"

"Now, imagine being in the middle. I never got any attention; no one ever noticed me, and I practically raised myself. Everything was always about my three older brothers. I would have needed to commit murder to be the center of attention. And then my youngest brother has the absolute *nerve* to come around and get whatever he wants because he's the baby! I never got to be the baby! Unspeakably unfair. I got to be the baby for exactly four and a half minutes; what is that?! Nothing, that's what."

She was sure they would be asked to leave, as hard as she was laughing again. He asked her if she had already designed her nursery, wrinkling his nose and shaking his head to dispute her choice of mint and grey with ducklings.

"Dinosaurs. Kids love dinosaurs. My nephew can play with dinosaurs for *hours*. You need to rethink your whole concept."

"*Kids* love dinosaurs!" she laughed in agreement. "Not newborns! That's too scary."

He was still shaking his head, face scrunched up in thought.

"No, I'm not so sure about that. Dinosaurs transcend gender and species. I don't know where you're getting your data, but I think it's questionable."

She had written down questions. She'd written down serious interview questions to ask him, but so far, he hadn't stopped chattering, and there wasn't a single thing on the little folded piece of paper in her bag that was worth interrupting him. It was the best first date she'd ever been on so far, and her questions were unimportant. *Too bad it's not an actual date. He's funny and charming and handsome. Which means he probably has a girlfriend.*

"So what made you decide to do this?" she blurted suddenly, her thoughts catching up

with her mouth, neck heating. "Is – is your partner okay with it?"

His cheeks pinkened adorably.

"No girlfriend, no partner. I genuinely don't know anyone here, not anymore. I didn't keep in touch with the people I went to school with here and I went to university on the coast. Before you ask, I didn't have a partner back in Tokyo either. With my lifestyle, it's hard. I'm gone so much, and I know that's not fair to the person left at home. Plus, I know myself well enough. I may look extremely intimidating, but don't let this tough guy exterior fool you. My heart is a little candy gumdrop. If I had someone I loved sitting at home waiting for me, I don't know if I would be able to do what I do, and I really love my job."

Moriah laughed again, squeezing her thighs together.

"I'm glad you said something because you're right. You are *extremely* intimidating looking." Lowell laughed at her words, dragging a huge hand over his not-at-all intimidating baby face. *Handsome, charming, and single. A little candy gumdrop. You love gumdrops! And this isn't a date. He's just your sperm donor. What are the fucking odds?*

"I probably look like I might rob you in the parking lot for spare change. I desperately need a haircut, but I'm worried that if I go to the guy who cuts my brother's hair, I'm going to walk out looking like him."

"Is your brother, like, super ugly or something?" she deadpanned, gratified by his immediate laughter. "Because I don't think they can do that with just a haircut, so you don't need to worry."

"He's actually obnoxiously handsome, but if we look too much alike, then I'll be the homely one, and I can't handle that sort of comparison."

"I maintain I don't think they can do that with just a haircut. Besides, I don't think they could make you look homely if they tried."

The tips of his ears reddened and her clit tingled in response. *He's so fucking cute.*

"Also, when you're having out-of-body nightmare adventures in sensory deprivation tanks, you don't need to wear pants, so this felt like getting dressed to go to the ball. I apologize if I look like I'm supposed to be replacing your air conditioner or something. I thought the tuxedo would be too much and the swim trunks maybe too casual, so I tried for the middle."

The middle, for him, had been artfully distressed jeans and a button-down, trendy and casual, she thought, the opposite of what she probably was.

"I think you did well, probably better than me. I think I tried on everything in my closet at least once while I was getting ready this morning, and that was only partially because of nerves. How does getting dressed work anymore? Have the trends changed since the last time I had to leave my house? Are trends still a thing? Or is everyone just wearing pajamas now?"

"I think you're gorgeous, but if you want to wear pajamas next time, we can coordinate that."

"Is there anything else I can get for you?" The goblin popped up at her elbow as Moriah turned scarlet, pressing her thighs together no longer providing enough friction for how turned on she was. *He thinks you're gorgeous?! You!* She wanted to crawl under the table and climb onto his lap, wanted to rock against him and feel his warmth again. The server frowned when she was waved away.

"What about you?" Lowell went on. "I'm sorry if it's inappropriate to ask, but is your partner okay with this whole process?"

She shook her head, hoping her smile didn't come off as the grimace she felt it was, not wanting to think about Sorben when her panties were getting damp from the man across the table.

"No, I-I'm divorced. My husband and I . . . We tried to get pregnant for a long time. We tried insemination and in vitro, but it didn't work. Our biologies just weren't compatible. I guess I should've known that it was foolish to waste so much money, but I just couldn't not try."

His eyes had widened, hands? climbing towards her. Moriah noticed then how much their positions had shifted. She leaned across the table on her elbows, and he had adjusted his chair slightly, leaning into her. *It might not be a date, but your body language didn't get the memo.*

"Your ex-husband isn't human then?"

"No. He's a lizard person. He moved away after the divorce, so he's completely out of the picture now."

She noticed that he stiffened at her words, his wide mouth pressing into a flat line. *Maybe he only wanted to help a married couple?*

"Is-is that a problem?"

"No, no. Of course not. Just seems like everyone I know lately is involved with a lizard person. Just to give you a heads up, I don't have two." He motioned at his lap, and her cheeks burned, laughter nearly choking her. "Just want to make sure you know that now so you can manage your expectations."

"You know, it's kind of surprising they didn't include a picture of it. They give us a *lot* of other information to make an informed decision, but not that. It feels like a wasted opportunity, to be honest. At least for this business model."

Lowell cocked his head, crossing his arms and leaning over the table. He made a face as if he was deep in thought, mulling over her words, and Moriah bit her lip. She couldn't remember the last time she had been so bold with a member of the opposite sex. Far before her marriage, that was for sure.

"Where do you think that photo would go? Right after the headshot? Don't you think that would lead to people making bad decisions? What if you pick your baby's father based on the size of his package, and it turns out he's a carrier of the asshole gene? Wouldn't you feel terrible?"

She giggled, relieved that he was playing along again.

"Well, I think the point is that it would feel great. At least for a little while."

His laughter was just as rich and loud as she had imagined the first time she saw his photograph. His shoulders shook, and he covered his face briefly, recovering enough to nod as if he was conceding the point to her.

"Fine, fair. I'll give you that one."

"You don't seem like you have the asshole gene. Is there a direct correlation between that and —?" She motioned to his lap with her spoon, gratified when he flushed, laughing again.

"I mean . . . I've been told it's very nice. I can collect references if you need them. I, personally, think it's great. But I don't know if that's entirely objective."

She dropped her face in her hands, her shoulders still shaking when the goblin came around with their meager bill. He whipped out a credit card before she had the opportunity to even gather up her bag, sighing in defeat when he waved away her attempt to rectify the situation.

"This is the most enjoyable afternoon I've spent since I left my apartment in Tokyo a million months ago. Would I be able to use the money I get from the clinic to pay you to have lunch with me at least once a week? Would that be weird?"

"Yes, it would be, Lowell. That would make me an escort."

He was practically doubled over as they exited the small café, the satyresses whispering and the goblin still glaring.

"Well? Did I pass? Despite the tragic lack of penile statistics on the website?"

She shrugged, grinning up at him.

"It really is an appalling lack of information. I'd like to see it, just to make sure I'm making an informed decision. This is my baby's future. Don't they deserve me having all the information I need going into this? When I'm doing a job, I always bring samples of the paint and materials I'll be using, and I give my client a 3-D render because they want to see the whole picture."

They had begun to walk along the sidewalk, following the path leading between the building that housed the café and the coffee shop, and a separate building that housed a gym. There was a small, gated park-like area with two wrought iron benches and a trickling water feature.

"I mean, if you really want to see it, I could technically whip it out for you right now. I'm pretty sure this town has some kind of legislation that makes clothing optional. I'll warn you, though, it's been stiff for the last forty minutes."

It was her turn to nearly hunch in laughter, wheezing at his audaciousness. Moriah didn't know what sort of magic bravery possessed her — maybe it was the thrill of being out with an attractive man for the first time since her divorce, possibly it was the knowledge of what they were going to do together, or perhaps it was a giddy combination of the two, for they had barely taken a few steps into the gated little park when she stopped before him and palmed the front of his jeans. She sucked in a breath between her teeth when he grunted in surprise, but did not remove her hand. He hadn't been lying. A long, thick firmness rested beneath her fingers, jerking when she squeezed it gently. A rush of wetness flooded her core.

The week of her heat had been agony. She'd held off touching herself for as long as she could. She'd read that it would only make the burning worse. The websites hadn't lied. Her first orgasm shook through her as she whimpered on her sofa, but it hadn't helped. It hadn't even taken the edge off. Instead, she had continued to twist, continued to ache, desperate to be filled.

She had swiped open her phone, typing in the web address for one of the multi-species porn sites with a shaking hand, alternating between Lowell's picture and videos of werewolves fucking human-looking women, both in their man skin and as wolves. It was something she had previously found distasteful in thought, the edge of being a bit too bestial for her, but which she now found wildly exciting.

It had been all she'd thought about for a week, and now it was twitching in her palm. She wasn't lying to him. She really did want to see his cock; wanted to ensure she was making the best-informed decision she could, and wanted to know everything about him.

"Someone needs to be on lookout duty because if I get caught this way, I really am going to walk into traffic, you have no idea."

Her breath came out in shallow gasps as he led her to one of the benches. The little park area was as empty as the coffee shop beside the café, and the only customers in the area were the two satyrs inside. Her heart was in her mouth when he undid his belt buckle, his eyes casting around continuously as he drew down his fly. It was hard to appreciate his full size under the conditions, but Moriah decided even like this — at an awkward angle, not fully pulled out, and not fully hard — she liked what she saw. *I like it very much.*

He wasn't quite as long as Sorben had been, at least not yet, but his shaft possessed a delicious thickness that would feel amazing inside her, she was certain. His cock head was covered in the thin membrane of his foreskin, but the flared edge of his glans was clearly visible, and his head dropped back, small groan vibrating from him when she traced the edge of it with her nail. She dragged the pads of her fingertips down his thick shaft until she reached the opening of his jeans, frustrated there was not more of him available to touch.

"We-we should probably go somewhere if you don't feel like you can make an informed decision yet. Clothing is optional, but I'm pretty sure hand jobs are not."

She wanted to protest as he tucked himself away with a trembling hand, doing up his fly and sliding the tongue of his belt through the buckle.

"I just don't think I can. You understand, right? I want to make sure I'm doing my absolute due diligence."

She couldn't take him home. She wanted to, and home was literally minutes away, but she couldn't. She knew that wouldn't be smart, it was a risk, and she wasn't willing to throw caution that recklessly into the wind. She still needed a tiny sliver of anonymity to feel good about this process, and she could not bring him home. She got the impression he lived in Bridgeton from the way he had referred to Cambric Creek initially, but she couldn't see this momentary burst of bravery lasting through a thirty-minute or more ride into the city.

Lowell sucked in a deep breath, exhaling slowly through his teeth before lacing the long fingers of his big hand through her own small ones, pushing himself to his feet a moment later and pulling her to follow. She didn't want to think about how well her hand fit against his, how neatly she molded against his palm, nor how his warmth sunk into her, heating her to the core.

"There-there's a place right around here, I think. Just around the corner. We can walk, if you want to leave your car here."

It was a hotel, she realized. On the other side of the industrial parkway, primarily used for visiting executives, dropping into the offices of the businesses populating the area. *You're the one who started this. What do you want to do?* She decided she would simply need to pick up an extra job this month to cover the cost of her afternoon fact-finding mission, for she was not ready to say goodbye to him yet. She had absolutely made her choice, but she still wanted to know everything about him, including every intimate secret of his long, lovely body.

"It-it just seems silly to wait until we're in an awkward, sterile lab setting to see each other for the first time, doesn't it?"

"I agree," he said quickly, nodding. "Super awkward. Performance anxiety. I might not even be able to get it up that way."

Moriah grinned up at him, knowing he was absolutely full of shit, but appreciated the effort.

"Something tells me we'll manage," she laughed, squeezing his hand. "Lowell, I-I'm definitely picking you. You're my choice. I want to do this with you. But it would be nice to get the awkwardness out of the way, don't you think?"

She didn't immediately know how to react when he gripped her chin with a gentle hand, tilting her face up and bending until he was able to reach her mouth. His lips were warm, so warm, like the rest of him, pulling a little gasp from her throat as he trapped her lower lip between his two, a soft suck, a featherlight brush of his tongue, and then an equally gentle release.

"Totally agree. Just wanted to get that out of the way too. No sense in making things awkward, right?"

She met his grin, feeling her heart lift on beating wings, threatening to levitate her fully. He sparkled. That was why she had chosen him, Moriah reminded herself, returning the squeeze of his hand. He sparkled, and she hoped her baby would too.

"One hundred percent. If we can leave our cars here, then lead the way."

* * *

Lowell

She was prettier than he'd been expecting. Not pretty, he corrected, crossing the cafe. *Beautiful.* She was beautiful, and he was shocked.

He wasn't sure why. Lowell thought that maybe he'd watched too many movies or spent too much time photographing the interior of that post-war orphanage. The austere building had been grey and squat, matching the old women who ran it; filled with children displaced from their families after the Rakshasa uprising, none of their dour-faced caretakers had been especially warm. One by one, the visitors from overseas who'd come to adopt them had largely been middle-aged, from the States and western Europe, and none of them had this lovely stranger's delicate, heart-shaped face and rosebud mouth.

Regardless of the reason, the petite young woman with the dark red hair and bright eyes was an unexpected but welcome sight. She had the kind of smile that spoke of sunny optimism, a contagious good mood, and his mouth ached as he mirrored her grin. Her thin sweater clung to softly rounded curves, and when she had risen to greet him, he noted that her skirt did the same. *If this were a blind date, you'd be thrilled.*

"Moriah? I'm Lowell. It's great to meet you!"

His brain acted on autopilot when he placed his hand on his chest, bowing slightly, freezing when he clocked her outstretched hand. *You don't even know how to act here anymore.* When he'd quickly course-corrected, she'd already done the same, a wholly bungled greeting thanks to his brain's inability to rewire itself depending on the situation. *Why are you worried about not touching her? You're literally going to be fucking her in a month!*

The previous week had been torturous. He'd underestimated the subliminal power of the urge to breed. Trapp had joked about having a guest room ready for when he inevitably wore out his welcome with Grayson, but unless the room was located within his brother's toolshed, far from the main house, Lowell had no intention of leaving the privacy and sanctity of Grayson's home. He'd been surviving up til that point, barely, despite the hometown-imposed celibacy, but now . . . now he could think of nothing other than the moment his body would cover this mystery recipient's, thrusting into her with a rising heat, nothing in his head but breed, breed, breed until his knot inflated, sealing her as he filled her over and over.

It was the only thought his mind could conjure, and the mindless drudgery he'd been calling a routine for months had been completely upended by his pent-up lust. He masturbated before he left his bed each morning, repairing to the shower to cleanse himself of the evidence and sometimes tug out another shuddering orgasm. His afternoon mope was bookended with self-pleasure, his evening swim replaced with a run, growling against the white-tiled shower wall afterward as his cock spit up the vestiges of the hour's lust.

It grew worse as the moon neared, knowing what he would be doing in one month's time, what he could be doing if the girl had understood the way calendars worked and got herself to the clinic two weeks earlier. As the waxing moon increased its fullness, his knot became more and more evident, and he wasn't sure if he even left his bed at all the day before the turn, stroking his cock until the base swelled, edging himself for hours by only stimulating the blood-engorged knot, thinking of the mystery woman he'd be buried within. Her appearance was indistinct, hair color changing from fantasy to fantasy, her features blurred; the only constant was the way she'd gasp and beg, squeezing him until he erupted.

The fire in his blood had eased up in the days that followed, the moon's waning energy depleting the ravenous lust within him, but the sight of this girl — petite and pale and oh so lovely — was a sharp reminder.

Her cheeks had flushed as he bungled their greeting, and he'd been unable to hold back a huff of laughter at the ridiculousness of the situation, pulling her into a hug instead. The gesture had been meant to comfort, to assure her that there was no reason to be nervous, despite the fact that he was an idiot who couldn't even shake hands like a normal person, but it had come with the benefit of providing him with the means to lower his nose to her hair and inhale. Orange blossom and jonquil, soft and floral and pretty, just as she was; appealingly feminine and coy, and Lowell let out a shuddering breath once he'd inhaled a second lungful of her. He wasn't sure how he was going to last the entire month.

"Tell me a little about yourself. The most dreaded question, I know."

He sucked in a deep breath, willing his internal monologue to stay firmly in place, lodged in his head. *I'm thirty-two years old, but I barely feel eight on my most accomplished days. I'm not even sure how I'm allowed to live on my own. I don't know how to make lasting connections or form relationships with people because I'm never in one place long enough. I'm afraid I won't have a career to go back to once this stupid pandemic is over. I'm so horny I can't breathe. There's a one hundred percent chance I'm going to cum in my pants just sitting here with you because this is the most interaction I've had with the opposite sex in months, I'm desperate for physical affection, and you smell amazing.*

"I'm a photojournalist. I have a fine arts degree from MAIA, that's the Mid-Atlantic . . ."

He wasn't sure what he had droned on about for the next hour, probably nothing interesting or intelligent.

All he was cognizant of was the sweet chirp of her voice, the way her nose wrinkled adorably as she talked, the expressive way her hands fluttered about like little white doves, and the soft, sweet smell of her. She was beautiful. Creative, funny and articulate, and he basked in the inner warmth she seemed to radiate from her pores, soaking up her undivided attention like the greedy little sponge he was.

This is instalove. Congratulations, you've just become the protagonist of one of those teen dramas you used to watch with Nikkia. Plot twist — you're just her sperm donor, and she's going to forget you exist the instant you do your only job.

Werewolves had enhanced senses, at least compared to humans. Their hearing was weak, their taste and olfactory palates unrefined, and their vision limited. Lowell watched Moriah's eyes flicker to the whispering satyrs in the corner several times, able to tell from the look on her face that she was assuming they were the topic of conversation. They weren't, not really. At least, not about her.

They had recognized him as a Hemming, of course, and had grumbled about his do-nothing father and steamroller mother, characterizations he did not at all appreciate. The one on the left asked her companion if she knew about the situation with Sulya Slade and one of the Hemming boys, both pausing to look over at Lowell and Moriah again, a lovely red flush creeping up his companion's neck as a result.

"Not him. It was one of the older ones. There were drugs involved, that's what Millie Tonguegrass said. She used to live over on Pear Tree, you know. Right across from Sulya, saw the whole thing go down. He talked his way out of lockup and left her there. Left her in jail! Jack made it all disappear, of course. Millie told me that Sandi showed up on Sulya's doorstep and threatened to rip her throat out if she didn't stay away. She ought to have known better, taking up with someone that young. But then again, they're all *so* handsome . . . Sulya and Jacob left the country not long after that, and well . . . you heard about what happened to *him*, right?"

Lowell winced internally. He had been in junior high when that happened. Shaking away the gossip, he closed his eyes to refocus on Moriah's smell. Under her perfume, he could pick out the cherry-almond smell of her shampoo, the warmth of her skin . . . he wanted to run his nose down the length of her, learning the scent of every inch of her body. *You'll not be able to do that rutting into her in an exam room. Besides, she's probably married.*

"Is your partner okay with this?"

He flushed as she asked her question, almost as if she were reading his mind.

"Um, no girlfriend. No partner. I genuinely don't know anyone here anymore," he laughed uncomfortably. And before you ask, I didn't have a girlfriend in Tokyo either."

Merely speaking the words made his stomach bunch and twist. During his forced Cambric Creek captivity, he had come to the uncomfortable realization that he wished he had a girlfriend. It hadn't felt like a pressing need before. As he explained to her, finding a partner with his lifestyle was difficult, and if some of his peers were to be believed, maintaining a relationship was nigh impossible. He'd made dozens upon dozens of friends in the industry, photographers of every species and gender. Virtually none of them were partnered, and those who were often cheated or had arrangements with their spouses or partners back home, that whatever happened on the road stayed on the road.

That wasn't how he wanted to live. Lowell knew himself better than that, based on the small handful of semi-serious relationships he'd had — he formed attachments quickly, and despite being a grown man with more sexual partners than he could count, his heart was a delicate thing. He wouldn't be able to have a serious partner at home and leave them for weeks at a time, and the mere thought of cheating on someone he loved made him tight with anxiety.

Now that he was home, though, everything felt different, and he wished there was someone with whom he could endure this. Those endless hours he had been stranded at the airport would've seemed like no time at all if he'd not been alone. He wouldn't have minded Jackson's guest suite if there had been someone there to share the empty bed, to quietly giggle with after the rest of the house had gone to sleep; someone to have shown around his hometown, the familiar routes he took brand-new to them, and thus exciting for him all over again.

Under those circumstances, he wouldn't have even minded staying with his parents. His mother loved nothing more than playing hostess, striving to get along with the various girlfriends and partners who were brought to their monthly after-moon brunches. Meeting up with Grayson and Trapp would have felt like a fun adventure, and reconnecting with Owen might have been a warm homecoming instead of the slightly awkward shuffle around each other they had done. He was a different person outside of Cambric Creek, someone he liked better.

He fell too easily into old habits when he was home, fell right back into the childhood dynamic that had always shackled him, and he would remember why he had run away as fast and far as he could. If he had to be back here, having someone with whom he could be someone different would be nice.

He tried to imagine himself sitting at the airport with this lovely girl, head resting in her lap instead of the familiar spot on his gear bag, planning their next adventure, instead of being stuck with a version of himself he didn't like, feeling like a third wheel for months on end. They could fly away somewhere together, her fingers in his hair and the soft smell of her perfume enveloping him in a sweet, gentle cloud . . . *now you're really dreaming. What happens next in this fantasy airport? Because it's all fun and games until her husband comes around the corner and kicks your ass. You've literally turned into a J drama. I hope you're happy with yourself.*

"What about you?" He swallowed hard before continuing. "I'm sorry if it's inappropriate to ask, but is your partner okay with this whole process?" *Where are they? Why didn't they come with you?*

He tensed when she grimaced, worried he'd made a grave mistake in asking. *She's going to tell you to mind your own fucking business because all you're here to do is ejaculate. Just be happy that you get to fuck something other than your hand.* Instead, she blushed prettily once more, shaking her head.

"No, I-I'm divorced."

Lowell listened, slack-jawed, as she described the fertility struggles she had faced with her ex-husband, a lizard man. *Fucking of course he was.* He stiffened as soon as the words crossed her lips, imagining Daiyuu and Nikkia, fury turning his insides all over again. *What kind of stupid, double-dicked asshole would leave this gorgeous, soft girl?*

He wished he could say the rest of their conversation had been short and innocuous. That he'd sat there like a perfect gentleman, sipping his lemonade with a completely flaccid cock, the thought of getting hard over the fact that she was single never even occurring to him. He wished she could say that, but he would've been a filthy, stiff-dicked, lemonade-sipping liar.

He'd never wanted to fuck anyone more than he wanted to fuck this gorgeous girl before him. Every drop of blood in his brain was fighting him, desperate to abandon the conversation and move south, like a snowbird fleeing the northeast winter. His balls throbbed, and his cock twitched every time she did something adorable, which was constant-ly. He was so focused on remaining upright that he nearly missed the moment she referred to his penis.

"You know, it's kind of surprising they didn't include a picture of it."

She didn't need to worry about a picture, he wanted to blurt, because he would've been happy to pull it out right there for her. He managed to make a joke about not judging her chosen donor based on size, but she'd made it very clear she was interested in seeing what he was packing.

"I mean, if you really want to see it, I could technically whip it out for you right now. I'm pretty sure this town has some kind of legislation that makes clothing optional. I'll warn you, though, it's been stiff for the last forty minutes."

They had left the small café by then and were passing between buildings, following the small path that led to a miniature park, one that was only ever populated during the commerce park's early lunch hour, which they were well past. He had expected his crass words to make her blush and quickly change her mind. He was shocked when her hand dropped to rest on the bulge at the front of his jeans, sucking in a breath when his shaft twitched in her hand. Lowell thought his knees would buckle when she gave his cock a light squeeze, sense leaving him as he pulled open his belt buckle.

"Someone needs to be on lookout duty because if I get caught this way, I really am going to walk into traffic; you have no idea."

He tried to imagine the scandal it would cause if some mother and her young child wandered through the little park on their way home from the elementary school, spotting one of the Hemmings boys with his cock out in public. He hadn't lied, not technically. The current town ordinance made clothing optional. There were unspoken rules, though, of course. His cock and balls rested on the outside of his body; therefore, he was expected to cover them the same as in any human town in the unification. There were other places in the world where he'd traveled where nonhuman species didn't wear clothing at all, regardless of their genitalia and if it would swing around in public, but here in Cambric

Creek, there were certain expectations — and as a Hemming, he was *expected* to lead by example. It would not do to be caught this way.

That didn't keep him from moaning when she touched him, the edge of her nail tracing the outline of his cock head. He wanted her to ease his foreskin back, tap her finger against his slit until it was slick and sticky with his pre-come, and wondered what the slide of her tongue would feel like against his frenulum. He wanted to pull his balls out and let her give them a bit of stretch, wanted her to suck each one in her mouth before kissing his sac and returning her attention to his needy cockhead. He desperately wanted to do all of the above ... but what he did instead was tuck himself away.

"We-we should probably go somewhere if you don't feel like you can make an informed decision yet. Clothing is optional, but I'm pretty sure hand jobs are not."

He could taste her arousal on the air. A slight, sweet tang on his tongue, he could taste her wetness. His mouth flooded, wanting to bury his face against her and lick her for all he was worth. He wouldn't stop until he was dripping in her and she was gasping in pleasure, filling her with his cock only after he had made her shake beneath his tongue.

"There-there's a place right around here, I think. Just around the corner. We can walk, if you want to leave your car here."

It was a hotel that catered to business travelers visiting their company campuses there at the Parkway, but it would be good enough just then. He wanted to take her home, lay her down in the middle of one of Grayson's sumptuous spare bedrooms and fuck her until she couldn't walk in a straight line, but he didn't want her to feel threatened or unsafe. She picked a public place for their meeting, and he could pick a public place for this. He had one of Grayson's credit cards in his wallet and there wasn't a single person in town who would say no to Hemming on sight. His name chafed and he disliked the heavy expectation he carried . . . but he didn't mind the open doors at that moment.

"Lowell . . . I'm definitely picking you. You're my choice; I-I want to do this with you. But it would be nice to get the awkwardness out of the way, don't you think?"

She could call it awkwardness if it would make her feel better; she could tell herself she was doing her due diligence in getting to know her chosen partner if that was what she needed to do to sleep peacefully later that night. He was relatively confident that none of the onboarding videos he'd watched said anything about sampling the goods before their appointed rendezvous at the clinic, but he wasn't about to voice that and spoil her illusion. She wanted this as much as he did. He could taste the evidence of that on the air and couldn't wait to bury his tongue in it.

It was his debilitating horniness that made his stomach flip and his lungs somersault at her words, though, that was what he told himself, heat burning up his neck in a way he knew made him splotch like a tomato. Horniness and not much more, he told himself, gripping her chin with a gentle hand, tilting her perfect little rosebud mouth to meet his in a slow, soft kiss. He wasn't meant to be kissing her; of that, he was sure. But they weren't at the clinic just then, she had opted to see him outside of the set parameters of their contract-dictated relationship, and she was just as soft and warm as he had suspected.

He was lonely and horny, and that was a terrible cocktail upon which decisions ought to be made, but it had been too many months of feeling both, and he no longer cared. If she wanted to do this, he was more than willing.

First, though, he had a wrong to right.

"Can-can we just move our cars real quick? Let me just ... Here, follow me." He quickly led her back up the little pathway between buildings until they had reached the café parking lot. There was a car on the far corner of the lot, which undoubtedly belonged to the cranky server, and another a few spots away that must've been the cook. There was a new car that had not been there when they had left, but that wasn't the one he was concerned with. There had been only one other car in the lot when he pulled in that afternoon, and it still sat there now. Lowell had no doubt the satyresses still sat at their little table, clicking like hens.

"Can you back into the spot next to this car here? I'll direct you."

"I think I'm too close to the line," she called him out her window a few moments later, doing exactly as he asked.

"Nope, you're right on the line, not even a hair over. Don't worry, you're perfect." She stood on the sidewalk, watching him with a furrowed brow as he quickly slid behind the wheel of the borrowed car he'd been using, Trapp's spare.

His mother was not a steamroller. She was terrifyingly competitive and viciously territorial, both traits Gray and Trapp had inherited, but no one was allowed to say that about her except for them. At least not in his hearing. She gave up copious amounts of her free time for this community, planning and executing festivals, parties, and picnics, one after another, putting in more hours and effort than people often did at a full-time job.

Perhaps, he thought to himself, climbing through the car to exit on the passenger side, taking in Moriah's slightly horrified expression, they might learn their lesson about being terrible gossips. He suspected not, though, which was why they were people like him in the world — malicious little shits, as Gray had called him just that week, a consequence of unplugging every single prostate massager in his brother's fancy drawer — adjusting the balances and setting things right.

The gossips would be unable to open either the passenger's or driver's side door more than a few inches, not enough to squeeze into their vehicle, at least not until Lowell and Moriah returned. She was beautiful. She was sweet and delicate, and he wanted to taste every inch of her skin. What they did and for how long they did it would be entirely up to her, but the fact remains that he would have the room for the night. *The old biddies ought to get comfortable because we're not rushing.*

"You know what?" She grinned from the sidewalk, the horror having left her face, "if this car belongs to that horrible server? I don't even care."

I think I'm in love. The thought came to him unbidden, and Lowell grinned as he gripped her hand, eager to have it back on his cock. *Maybe it's true. Either way, it's going to be a real long fucking month.*

* * *

Moriah

Moriah felt as though she were falling.

She'd stood near the small fountain in the hotel lobby, giving him some distance at the check-in desk, not wanting to appear too eager at his side. She was sure it didn't matter. You're checking in the middle of the afternoon with no luggage; what do you think the hotel staff is assuming? She was sure she ought to be the one checking them in. After all, wasn't she the patient? Wasn't this her interview? He was merely the donor and would already be doing his part come the full moon, but he had insisted.

"It's fine, don't worry. You want to keep a little bit of anonymity, right?"

His words made her smile, and the decisive action sent a little bubble of warmth rising through her. She got the feeling it wasn't his forte, but he was making an effort for her, protecting her from the judgmental stares of the counter staff, and she appreciated that more than he knew.

He'll never have to see these people again, but you might run into them at the grocery store.

She appreciated him taking charge at the desk and enjoyed it even more when he pulled her into his arms the second the elevator door closed behind them. His mouth was hot against hers, his whole body hot to the touch, and she melted into his warmth as he kissed her.

She was barely aware of how they managed to get from the elevator to their room on the eighth floor, didn't remember him ever releasing her long enough to pull out a key card, but before she was fully cognizant of how they had moved from one place to another, the door was closed behind them, and he was backing her up to the bed in the center of the room.

This was not how she expected the afternoon to end, Moriah thought to herself, staring at the ceiling as his hungry mouth trailed from her jaw to her throat, kissing over a sliver of collar bone exposed by her dress. *Drea said it was important to interview him, and it's wise to be as thorough as possible. After all, this is going to be your baby's father. You want to make sure you're making the best decision you can.*

"I have a confession to make." His voice was a ragged gasp, breaking contact with her mouth so suddenly that she floundered for a moment, unable to even open her eyes. She was positive she probably looked like a fish, mouth gaping.

"What – what is it?" Pushing herself back to a sitting position, she expected him to say something horrible. That he had lied on his application, that he wasn't actually a werewolf, that he was just some human, and his name wasn't even Lowell. Both of his big hands dragged down his face, pulling his eyelids comically as he did so, and she braced for the worst.

"I-I haven't had sex since I left Tokyo. I've been staying with family, and it's been really hard, and I am so, *so* horny. Like, it is a *medical* condition at this point. Sometimes I can't even stand up because there's not enough blood in my brain to keep my balance. I'm going to die if we don't have sex, and I will probably explode like a geyser the second you touch me. We're going to need to ring down for extra towels. I just need you to know that I'm not normally a pump-and-dump one-minute-man. These are extenuating circumstances. So-so if you're planning on making a decision based on how this goes, I just . . . Can you please at least give me a round two?"

The words came tumbling out of him. He was frantic, verging on hysteria, gesturing to his crotch as if it had committed a bank robbery without him, and he was caught holding the bag. Moriah was obliged to bite back her grin as he went on, dramatic hand gestures punctuating his words, exhaling on a *whoosh* when he was finished, breathing hard. She gave him her best smile, beaming beatifically before opening her arms, waiting for him to come back to her.

"Poor baby," she crooned into his hair, pulling him against her, grinning as she felt his shuddering sigh. She'd noticed at the restaurant the way he shivered every time she complimented something about him, be it his bravery for moving overseas alone or her admiration for the amount of traveling he did. She thought she understood why.

He lived alone, was far away from his family, and his friends sounded as if they lived similarly transient lives as he did. He said he felt lost amongst his giant clutch of siblings when he was home. He may have teased her position as an only child, but she'd not grown up at a loss for attention. She had always lived with friends once she was out on her own, usually in groups, strength in numbers, always someone there to keep her company. She moved from a shared University flat into the apartment she'd shared with Sorben before they purchased their house, and she had never needed to know what it was like to be alone in the world.

Moriah pulled herself up to her knees. His wide eyes were full of earnestness, eager to please, like an adorable spaniel, and she had no doubt in her mind that if he did prematurely explode like a geyser, he would fall over himself to make it up to her in a way that would leave little room for complaint. She hoped her baby would also have his wide-eyed earnestness, mentally promising that she would shower them with all the love and attention she had to give. In the meantime, though, she would put her observations to work.

"Poor Lowell," she murmured again, pressing her lips to his temple and scoring her nails down his back. "You don't have to worry. I've already made up my mind, and I pick you." She punctuated her words with a small kiss to the juncture of his neck and shoulder, feeling him shiver once more. "And if you need a round two, that's fine by me. I'm not in any hurry. I'll bet you'll do your best work come round three. But first, though, I want to see what the clinic isn't showing."

Her fingers were nimble, opening his shirt buttons, pushing the T-shirt he wore beneath the button-down up his body and over his head, revealing the long expanse of his toned arms and chest. His pectorals were dusted in dark hair that moved to the line down his body, leading her fingers to his belt buckle once more. His breath hitched as her nails grazed his sides, and she filed the information away later with a grin. *Erogenous zone? Ticklish? Maybe both?*

He was broad-shouldered but leanly muscled, his arms enveloping her with a strength that made her dizzy. She imagined him hiking through jungles and climbing the craggy rock face of mountains, hauling his heavy camera equipment wherever he was, in places she had only dreamed of. His kiss was hot and insistent. Lips and tongue and teeth, demanding entrance into her mouth before pulling back again with another shuddering gasp, pacing himself as best he could.

She caressed his chest slowly, mapping his musculature with her fingertips, dragging her fingers down his sternum, and detouring to each of his nipples, paying attention to the way his stomach muscles jumped as she teased each pebbled peak. *You're going to make a baby with this man.* The idea was oddly thrilling. She let her nails scrape down his hard abdomen until she reached the barrier of his jeans, running a quick hand over the bulge tenting the front.

Now or never. Isn't this what you really wanted to see?

His breath was practically wheezing when she pulled open his belt and undid his fly again. Moriah decided not to tease him here. Hooking her thumbs in the waistband of both jeans and the boxer briefs beneath, she pulled straight down, letting his cock bounce free. She let him do the awkward shuffle of kicking off his shoes and socks, freeing each leg from the distressed jeans before she left the bed, kneeling before him, wanting to get the best view.

His cock was magnificent. At least, she thought so. It was entirely possible that her opinion was born of a decade of marriage to a man with altogether different anatomy and fed by the fact that she hadn't seen a penis this up close and personal since her divorce, but the thick length of him made her mouth water. He had a slight upward curve, one she knew from experience with similarly-shaped toys would feel delicious inside her. His foreskin was partially retracted, just enough to show her the shiny skin of his cockhead, so swollen that it held a bluish tint. His slit was already leaking, a clear, viscous fluid, and she wanted nothing more than to press her tongue to the opening and lap it up. *Finish exploring first. Like he said, he might erupt. And you haven't even reached the grand prize.*

His cock was necessary, of course, but considering this was a fertility match, Moriah couldn't help but feel that his balls had earned the central place of honor. Her ex-husband's testicles were inside his body, and it had been a long time since she felt the weight of a partner's scrotum in the palm of her hand. Lowell's was fat and heavy. Like his cock, his balls were swollen and tight, his sac forming a perfect heart shape, and she couldn't resist leaning in and giving each one a soft kiss. *After all, this is where the magic happens.* He shuddered when her lips pressed to the first, its twin raising in expectation before her mouth shifted.

"You should put on a raincoat. They're *so* full right now, and you're in the splash zone."

She slumped against him in laughter, scratching his thighs.

"Thank you for being a good sport. I just want to get this out of the way. I can't imagine seeing you for the very first time the day we're supposed to perform at the clinic! Okay .. tell me what you like. Are-are they too sensitive to touch?"

He shook his head, breathing raggedly. Reaching a hand down, he tugged on his sac, giving each of his balls a stretch, allowing her to replace his hands with her own. Testing their weight, deciding to add large plums to her shopping list, she rolled them in her palm, mirroring the stretch. *Extra large eggs, put them on the shopping list as well.* Gently pulling her finger down the seam, Moriah watched as his balls separated, pulling back up as he groaned, the sound a vibration that rippled through his body. Cupping his sac once more, she continued to caress him until his cock bobbed insistently, waving down her attention.

"Poor baby," she laughed again, taking a deep breath before gripping his shaft for the first time. He was right. He was too far gone for her to explore his shape and learn the snaking path of each vein with her lips. She had only been with an uncut cock once before, and that had been when she was too young to fully appreciate anything more than a fast climax. She wanted to examine his foreskin and learn the way it stretched, wanted to practice stroking it in her hand and easing it back over the flared edge of his cock . . . but a quick glance up showed her that he was hanging on by a thread.

His jaw clenched, his eyes squeezed tight, and she would have laughed if she wasn't afraid of hurting his feelings. He was the most adorable man she'd ever met in her life, and she wanted to take her time learning every inch of his body . . . But first, she thought, carefully easing back the membrane of skin until his head popped free, she wanted to let him have a bit of relief.

He didn't resist when she pulled him back to the bed. Her panties and skirt were peeled off easily. His fingers were clumsy at her back once he had pulled her sweater up over her arms and head, finally undoing the clasp of her bra, gently pushing her to lay back against the bed. When his lips met hers again, Moriah melted. It had been too long since she'd made out like a teenager. Towards the end, all the intimacy she and Sorben shared was dictated by her temperature and the day of her cycle, tracking her ovulation obsessively. It had been too long since someone kissed their way down her body, the way Lowell did just then, breathing against her skin reverently as if she were a goddess and not a suburban divorcee. She hadn't been naked in front of another person in two years, hadn't been naked in front of someone other than Sorben and what felt like forever, and she had forgotten how vulnerable the reality of being so was.

"Fuck, you're so beautiful . . . I'm going to kiss every inch of you once my balls stop vibrating, I promise."

"Do-do you want to go ahead and . . . you know, I just want to make sure that everything feels okay."

"Of course, this-this is important; you have to make sure you're making the right decision," he gritted out, his eyes nearly rolling back in his head when she gripped his cock once more, relieved that he was still following her train of thought. "Do you want to see how it feels inside . . ."

"Yeah," she breathed, "yeah, I think that's important. You know, just to make sure."

The first bump of his cock head against her clit made her see stars. He stroked back and forth, his eyes heavy-lidded and glazed in pleasure, coating himself in her slickness until she urgently gripped his shoulder.

"Go ahead. I just want to see how you feel inside me, don't worry about lasting long."

He groaned when she gripped him again, leading him to her opening.

"I feel like a fucking virgin," he laughed. "Just don't hold this against me."

Her own laughter cut off with the first push of his cockhead, the flared edge catching at her inner lips, and her breath caught as he slowly pressed into her. He was so deliciously thick, more than making up for what he didn't possess in her ex-husband's length.

"Is that okay?" His voice was strained, and she could tell he was holding himself steady, an effort she appreciated.

"It's good. It's *really* good. You feel amazing."

His hips pulled back slowly, the backward drag of his cock making her toes curl, before he thrust forward, a solid thump that made her wheeze. Once, twice, on the third thrust of his hips into her, she moaned, digging her fingers into his thick dark hair.

"Good?"

"Yes," she wheezed, "*so* good. That feels fucking incredible. Okay, yes, you're definitely hired. I want your cock in me for the full moon. Do-do you want to come inside me? Just so we can make sure that's good too?"

The noise he made was a strangled gurgle in his throat, but his hands lifted her hips, pressing her against him snugly before he began to pump into her once more.

The slight change in position nearly made her go cross-eyed. She would let him fuck her every day for the rest of her life if it made him happy, if it kept his fat testicles healthy, if it would always feel this incredible, for suddenly, she was also only hanging on by a thread, desperate to come with him.

"You can go harder if you want," she murmured against his neck. Moriah had wrapped her arms around his back, her nails digging into his shoulders. She wanted him to have her up on her knees as well, thinking about what Drea had said about getting in deep, although Lowell felt plenty deep inside her. The thickness of his shaft dragged against her G spot, and with every thrust, he bottomed out, his heavy balls slapping into her, the head of his cock hitting a place inside her that made her wheeze. She wanted him to go harder, deeper, faster . . . But then she also had a fast vision of him spooning against her, kissing her body as he pumped into her slowly, more intimate than was appropriate for her sperm donor, she reminded herself.

"*Fuck*, you feel so good," he groaned against her. "Are you sure you want me to finish inside?"

His hips had picked up speed, the percussive slap of his balls against her skin seeming over loud in the room, the rub of his pubic bone against her clit making her vision go spotty on every backward drag.

"Yes," she assured him decisively, tightening her hand in his hair. She'd decided there was no point in letting him finish anywhere else. *That's the whole point of this.* "Come inside me."

"I can't wait for you to take my knot. You're so fucking tight. You're going to feel so good squeezing me." Her head lolled at the thought, his tight press already nearly too much. "Fuck . . . I'm gonna come."

She felt the tension in his shoulders, the vibration in his back, and when his hips faltered, surging forward, she gasped.

"Fill me up," she gasped, the spread of heat within her letting her know he was doing precisely that. She wasn't sure what possessed her to do so, but her arm stretched, her fingers seeking until she was able to grip his scrotum once more. Pressing her thumb into the pulsing muscle she found, she thrilled at the way he rhythmically spasmed as he emptied. The noise he made as she did so made her clench, tightening around him as best she could, the pressure of far more semen than she was used to filling her like a balloon.

"Good boy," she crooned against his hair. Lowell seemed to ripple at the endearment, moaning against her neck, his hips refinding their rhythm, pumping against her. She wasn't sure if it was normal for a werewolf to ejaculate so much, his hips stuttering to a stop and restarting twice more, and she was positive if she could see her belly, it would be bulging with his release. *And in a few weeks, he'll come in you this hard again and fill you with his knot. He'll be able to give you a whole litter of werewolves at this rate.*

When he slid a hand between their bodies, Moriah wasn't sure exactly what he was about to do, and she nearly arched off the bed when he trapped her clit. Tight, precise circles, his cock still stretching her, and she was sure the only way it could have felt better was if he were using his mouth. When she came with a cry, all she could think of was what Drea had said about it being necessary that she orgasm after him, sucking his seed further into her body.

He was solicitous in the moments after. She felt the gush of his release leaving her as soon as his cock softened, slipping out, and he scrambled. Jumping from the bed and returning a breath later with towels, he made sure she was cleaned and tucked under the covers with enough pillows, sliding in beside her only after he'd seen to her comfort. *Why couldn't you have met him at the grocery store or the post office? He's sweet. He's funny and interesting. This is such a fucked up situation.*

"Well, I don't know about you, but I'm extremely proud of myself. That wasn't nearly as embarrassing as it had the potential to be. Still not a great showing, probably not going to put that in the family Christmas card, but not nearly as tragic as I'd anticipated."

His chest absorbed her laughter as he curled around her, the warm smell of him enveloping her until her head dropped to rest against him, knowing as soon as she did so that it was unwise.

"Not a bad showing at all! If that was you embarrassing yourself, I can't wait for round two. And thank you for helping me break my dry spell. Feels like things can only go up from here."

He gasped comically, and she laughed again.

"You too?! How long? You have to tell me, I told you my embarrassing secret. And by the way, thank you for not trying to suck me before, I thought you were about to, and that was going to be the end. Splooge in your eyes, in your hair, on the rug. I would have been fired three weeks before the full moon, end of the story."

It was hard to imagine how devoid of laughter her life had been for the past several years when she had laughed so much since arriving at the café that afternoon.

"Um, well . . . let's see . . . It's been two years since my divorce."

He nodded earnestly, his dark eyes sparkling, waiting for her to continue.

"And I guess . . . I don't know. I guess it had been maybe a month or two before he left? Maybe only a few weeks? Honestly, I don't even remember. He was so withdrawn by then. More than two weeks, less than two months."

Beside her, Lowell blinked. Nodded again. Waited. When he realized she was done talking, his eyebrows came together again, two dark caterpillars, angrily conversing.

"Two . . . Years? Two *years*?! But . . . but, but you're beautiful! That doesn't make any fucking sense! Is everyone you know *blind*? And you're interesting! You're artistic and funny, and you have a Parisian cafe! I mean, *look* at you! Do you literally live in a monastery or something? Wait . . . are-arere you a serial killer? I feel like they probably should've screened for that, but are you going to cut out my liver? Am I gonna die in a business class hotel? I need to protest if that's your plan because if I'm going to die at the hands of a beautiful stranger in a hotel room, my brother will be *mortified* if it's not at least a five-star resort. I won't be able to answer to him from the afterlife if I die in a business class hotel. I'll have to come live with you as a ghost because *he* will haunt *me*. How were you not tripping over interested parties the second you were single again?!"

Incontinence had never been something she had worried about before, but she was laughing so hard that she was concerned she might wet the bed.

"Wait a minute," she wheezed, "I need to use the restroom. I should've done that immediately. It is a testament to how absolutely not *tragic* round one was that you have me forgetting my UTI management."

When she returned to the bed, he watched her with narrowed eyes, the covers drawn up to his chin.

"I'm on to you. Just be aware of that before you pull out a knife."

She giggled again, clambering ungracefully onto the bed, gratified when he threw back the coverlet for her, pulling her against him once more.

"This is the brother you live with? The one who's going to be mad at your ghost?"

"Mmhm. He is what you might call a bit of a huge fucking snob. The only plus to that his house is awesome, it's like staying at the poshest hotel you can imagine. There's laundry service! The groceries get delivered, and he buys the best stuff. And If I want something specific, I just need to ask the refrigerator, and it's added to the order. It's restaurant quality for every meal, with the bonus that I don't need to put pants on. Plus, he gives excellent presents at Christmas, so please don't take my liver yet; I've already been dropping hints about the lens I want."

"So what you're telling me is you're a bit of a brat."

He huffed in outrage, sputtering his denial, and Moriah laughed, positive it was not the first time he'd been told that.

"You said you like staying at your brother's house because he has nice stuff and you like eating all his food. *And* you're already angling for your expensive Christmas gift. That sounds pretty spoiled to me."

"I am the opposite of spoiled! You don't know what you're talking about."

She continued to giggle against him, her eyes turning up in interest.

"You celebrate Christmas, then? Not Solstice?"

Sorben had celebrated neither, begrudgingly attending the community-wide Solstice night celebration with her for a handful of years until she'd stopped suggesting it. It had become a theme in their marriage — she wanted to do things he did not, him going along grudgingly and making it known that his participation was only grudging until she simply stopped asking to do the thing at all. She'd spent two years in therapy trying to root out if she'd *ever* been happy in her marriage, coming to the determination that they'd simply been too different right from the start.

She had grown up celebrating Christmas, but it was hard to feel festive when the majority of the community did not, and she was so far from her family. *You should go to the Christmas party this year,* she told herself. There was a secular celebration of the holiday, with several family-friendly events organized by the community planning committee, one of the many community-wide events the town hosted that she'd never attended, one more reason she felt so disconnected from her neighbors. Sorben had always grumbled about the crowds, and in the two years since she'd been on her own, she hadn't wanted to go and intrude on the happy family celebration, knowing herself well enough. She would see little kids opening presents and proud parents holding their hands, and she would fall to pieces in public, one more mortifying thing to contemplate.

"We do. My family does, at least. A lot of the werewolves we know also do the secular side of the holiday. There are plenty of wolvish families who follow human religions, we're not really one of them, but yeah, we do Christmas. My mom loves doing the whole decorations and tree thing. She didn't grow up with that, so she goes all out. And my brother is *always* extravagant; that's not me being a brat! Spending money is his love language. But if you kill me in a business class hotel, I'll never have a chance to find out what he would have bought me, so please don't."

"I grew up celebrating Christmas," she murmured against his chest, pressing her cheek to his warmth. He was *so* warm, as if there was an inferno under his skin, heating him from the inside out, but rather than be uncomfortable, she snuggled into him, feeling cozy and comfortable and complacent. "My ex didn't celebrate anything, though, so we really didn't do anything during the holidays. I guess I've fallen out of practice."

Lowell's dark eyebrows drew together, but he said nothing.

"Do you live in a human neighborhood?"

Moriah swallowed. She wasn't ready to take that step, cross that line. It had less to do with feeling unsafe or not trusting him and everything to do with the fact that if she told him about her home and her life and invited him in to see her office and her little French café breakfast nook, she would want him to stay forever, and she'd only just met him a few hours ago. It felt impossible to believe. *It's the situation. It's forced intimacy. You're doing something huge with him, and you will be connected to him forever, whether he's in your life or not. That's why it feels this way.*

"It's not all human. I have a lot of neighbors of different species, so there's a pretty good mix. It's weird, though; I don't feel that connected to the community, even though I love living there. I don't know if I really belong there. Especially now. When my ex left, he literally just picked up and left. He left me the house, no contest. But in all the years we lived there, we never really did much *in* the community, so . . . I don't know, it's odd. And it's a super gossipy place, everyone is very into the community and everyone else's business and local politics, and I feel so removed from all of it. I don't leave my house enough to keep up with the who's who. I love it, I don't want to leave. But I feel very disconnected at the same time."

"That's how I feel about the town I'm from."

She hadn't expected the confidence from him, but she supposed he was feeling their situation's forced intimacy as well.

"There's just so much expectation built into living there. Everyone I know hopes I'm going to be something I'm not. It's how I feel about my family half the time too. I love them. I miss them, desperately sometimes, but they're just living their lives, and me not being there is the norm. I don't think they notice I'm gone most of the time, and then when I'm here, it's like . . . I don't know. An annoyed surprise. The brother I'm staying with right now is the only one who ever checks up on me; he's the only one who remembers I exist. And I'm pretty sure that's just out of obligation."

She turned her head up as he spoke, noting how his dark eyes were fixed on a point above their heads, his eyebrows still drawn together. She wanted to reach up and kiss away the furrow between his eyes and had to remind herself that was the action of a girlfriend and not someone who'd only met him hours earlier, who was only sharing a temporary medical procedure with him. Instead, she dragged her nails lightly down his chest.

"I don't think that's true at all. If he checks up on you, it's probably because he misses you and is thinking of you. He wouldn't care about you dying in a business class hotel if he didn't miss you. So sorry to burst your bubble, but you are not someone I would consider easily forgettable."

When he tilted her chin, she was ready to meet his lips. The slow drag of his mouth against hers, her tongue meeting his, and their teeth glancing off each other as their bodies molded together, the long, hard line of him against her slight frame . . . it was, without question, the most intimate thing she had shared with another person in at least a decade. *And none of this is real. He's your sperm donor. He signed a contract, and so did you.* Moriah tried to memorize the silky heft of his slightly over-long hair between her fingers, the heat of his skin pressed flush to hers, the soft tickle of the hair on his chest against her nipples.

She was lonely. She'd been lonely for the last two years, and she'd been lonely in her marriage for countless years before that. *That's all this is.* She was lonely and desperate for a connection with someone, and he was sweet and lovely and eager. *It will be different when you have a baby,* she reminded herself. She needed to refocus and remember why she was doing this. His cock was hard against her, and her heartbeat pulsed between her legs. When he turned her, her legs fell open easily, more than ready for round two.

C.M. NASCOSTA

* * *

Lowell

By the time he got home that night, the sky was black.

"You know we have the room until morning," he'd hesitantly offered as Moriah searched for her underwear on the hotel room floor. "I-I don't mean that we have to stay, only if you didn't want to —"

"We should probably go, don't you think?"

He'd enthusiastically nodded his agreement, even though he wanted to shake his head no with vehemence. He didn't want them to ever leave the hotel room, but as she slipped her arms through the straps of her bra, he resigned himself to getting dressed. She was right. They had only met for the first time that afternoon. It was premature to be spending the night together. It was stupid to do so in any case, and it wasn't as if this was a relationship, no matter how close he already felt to her, despite the intense attraction they clearly shared.

There were specific memories emblazoned on his brain, every detail captured in crisp perfection. The advice he'd been given by his brothers nearly two decades earlier, on a Friday night when he'd been leaving to pick up his girlfriend for a school dance, was one such moment.

"Any pointers?" he'd asked Gray and Trapp, both in their twenties, home for the weekend to attend a mutual friend's wedding. He'd been at the kitchen door, the sun shining as brightly that spring evening as it had done in the middle of the day, hardly a romantic backdrop for a dance. His brothers had been musing over their plans for the evening, debating over where they would go if the wedding festivities were deemed boring.

"When you lick her pussy, don't act like you're doing her a favor. It's a five-course meal and you've been starving. That's how you treat it."

Trapp had nodded his agreement with Grayson's pronouncement, and Lowell had stood there dumbstruck, doing what they had advised never even occurring to him until that moment.

"A-anything else?"

"Yeah. Don't be bad at sex. You'd be shocked at what a low bar that is."

He had rolled his eyes, hand already on the door.

"That's not real advice!"

"It is, though," Trapp had cut in. "Most guys don't care. Put in the effort, build out your skillset. We have reputations, don't embarrass us."

"What are you now, like, nineteen?"

"I'm sixteen, you asshole!"

Grayson had shrugged. "I was fucking your babysitter when I was sixteen. You've got some catch-up work to do, kiddo."

"Don't embarrass us!" Trapp had called to his back, the sound of their laughter following him to the dance.

It was odd how things from the past crept back in at inopportune moments, for he'd thought of Gray's words and the way Trapp nodded solemnly beside him every time he was with a new partner, every time he went down on a girl for the first time. Moriah had been no exception.

Lick her pussy like it's a five-course meal. Don't be bad at sex. He licked her from clit to slit and back up again, slow and steady, not missing an inch. He savored the taste of her, the silken slipperiness of her slick folds, and the way she moaned softly, tugging at his hair as he suckled the little pearl at the apex of her sex. It wasn't what he was meant to be doing, wasn't the point of their little bedroom interview. She wanted to know how his cock would feel inside her, and he'd already shown her . . . but he wanted her to come against his tongue, to hear her moaning his name and feel her nails digging into the back of his neck; wanted to pleasure her over and over again, her soft little gasps and moans the sweetest music he'd ever heard.

He'd groaned against her, his tongue working her clit steadily, his cock twitching every time her back arched, which it did every time his lips fastened in a sucking pucker. She had moaned with her whole throat when he slid 2 fingers into her, her toes curling when he curled his fingers to stroke her from the inside. He was used to hauling his gear bag up mountains and across rocky terrain, never letting it fall, holding his camera for hours at a time, catching shot after shot, and he had built up solid endurance in his upper body. She was going to fall apart before his arm got tired, he thought as he sucked on her clit once more, smiling when her fingers tightened in his hair, he was going to make sure of that.

Her G-spot was not difficult to find. She cried out as he rubbed it, letting him know he had the right spot, and when his arm began to piston rhythmically, the pads of his fingers doing the work inside, she was lost. His arm moved in tandem with his tongue, and he felt the moment her orgasm shook through her. Her pussy clenched, tightening around his hand, but Lowell kept going, intent on giving her as much pleasure as he could. She was so lovely, so sweet, and he loved her laugh.

It was loneliness, he reminded himself. He was horribly lonely and that was affecting his judgment, but the knowledge didn't prevent him from wishing this was more than just a transaction. He didn't know if he would ever be able to return to work in the same capacity, where he would live if not, and he didn't know how to meet anyone in Cambric Creek. But he had met her, and she was sweet and lovely, and he wanted to make her come over and over again.

He continued to lick and suck on her clit through her orgasm, only slowing when the hand in his hair tightened, a silent plea to ease up on the pressure, which he quickly obliged. His hand, though, never stopped moving.

"Oh gods . . . What are you *doing* to me, oh fuck . . . I-I'm going to come again . . ."

He was going to need to use every last dollar in his wallet as a tip for the cleaning staff, he thought, grabbing the towel that was already smeared with his semen when she released in a spray of fluid. The way she moaned was worth it, though, he thought smugly. *Be good at sex.* It was a lesson he had taken to heart.

"What-what the fuck are you? I've *never* done that before. Are you even a werewolf?! Or are you actually a succubus? Or a wizard?!"

He'd shrugged and given her his most winsome smile.

"Just good at sex, I guess? Are you ready for round two?" He stroked himself from root to tip, letting his solid erection slap back against his belly. "Because I sure am."

The third time he'd fucked her — and there could be no pretending that they were doing anything other than fucking at that point, no matter how many times she said she *just wanted to make sure she was making the right decision* for their doings at the clinic — she asked to be taken from behind.

"My friend used the clinic a few months ago, and she's pregnant now. She said her partner told her he could get in deeper that way."

He could get in deeper if he fucked her as a wolf, he thought to himself. His cock was bigger, a completely different shape, with a tapered tip designed to fit over her cervix and fill her until she could taste him on the back of her tongue, but he had a feeling that was likely outside of the clinic's parameters.

"I can go deeper if you want."

She pulled herself up to hands and knees in the middle of the bed, and he knelt behind her, holding her hips and pulling her back onto his cock. She didn't protest when he pushed down on the center of her back. Lowering herself obligingly to her elbows, with her cheek pressed to the mattress and her ass high in the air, it was a better angle for his balls to slap into her clit as he pumped into her. Lowell ultimately knew he could get the deepest angle if he covered her with his body, rutting into her like the wolf he was, and her moans of pleasure when he did so told him when he hit just the right spot.

. . . And then she'd pulled on her clothes and straightened up the bed as best she was able, wrapping the soiled towels in the sheet, leaving it knotted like a fat, shameful dumpling on the bathroom floor. He'd watched from the bed as she fixed her hair and straightened her sweater, realizing he, too, needed to get up and get dressed unless he was planning on staying the night. He could. The room was paid for until morning, and he did not need to rush out . . . But the thought of staying there without her made his stomach twist, and he'd pulled on his jeans hastily, just as eager to leave as she seemed to be, feeling foolish for fantasizing that this was anything more than a prelude to a transaction.

Grayson's car was in the driveway when he pulled in, noting with a sinking stomach that Vanessa's was as well. He could go straight to the pool house, he thought. He could go straight to the pool house and avoid seeing them looking happy and complacent together, a sharp reminder that he had no one to share either of those emotions with, not that either of those emotions were things he was terribly familiar with anymore. His laptop was in the house, though, and if he went to the pool house now, he would have nothing with which to amuse himself. His phone battery wouldn't last much longer, and his charger was in the bedroom. He could try going to sleep, but he'd always been a night owl, and the previous few hours had done nothing to make him drowsy.

You can go for a run. You can climb under the pool cover and go for a swim. No one would even notice you're gone. It probably wouldn't matter if you ever came out. You could stay in there until you grew gills or expired.

He waffled indecisively, realizing that Grayson had probably already been notified he had pulled in the driveway, the camera doorbell catching all. *Or you can act like an adult and go into the house. They might not even be up. Or maybe they are, and it doesn't matter. You can just go to your room. Or go get your laptop and charger and come back to the cabana. Act like a fucking grown-up for a change and not a little kid.*

Luck was not with him as he shimmied past the two cars, pulling open the side door through the kitchen to instantly hear voices.

"See, here he is now! I told you it was him."

Vanessa was leaning on the kitchen island, wielding a pair of chopsticks she used to wave in his direction and holding a takeout container in her hand.

"Lowell, please, *please* eat. I ordered so much food, I don't know what I was thinking."

He hadn't planned on slowing.

It wasn't that he disliked Grayson's girlfriend; he'd not taken the time to get to know her, quite honestly. But everything about her confounded him. She had thick dark hair, bright, wide eyes, and a girl-next-door prettiness that didn't quite align with his brother's extravagant luxury tastes. He wasn't sure what exactly she saw in Gray, for Lowell knew well that beyond the handsome, muscular exterior, he was argumentative and petty, and this woman looked far too nice for his combative, egotistical bravado. He could only assume she was temporarily addicted to the sex, an affliction that would surely pass. His stomach growled, reminding him that all he had to eat that day was the less than stellar fruit plate at the café, and he was, in truth, starving.

Grayson entered the room, taking in Lowell with a long hard look, causing him to clench in panic, uncertain of what he had done to earn his brother's ire this time.

"If you finally got laid, I don't even care."

His relief manifested as a choked laugh, gladly taking the container of beef and broccoli Vanessa offered him. He'd been tasked with taking the Truck for an oil change the previous afternoon, and the credit card he'd been left for that task had been the one he'd charged for the hotel room. Gray must have alerts sent to his phone when his cards are used.

"I did," he admitted before stuffing his mouth, talking around the broccoli a moment later. "My balls feel ten pounds lighter."

Grayson's laugh was a rich, deep scrape, and it would always sound like home, no matter how old he was or where he was, Lowell thought, warmth pooling in his belly as he remembered Moriah's words. He lashed out when he was mad, but she was right. He called him because he cared. Grayson's deep laugh and biting sarcasm and Trapp's bright smile and bark of a laugh would always be home, a testament to how much time he had spent trailing after his two older brothers growing up instead of playing with his twin.

"Well, thank fucking stars for that. I can only hope you won't be such a mopey bitch now."

Instantly, the warmth froze over. *So much for that.* Grayson was an asshole, and he always would be. *And what did he call you? A malicious little shit?*

"Yeah, I met her for lunch this afternoon by the commerce parkway. You know that place next to Burgess Coffee? Some satyrs were gossiping about you, actually."

Lowell realized he was holding the mail, a thick stack from the box at the curb that no one ever checked.

"What else is new?" Grayson grumbled, shuffling through the envelopes and tossing junk mail onto the island. "Probably all a'twitter over Jackson officially running. How do we have this much mail if we have post office boxes? I don't understand it."

Lowell shook his head. "Nope. You specifically. You and Sulya, actually."

Grayson's head lifted, dark eyes narrowing to slits in Lowell's direction, but the damage was done. Lowell took another bite of his beef and broccoli, savoring the sauce as Vanessa perked up.

"Sulya Slade? She's one of the owners of the Greenbridge house with you, right? What about her?"

"Mhm, her and a handful of other people. The charity document is registered in her name. Harmond mentioned something about opening it for tours after the holidays. I think that's a good idea. Let people see what we're preserving."

"That is a good idea! You should start it before the holidays, actually. Get everything all festive. People love that shit."

Grayson was a professional. Lowell understood why he was so successful, for there was no trap he didn't see a mile away, sidestepping with ease. Vanessa was talking about pine boughs and uplighting at the front of the Greenbridge Glen house and how nice it would look in the snow, wholly rerouted, with a few mildly spoken words from his brother. It was a superpower Gray had inherited from their father, one for which Lowell had missed the gene. Fortunately for him, what he had missed out on in strategizing, he earned back double in shit starting.

"No, they weren't talking about a house. It was about the car accident. And how you left her in jail that one time, remember? With the cocaine?"

He was feeling poorly about the way the evening had ended with Moriah. He'd laced his fingers with hers as they walked back to their cars, laughing at the sight of the satyr's vehicle still sandwiched between their own, opining that someone probably had to call for a ride. He kissed her at her car door, rubbing a strand of her dark red hair between his thumb and forefinger, trying to memorize the silky glide of it and the soft, sweet smell of her, before she pulled back first, giving him a smile that melted a piece of him.

"Well, I guess I'll see you in a few weeks. Thank you again for taking the time today, this was . . . this was really nice. I'm so glad I picked you. I'll see you before the full moon."

She hadn't said anything wrong; hadn't said anything offensive or upsetting, but each word had reminded him that was all he was; her donor. An instrument of insemination. This was a transaction. She was a patron, not his girlfriend, not even a date. Even though it had been the best date he could remember having in years, despite the fact that he felt an actual connection with her beyond his loneliness and desire for attention . . . she would see him in several weeks when he would be fucking her again in the clinic, and that would be that. He didn't like the heaviness in his head and the ache in his heart, and Grayson was mean and an easy target.

Vanessa's mouth dropped open, and the look his brother gave him was positively murderous.

"The *what*?! What car accident? Jail?!"

Grayson sighed heavily, already playing it off as nothing.

"It was a long, long time ago. I was a stupid kid, like 23 years old. You know what law school is like. Cocaine is actually an extremely effective agent in migraine control; did you know that? It's human purity culture bullshit that keeps it off the market as a viable drug when it used to be used for everything! Have a headache? At the dentist? Take some coke. Fucking ridiculous, to be honest."

Watching him in action was like a master class in diversion tactics, but Lowell was reminded that Vanessa herself was an attorney and wasn't falling for it.

"What does she have to do with it, though? Was she selling you cocaine? Even though your families have been friends for, like, ever?"

Lowell grinned broadly. It was so much worse than she could possibly guess. When their parents had found out that Grayson had been fucking Sulya Slade since the summer he'd come home to prepare for the LSAT, it had been enough of a scandal. Their mother had been furious. When it had come out that Sulya had been supplying him with cocaine since then, often flying him home for sex and drug-fueled weekends, they had nearly lost their minds. It had been one such weekend when they hadn't even known Grayson was in town, when he wrapped Sulya Slade's car around a telephone pole, enough drugs and alcohol in both of their systems to ensure his legal career would have been over before it started.

Gray, being Gray, had somehow managed to talk his way out of lockup that night, convincing the arresting officers that he was too young to know what he was doing, wasn't that inebriated in the first place, and would very much like to speak with his father. He wouldn't have been afforded the same courtesy had he been someone even an ounce less privileged, a fact they all knew well. Invoking Jack's name had been enough to spook the rookie officers, and Grayson had been let go, showing up at home in the middle of the night to inform their father that he had fucked up. Lowell and Owen had watched from the stairwell as Jack ranted and raved, a rare comeuppance for their elder sibling who thought he could get away with anything.

Although, Lowell thought with a huff, Grayson *had*, in fact, gotten away with it. He'd logicked his way around their father's anger, pointing out that he was sitting at the top of his class at the competitive, prestigious law school he attended, that the drugs genuinely *were* helping with his migraines; that he wasn't stupid enough to have unprotected sex with women his own age, let alone a married shifter fifteen years his senior; that the car accident had happened in the middle of the night when the suburban streets were empty and no one had been hurt, and most importantly, he'd learned a valuable lesson about mixing alcohol and stimulants, a mistake he'd never make again. Lowell privately thought their father had been amused by the situation once his surface anger had faded, particularly with Grayson's slippery ability to extract himself from trouble.

Sulya was the one who had to contend with Sandi's fury, the embarrassment of being first caught out with and then jilted by a man more than 15 years her junior, and stuck paying a hefty fine for the accident itself. Lowell had no idea how it was that the two of them had come to own property together all these years later, but apparently, the whole ugly incident was water under the bridge now.

But Vanessa knew nothing about that, hadn't had years to digest and come to terms with her feelings, and Lowell bounced on the counter merrily, watching her eyes narrow further.

"Were you *fucking* her?! Isn't she like, sixty?"

"She's not sixty, for fuck's sake. She's barely fifty-five, I haven't spoken to her in probably six months, and before I got pulled into the thing with the house, it had been years. This literally happened when I was 23 years old, I can barely remember two weeks ago. What the fuck is Moon Blooded Breeding? There's no addressee name." He was holding up a piece of mail, having deflected the conversation away from his misdeeds once more.

"That's mine."

Lowell and Vanessa had spoken simultaneously, and the mirth he felt over raising Grayson's hackles quickly dissipated.

"That's mine," she repeated quietly as his brother's brows drew together. "That's the place where I had the-the thing. Wait, that had better not be a fucking bill. Insurance paid that months and months ago."

As Lowell watched, his brother's face rapidly cycled from triumph at having turned the conversation to a brief look of confusion, landing at understanding, his eyes closing briefly as he nodded, handing the envelope to his girlfriend. Lowell's hands bunched into fists as he watched her tear *his* letter open, reading a few lines before her eyes lifted to his, squinting in confusion.

"This is yours?"

"Yeah, like I said," he muttered, heat burning up the back of his neck as she crossed the kitchen in two strides, the envelope in her outstretched hand.

"Whatever. I want to hear the rest of this cocaine story, don't think I've forgotten. And if you don't want to tell me, that's fine. I'll just ask your dad. I'm gonna get ready for bed; if Trophy Wives starts, make sure you pause it for me."

Grayson waited until her footsteps padded down the hallway, listening as she climbed the staircase. The second the door to the master bedroom clicked shut, he pounced. Lowell should have been ready for it. He'd forgotten how fast his brother was, despite his huge size. There was a crushing hand around his neck, the back of his head thumping into the cabinet, Grayson glowering inches from his face.

"If you ever pull a stunt like that again, I will cut out your fucking tongue and eat it for breakfast. Do you understand?"

Lowell wheezed when he was released, sucking in a lungful of air. He *should* have known better, but he would take his chances. One of the benefits of being the junior toadie little brother was that he knew where all of the metaphorical bodies were buried, for Grayson and Trapp both.

"Are you trying to have a baby?"

Gray's dark eyes squinted, his face screwing up in disgust at the thought.

"What? Why would you think that."

"That place. It's a fertility clinic."

"It's a family planning clinic, actually. For werewolves. I'm sure they offer a whole range of services."

"So . . . you guys didn't go there to try to get pregnant?"

Grayson paused, pulling open the refrigerator, taking his time answering. Lowell watched as he refilled Vanessa's glass from the strawberry-mint-infused water decanter on the center shelf before filling a second for himself. It was a tiny, inconsequential thing, but watching the action made him feel impossibly alone.

"We terminated a pregnancy there, actually. Last year."

Lowell's stomach flip-flopped at the thought, and the room suddenly seemed too bright, too close. He regretted saying anything at all, but Grayson only shrugged lightly.

"That's not in the cards for us, not anytime soon. Probably not ever. We weren't in a good place anyway, it was the right thing to do. It's a good thing Jackson is doing his part to keep the family line going. I don't know how you lived there as long as you did. Every surface in that fucking house is sticky . . . I guess you and Owen need to step it up."

"Are you in a better place now?" he asked, ignoring the dig.

"We are, actually. Hard to believe, but we are. I'm not her boss anymore, for starters. Turns out that was sort of a big fucking obstacle, who knew? Hard to keep a balance when . . . well, it was just hard. Now we can scream at each other about all manner of shit and not worry about it being felt at work the next day. Highly recommend. What are *you* doing receiving letters from this place?"

Lowell stammered, possessing none of his brother's loquaciousness.

"It's-it's um, a volunteer thing, for um, genetics, werewolf reproduc-tive, ah—"

"You know what, never mind. I just remembered that I don't actually give a fuck. You ever pull something like that again, you'll be back at mom and dad's house, taking orders from Liam. Make sure you lock the side door."

The letter was a confirmation that he'd been selected and that his information had been given out, reminding him that if he wished to not be contacted by patients in the future, all he had to do was change his privacy settings on the website with his access code. He climbed into bed a short while later, dropping the envelope in the trash. He didn't need a reminder that he had been chosen as a donor. After all, a donor was all he was, and it was a hard thing to forget.

* * *

Moriah

The count was on. Obsessively tracking her ovulation for years had given her an advantage when it came to waiting down the month for the full moon. She was used to checking days off a calendar, tracking her temperature and cervical mucus, jotting down notes about breast tenderness and how much sleep she was getting in her little tracker journal. She knew the routine. But that didn't make it any easier.

She had twisted in her sheets for days after meeting Lowell for the first time. She was able to feel the phantom whisper of his big hand encircling her waist, the heat of his breath on her neck, and the fresh, minty smell of him. In her dreams, she could feel the glide of his thick hair through her fingers, holding onto him for dear life as he pressed his face between her legs. She could still feel the scrape of his even, white teeth on her shoulder, braced around her as his thick cock pumped into her from behind, could still feel his fingers rolling over her clit and the shiver of his body beneath her hands as he orgasmed.

Worse, though, were the soft dreams she had in the hour just before waking, the ones that never failed to make opening her eyes a disappointment. They were the ones that left her hunched in longing, hugging a pillow tightly to her chest, alone in her bed. Those soft, rosy-colored fantasies of the predawn hours were built on the bedrock of his smile and infectious laugh.

She loved his sense of humor and wanted to entwine her bare legs with his and hear stories of his travels to places she'd only ever dreamed of seeing. In her dreams, she would be in bed, exactly where she actually was, but instead of a smooth, cool expanse of empty streets beside her, his warmth could be felt, and she would inch her way closer, invading his space, slowly taking over his pillow until his arms opened and he pulled her against him, never fully waking.

Whenever she had one of those soft, domestic little dreams, she would wake with a stone in her stomach, heavy and full. It would turn as she made coffee at her French press, having envisioned him bending his long frame into one of her little chairs, sitting in her pink and cream breakfast nook with a grin on his face and a sparkle in his eye.

She wasn't supposed to like him as much as she did. It was foolish to form an attachment, and she knew that. *What good does having a crush on him do? It's not like this is going to turn into a relationship. It's not like you'll ever see him again once this process is over. Who knows, the borders could reopen and he might fly back to the other side of the world tomorrow.*

Moriah was aware that her head knew what it was talking about. It often did. Her heart, however, didn't much care. She liked the dark-haired werewolf with the sparkling smile and wanted to see him again.

She walked into the Black Sheep Beanery a week and a half after that first afternoon with Lowell, waving across the dining room to Drea. It was early, the work crowd not having yet given way to the breakfast crowd, and she was relieved they had a table. *A week and a half.* A week and a half since, and a little more than two full weeks to go.

"Are you so excited?" Drea squealed as soon as she slid into the chair across the table. "Just a few more weeks!"

"I am," she agreed, "but I'm nervous too. And the doctor mentioned that it usually takes a few months, so I don't want to get my hopes up crazy high or anything."

"Oh, of course not! Still, though, it's exciting. Have you been doing your research? Have you thought of more questions for me?"

Drea was also the mom friend, the fixer, the one who always wanted to solve everyone else's problems. They would talk about Moriah's full-moon appointment, but she wasn't letting her friend off the hook that easily. Moriah fixed her friend with a pointed look.

"Of course I do, but first, how are you feeling?! What are you at, thirteen weeks?"

Drea grinned broadly, resting her hand over an imaginary swell, for Moriah could see no bump in her friend's abdomen, still as fit and lovely as she'd always been.

"Fourteen weeks, almost fifteen. Still throwing up my guts. My regular doctor thought I might be past that point by now, but nooooope.

Overall, though, good! A little sore, a little cranky. Not nearly as run-down as I felt last month, though. Still too early to really feel any sort of movement, but soon. Elijah is going to wet himself the first time we feel the baby move; he's so excited." She leaned in over the table with a knowing smile. "Okay, enough pregnancy talk. You're not going to trick me that way. It's all my mom wants to talk about, and I'm so tired of telling other people about my bowel movements and heartburn. It's honestly so boring; you'll see soon."

She appreciated her friend. Drea had taken pains not to go on about her pregnancy, something she didn't need to do, for it wasn't as if it were a secret, but Moriah appreciated the consideration, even if it was unnecessary.

"I *do* want you to come over sometime in the next few weeks so we can talk about nursery stuff, though, I'm giving you free rein. You just have to stick to Elijah's budget." She grinned widely. "Now, I want to hear all your questions. You picked your wolf?"

Moriah nodded, feeling her ears heat. She couldn't have picked a better wolf.

"Excellent. And you did an interview with him? You feel good about your choice? You know it's not too late to change your mind, don't feel like you have to pick one guy and stick with it. You know part of this is just a numbers game. If you're not feeling it with one, you can choose a backup."

Drea's words made her stomach swoop. She couldn't imagine choosing someone else, not now. *Not when you want to make him breakfast and watch him sleep and find out if he's really ticklish on his side or not.* They would be snuggled in bed, nose to nose. She would wake him up with a soft kiss, giggling as he rolled them, able to *feel* the silky weight of his hair in her hands as the warmth of his body settled atop hers, her soft sigh as he slid home, hitting himself within her. She would make him coffee, and he would fill her empty house with his chatter and laughter.

They would sit in her little French café breakfast nook while he told her about Paris, or better yet — while they made plans to visit together. She would show him the aesthetic boards she had already created — soft, muted colors, a dreamy wash of pinks and grays and blues, crushed velvet and watercolor flowers. She imagined them strolling down the Champs-Élysées hand-in-hand, kissing on some scenic bridge at sunset.

"I-I feel good about my choice. I don't think I need a backup . . . well, we'll see."

She cleared her throat, jumping when her name was called. He had been tap dancing at the forefront of her mind for so long that she spun in her chair, expecting to see Lowell behind her, realizing a beat later that her coffee order was up.

Pull yourself together! What is even wrong with you? You should be thinking about this clinic process, not daydreaming about feeding him beignets and him giving you a piggyback ride around the Louvre.

"Okay, I do have a big question," she announced upon returning to the table. "What on earth did you wear? I've been racking my brain trying to figure out if I'm going to be in a hospital gown. Or do I wear my own street clothes? A dress for easy access? Help me out; what should I do?"

"Ooo, okay, yes! There's a changing area, and you'll have a chance to change into something else for the drive home. I wore a comfortable dress and packed underwear. But yeah, I did an easy-access dress; that was exactly where my mind was as well. I think I made an effort to look a lot cuter the first time, but by the third, I knew the drill. Don't wear anything too nice, nothing that's not machine washable."

Drea paused as a group of students passed on the aisle, waiting and ensuring no passersby were lingering too close to their table, before leaning in conspiratorially once more.

"So, once it's done, he leaves. Then a nurse will come in and fit you with a plug. You'll probably already be leaking by then. You can clean yourself up in the changing room if necessary, but even with the plug, everything is still on the messy side. I made the mistake of wearing cute underwear the first time and threw them away. After that, it was laundry day cotton granny panties. You'll be leaking the whole way home, so just keep that in mind."

The thought of driving home to Cambric Creek with her panties full of Lowell's semen made her whimper. He was going to come inside of her over and over again, and if she had thought the mess of towels at the hotel room had been embarrassing, Moriah realized then that she had no idea what she was in for.

"What-what kind of plug?"

She knew it was likely an entirely respectable, run-of-the-mill medical device, but she couldn't help the way her mind instantly attempted to conjure a vision of something akin to a knot, squeezing her thighs together at the mere thought.

It had been a week and a half since he'd kissed her outside her car door and she had left him in the twilight, and she had not stopped thinking about his cock in all the days since.

She wanted to make him breakfast and kiss his nose and fall asleep in his arms, pressed to his chest . . . and she wanted him to fuck her hard and deep enough that his cock brushed her tonsils. She contained multitudes, Moriah reminded herself. She found that she could not stop thinking about the shape he would take as the full moon neared, the base of his cock swelling, forming the knot that would seal his seed within her, increasing the likelihood of conception. *Also, it's going to feel fucking amazing.*

Round two had been an excellent preview of what going to bed with him would actually be like, if they were dating like an average couple. She couldn't stop thinking about how cute he was, how funny he was, how much she wanted to get to know him better . . . But she also couldn't stop thinking about how well he had fucked her.

He had held his shaft, rubbing the thick head up and down her dripping folds, pressing into her shallowly but never going farther than just the tip. Over and over again, he held himself back until she begged him for more. He knelt upright on the bed, pulling one of her legs flush up his body, her ankle beside his ear as he fed his cock into her slowly. Once he bottomed out, the curve of his balls kissing the curve of her ass, he'd groaned, turning his head to graze his teeth over her ankle.

"Still feel good?"

She'd answered on a wheeze, her eyes rolling when he began to undulate his hips, his cock moving within her like a wave.

"Just making sure. We want you to make an informed decision, remember?"

She'd realized then, gritting her teeth and fisting the sheets, taking in his serene expression, just how on edge he had actually been for their first to go round. Round two was completely different, and he had been entirely in control. His focus was laserlike and pointed, rolling his hips against her in a way that made her lungs quake, and she wondered if that was how he was when he worked as well. Focused and precise, an expert at his craft, and completely in control. His teeth had found their way to the arch of her foot, biting down gently before chuckling against her skin, and she'd been reminded that he was a wolf.

"Well, I hope I still feel good inside you because you feel fucking amazing around me."

By the third time he'd had her, Moriah had realized she was utterly outgamed. She had been a fun girl once. Not quite a party girl, but she had enjoyed her time at University, sometimes a bit too much. She thought she had been good at sex, and that it was the long years of her marriage that had made her rusty, but she understood then, as he rearranged her body to better allow his fat, full testicles to slap into her clit, that she was a mere novice. *That* was what being good at sex looked like, and there was no other way around it. She had never come quite so hard in her life, had never *squirted* before, and the fact that she had done so with him, in addition to orgasming more times than she'd been able to count by the end, had been enough to leave her chastened.

"You know those candy rings that kids wear? That's kind of what it reminded me of. Like, a big squishy bulb attached to a little ring, so you can pull it out. And you're gonna want to do that in the shower, by the way. It is a *mess*."

Her cheeks heated, and she nodded quickly. She already knew what a mess it would be. Once Lowell had slipped from her, the deluge had been nearly immediate. It took several towels to mop things up, and then she had made her own embarrassing mess a short while later. She had been shamefaced, gathering all the soiled cloths together and scooping them up in the damp bedsheets.

"Okay, so . . . A comfortable dress, not cute underwear, take the plug out in the shower. What happens after . . . well, *after*?"

"After you're finished, like I said, your wolf will leave. He'll tell you when you're done. Obviously, if you're feeling uncomfortable, you can call it quits at any time, but as long as you're okay to keep going, wait for him to tell you he's done. You know they can just keep going, right? It's like they're wearing a backup battery."

Moriah nodded weakly, squeezing her thighs together again. Lowell had already displayed impressive stamina, and that was without the benefit of the moon. *He also said he was super horny. It'll probably be different the next time.* For as surprised as he had acted over her own two-year dry spell, Moriah couldn't fathom how someone as handsome and cheerful as him wasn't getting his dick sucked every time he stepped out the door.

"The one thing I will say, this will completely change the way you look at werewolves. There's a guy getting his order right now; I always see him in here. I think he's a fireman or something? He's *so* sexy, and now all I can think about every time I see him is that he is probably fucking his wife into the following month every full moon."

They dissolved into giggles over their cups, and Moriah held her breath, counting to three before she turned around. She was always hyper-conscious about being caught staring at people, being a human in a mostly nonhuman environment. She never wanted to cause offense, and erred on the side of caution.

She'd waited a few beats too long, for the man was already walking out the door, carafe boxes in either hand. He was tall and broad-shouldered, thick with muscle and dark-haired, and she couldn't help but agree with her friend's sentiment. It seemed like every werewolf she knew was tall, dark, and handsome.

"Just remember, they want you to be comfortable the whole time. I know it's awkward and embarrassing to think about, and I'm not going to pretend that the first time wasn't absolutely mortifying, at least at the start. That's why the interview process was so important for us, to make sure we felt good about the donor we picked."

"Oh, for sure," Moriah sighed in agreement. "I'm *so* glad we got the awkwardness out of the way. And he's just so nice and sweet . . . I haven't been able to stop thinking about him, actually." She laughed, ducking her head, raising her eyes in time to see her friend's brow furrow. "But you're right. I know the atmosphere itself is going to make it super awkward. I keep thinking about people watching us."

Drea nodded. "You forget about it eventually, but that made me a little paranoid too. Sooo, did you pick someone who looks like you? Or at least looks like someone in your family?"

Moriah blinked. She was ashamed to admit the thought hadn't even occurred to her. She hadn't even paid attention to see if there was a wolf in the pages of the clinic's catalog that resembled her physically, someone who may have possessed fair skin and red hair, or someone who had her green eyes. Lowell's eyes were dark, nearly black. His hair was equally thick and dark, and his skin held the golden, sun-kissed glow of someone who had spent their summer poolside.

Or at least someone training for the Olympic swim team. Medaling twice, blowing it on his backstroke. She grinned just thinking of his quirky humor, wondering if it would be egregiously inappropriate to call him before the full moon. *Maybe we could get together one last time and discuss the clinic procedure . . .* or perhaps they could just spend time getting to know each other better, she thought.

In either case, he didn't look at all like her, and she wondered which of their appearances their baby would favor. She tried to imagine a little girl with red hair and sparkling dark eyes or a little boy with her green eyes and his mischievous smile, and found it surprisingly difficult. In all the years she'd tried for a baby, she pictured herself with a bundle pressed to her chest, but very rarely was her mind's eye able to articulate exactly what she would find once the swaddling was pulled back.

"Oh, um, no . . . I-I guess I didn't. He doesn't look anything like me," she laughed weakly.

"Well, I guess that's okay, right? How did you pick him? Something in his bio?" Drea grinned broadly. "Secretly hoping for a future surgeon?"

"No," she murmured, letting out another awkward chuckle, "I-I guess I picked him because of his smile."

"His smile?"

Drea sounded skeptical, and instantly, Moriah felt her hackles raise.

"Yes," she said a bit more decisively, sitting up in her seat. "He has a gorgeous smile. It made me feel good as soon as I saw his picture. Too many of those guys look hard, like it was their corporate photograph. Are they too manly to smile or something? Are they still going to be pulling the tough guy routine when I'm with them? Why wouldn't you smile for something like this?! You want some strange woman to pick you as the father of her child; why would you go out of your way to look as surly as possible? Why would I want to procreate with someone who looks like they're going to yell at me through their picture? Sorben was hard enough for a lifetime. I can't do something like this with someone like that; I just can't."

Moriah sucked in a long breath through her teeth, flushed from her outburst. She needed to start seeing her therapist again. She had initially thought she would need to go back to Bridgeton to find a human who would understand her and everything she was going through, but she'd decided to try someone local first, and it had been a perfect fit. She realized she picked people to be in her life based on ancillary traits, for her therapist had a wonderful, honking laugh, like a great goose, and it was what had sold her on seeing the Sphinx beyond their first appointment. All of this baby business was kicking up old feelings and fears again, and she ought to have someone with whom she could talk through things. *You can call and make an appointment tomorrow.*

"So yes, I picked him because of his smile. And it turned out to be a good choice because he's wonderful. He's funny and artistic; he's traveled all over the world. He's a little bit of a troublemaker," she added with a laugh, thinking of the satyr's car and Lowell's utter delight at finding it still sandwiched between their two vehicles when they returned to the café's small parking lot. "He lives overseas normally; he's only here in the area because of the pandemic. He's staying with family right now. No, he doesn't look anything like me. I didn't even think about that being a factor. He's not a surgeon and didn't go to an Ivy League school. He's just . . . a sweet, normal guy. And he made me laugh more in the few hours we were together than I have in the last decade, so I think I made a good choice."

"Whoa, what?" Drea cut in, her brows coming together. The gold markings around her eyes glittered in the overhead light, and Moriah felt heat creep up her neck again. "What do you mean the few hours you were together? You just interviewed him, right?"

"Yes! I did exactly what you said. I wrote up a whole list of questions for him and everything! We met at a little café; I made sure it was a public place, and—"

"You *met* him?! In-person?"

Moriah felt as though she had suddenly lost her ability to understand the common tongue.

"What?! You're the one who told me to interview him! What do you think *interview* means?!"

Drea was holding her head, eyebrows still drawn together, her mouth hanging open.

"Okay, so let me get this straight . . . you *met* him at a café, like physically in person, to interview him. I mean, great, I'm glad to hear that you wrote down some questions, that's good, but you said you were together for *hours*?"

She wanted to fall through the floor.

She had done *exactly* what Drea had recommended. Her friend had said to be sure to interview her donor, which she had done. She had prepared questions; she'd gone in prepared to determine whether or not he was a suitable donor candidate. Everything that had happened after they had left the café had been . . . well, a bit off script, she was willing to admit that. But *she* was the one who had started it while they were still at the table, she was the one who touched him first. *But it was necessary!* She bristled at her friend's horror-stricken look. If she was going to be making a baby with this man, it was necessary to know what sort of *everything* he was packing.

"Oh my stars, Moriah, what did you *do*?"

"I didn't mean for it to happen!" she yelped, face flaming. "I mean, I *did*. I didn't do anything I didn't want to do. I wasn't forced into anything. But . . . he was so nice! And he's so cute, gods, he's so freaking cute. He's super hot, he's got a great body, and he's handsome, you know? Like, from across the room, you see him coming and stop and think, 'wow, that's a handsome man.' But then, up close, he has such a baby face. He looks like he's ready to get into mischief at any moment, and I love that. He's got such good energy, and I think he's pathologically incapable of holding still, but . . . He made me laugh *so*, so much, Drea. I haven't laughed like this in years. Years! And he's so interesting, he's been all over the world! He's a photographer, and he's seen all the places I want to visit. I loved talking with him. He made me feel good. And I haven't felt good in such a long time . . ."

She was mortified when her voice broke and her eyes flooded with tears. It was the hormones, she reminded herself. The hormones from the shot were realigning her system and wreaking havoc on her emotions and judgment. Drea's hand reached across the table, long slender fingers knitting with her own, as she breathed in, steadying herself.

"I was just worried about how it would be at the clinic, and it seemed like a good idea to get the awkwardness out of the way first, right? So we . . . sort of fooled around a little in the park behind the coffee shop, and-and then we went to a hotel."

"Moriah!"

"*You're* the one who said to interview him!"

"That meant on a video call or something! Not a 'pleased to make your acquaintance' blowjob behind the coffee shop!"

Their heads both swung around, checking to see if one of their neighbors was standing nearby gawking.

"Do you remember when I told you not to hand wave through your explanations?" Moriah demanded. "You're the one who was willing to fuck a stranger sight unseen; you don't get to be bashful explaining the process to someone you're trying to rope into doing this with you! I told you that weeks ago! You didn't say, 'make sure you call the wolf you pick and set up a video interview while you're wearing a turtleneck and a winter parka.' You said to interview him! Why would I do a video call interview if he's going to be sticking his dick in me in two weeks?"

Drea moaned in horror, covering her face with both hands.

"No! No, no, no," Moriah huffed. "You don't get to pull that again. See, this right here? *This* is the problem. You're a huge prude! If you want to call your friend and tell her all about the werewolf fuck factory and that she should totally buy a ticket, that's fine. But don't leave out the fucking part."

"I don't know about you lot, but *I* would love a ticket to the werewolf fuck factory. If they've a mailing list, help a girl out and pass it along."

The girl who had paused beside their table had asymmetrical platinum blonde hair, and frosty lavender eyeshadow winged out from her pale blue eyes. Her British accent was cheerful and upbeat, and she winked before continuing on, a giant bag swinging from her shoulder.

Moriah and Drea dissolved into mortified laughter.

"Are you happy with yourself?" Drea hissed, hiding her face in her arms upon the table, shoulders quaking. "This is the reputation we're going to get around town now. We'll probably get invited to one of those werewolf sex parties."

Moriah was wheezing. It was the hormones, she reminded herself, that were causing these mood swings. The hormones and the certainty that she wanted to see him again, regardless of the moon's fullness in the sky.

"I only know about the parties from you! You're the one who seems to have the drop on all of these X-rated werewolf affairs. You've got a lot of nerve, lady."

"Please just make sure you stay safe," Drea sighed, finally sitting up. "I have no doubt they screen these guys as best they can, but you don't want to do anything reckless with a stranger."

They parted shortly after, and Moriah turned her friend's words over and over again in her mind. The disconnect, she thought, was mind-blowing. *You don't want to do anything reckless with a stranger.* Nothing reckless. Nothing reckless, nothing reckless at all.

You know, like make a baby with one.

* * *

Lowell

Everything about the room was too much. The lights overhead were over-bright, stinging his eyes. The ticking of the clock on the wall was too loud, each second bringing him closer and closer to an inevitable end. Lowell sucked in a slow breath, holding, trying to calm his nerves and quiet his mind, releasing on a measured hiss. He was freezing. He had been running a low-grade fever the past 24 hours, normal at this point in the month, but the gusting air conditioner against his heated skin felt frigid, and his arms were prickled in goosebumps.

It felt like hours before the doctor finally entered the room.

"Looks like cool but sunny weather the rest of the week," the doctor said conversationally, his fingers prodding his throat and down his neck, checking the size of his lymph nodes and any swollen glands. "Nothing I like better to see in the forecast. I don't know about you, but I can't tolerate getting wet during the change. I don't know what it is about it, but it's like I can't get dry for a week after."

Lowell gave a short bark of laughter at the doctor's words as the man ran gloved fingertips in a straight line down his chest, pausing to prod his pectorals, palpating around each nipple.

"Oh, I understand that all too well. I was in Vietnam for a few months a couple of years back, and it rained every day. Every single day. Three moons in a row — downpour. I didn't think I would ever be dry again."

The doctor chuckled, pressing on his abdomen, feeling down to his naval before working his way around his back to poke at his kidneys. Lowell tried focusing on what he would do *after, as* the examination continued. They would each go their separate ways. He would exit first, leaving the premises. The clinic was very clear about that: he was not to linger. The donors were to depart once they and the patient had ceased relations, and then they were to leave. It was closely monitored, with tight security. He would go home alone that day, and there was no way around it.

"Big breath in . . ."

The stethoscope with an icy kiss against the inferno of his chest, and he attempted not to flinch away. *Why does it matter? This is a transaction. You're just a donor. She's a patient. That's all this is. Altruism, remember? Isn't that why you're doing this?*

". . . And out."

His inner voice spoke truly, and he knew he ought to listen. His squishy gumdrop heart, unfortunately, didn't seem to care. He had been unable to stop thinking about Moriah since the afternoon they'd spent together.

He couldn't stop thinking about the brightness of her smile, the sparkle of her emerald eyes, or the flush that spread up her lovely face every time their eyes met for more than a second or two. He couldn't stop imagining her graceful hands, like small white doves, still able to feel their warmth engulfed in his larger one. His mind could not stop re-creating the way her dark red hair had caught the sunlight as they sat in that small park, making it burn like fire, and the soft sigh she had made when he had kissed her for the first time still echoed between his ears.

"Drop your shorts, please. Don't worry, we're almost done."

He'd been semi-erect for the past several days, a side effect of the approaching moon and his twisted, tangled thoughts and dreams, but if the doctor had any issue with the sight of his thickened cock as Lowell hooked his fingers in the waistband of his boxer briefs, tugging them down far enough over his ass that they slid to his knees on their own, the man had the good grace to keep it to himself.

He couldn't stop thinking about the softness of her skin and the sweet smell of her. He couldn't stop mentally recreating the way her breasts fit so neatly in the palm of his hands, the way her fingers tightened in his hair as he licked her, couldn't stop thinking about the delicious taste of her cunt, and how perfectly it had squeezed his cock. His mind couldn't forget the sight of the long, white column of her throat, presented to him as her head dropped back while he fucked her, and he was sure he would never be able to stop hearing the high-pitched little noise she made when she came, her muscles clenching around him.

His cock twitched, and he had to remind himself the hand holding it belonged to this white-haired doctor, not the woman he was pining over like a teenager. His rational mind knew he was being checked for a visual indication of an STI, but as his foreskin was drawn back over his cockhead, his eye twitched, wishing it were a smaller, softer hand doing the prodding.

He couldn't stop thinking about Moriah, and perhaps more insidiously, he couldn't stop dreaming of her either. He revisited everything they had done together in that hotel room bed numerous times, his mental masturbation fodder for the past week, but the soft REM cycle dreams he had in the hours before waking were much more dangerous.

He imagined waking with her in his bed — *his* bed, his actual bed, back in his apartment in Tokyo. Of course, the apartment was no longer his, but in the dream, it didn't matter. He would wake her with a trail of soft kisses up the side of her neck and across her rosebud lips, finishing at her upturned nose. He made excellent egg and miso soup, which he would make for her, and scallion pancakes, full of vegetables and fried crisp, and in his dream, she sat watching him in the tiny kitchen, happy and complacent as he waited on her. They would be hand-in-hand as he pulled her through a wet market or a bazaar, up the steep rock face of a mountain, or through the thick underbrush of a jungle, all places he'd been, places she confessed to only seeing in pictures. She wanted to see the world, and he desperately wanted to show it to her.

Jackson, Grayson, and Trapp all had cabins on Shadowbend Lake, deep in the woods, secluded and peaceful, and their father had bought up a chunk of the surrounding land a few years back, intending to build similar structures for the three sons who had not yet been born when their grandfather had willed his possessions and legacy to the eldest three Hemming grandsons. Lowell had no idea why the project had stalled, but the cabins had not yet been built.

That didn't stop his dreaming mind from creating a scenario of him and Moriah in the woods together. She would baby him after the change, keeping him in bed, wrapped in her arms as muscle and bone knit themselves back into his familiar form, the soreness that always accompanied the day after the moon a bit less sharp snuggled against her warmth. Waking up in his bed in Grayson's house was always a disappointment, and his throat would stick when he remembered that he was merely a donor, a third wheel under his brother's roof, an aggravating, often troublesome footnote in his family, and ultimately a stranger to her.

When he wasn't dreaming of her, he was turning over this entire situation in his mind, still unable to make heads or tails of her reasoning or rationale. He didn't understand why she was doing this when she had expressed her desire to travel with so much longing. She was young, beautiful, and had nothing tying her down.

He didn't understand why she was choosing to do *this*, choosing to have a baby with a stranger to raise entirely on her own, particularly as it didn't seem that there was any issue with fertility on her end. She'd not been able to conceive with her ex-husband, and on more than one occasion during a conversation, Lowell had to bite back the impulse to remind her that he was out of the picture, and a good thing, from the sounds of it. His hands had clenched the sheets in annoyed frustration when she casually mentioned the fact that she'd not celebrated holidays because her ex-husband hadn't, even though she had grown up celebrating Christmas and had seemed to enjoy her community's Solstice celebration.

She should have left the cranky fuck at home and gone out on her own to have a good time. Who knows, maybe she would have met someone sooner. Lowell tried to imagine meeting Moriah at the spiced brandy-soaked festival, the cold leaving the apples of her cheeks and the tip of her nose red, her lips begging to be kissed by someone who would appreciate their softness. He wasn't Grayson and had no desire to be a homewrecker all over town, but if the power to go back in time with his current knowledge was one he possessed, Lowell would be propelling himself backward without a moment of hesitation. He didn't fancy the idea of being the cause of someone else's unhappiness, but if he had run into Moriah at whatever community's solstice festival she was attending alone, he would've been more than happy to kiss the frown off her face and fuck a delirious a smile on to it, her miserable double-dicked asshole husband be damned.

She hadn't mentioned there being any issue beyond their biological incompatibility. Lowell hadn't wanted to ask, knowing that was the height of rudeness and that his mother would probably feel the phantom ripple down her back from wherever she was, seeking him out to thwack him upside the head with a rolled-up newspaper. He couldn't fathom why she had been single since her divorce, particularly if she wanted a baby so badly; he wasn't sure why she hadn't simply thrown herself back into the dating pool to find a partner to share this experience with. It seemed to him there was no better time to go out and see the world, have a baby with someone she loved when she came back from a real adventure in a year or two . . . But that wasn't his business. *Nothing that happens outside of this room concerns you.* You're just the donor.

"Turn your head and cough," the doctor instructed, cupping his testicles and probing to ensure there was no danger of herniation. "All right, we're all finished here. Chart looks good; I think we are ready to proceed. You certainly seem ready for it," he chuckled, pulling off his gloves as Lowell's half-mast erection bobbed indignantly. "You'll be notified over the intercom when you can enter the room, and when you're finished, you'll come back through these doors, collect your things, and exit through the security hallway. It *is* monitored. Best of luck, and a good turn to you this week."

"Yeah, um. Same to you. Have a good turn. Stay dry out there."

The doctor laughed again on his way out the door, leaving Lowell alone. *Almost time to do your only job.* He had no idea what he was supposed to have worn, but he had a feeling his distressed, button-fly jeans had been a poor choice. He nearly put his foot through the opening at the knee that morning, hopping on one foot to keep from stumbling over into the television in his bedroom, low-key relieved that Grayson and Vanessa were at their apartment in the city and there was no one to witness or overhear his yelp of panic when he nearly toppled, stubbing his toe in the process.

Lowell realized that every time he had imagined this part of the process, he had been wearing a sterile hospital gown, he and Moriah both. It seemed almost comical now, but it was the image his mind had conjured and the one he'd not let go of. Finding himself without the paper covering now was quite honestly a bit of a letdown.

His only choices seemed to pull his boxer briefs back up or forgo them entirely. *You're going to be fucking her in a few minutes. What difference does it make what you're wearing? You're going to be taking it off!* He had always looked for the straightest path forward. Shaking his leg, he let the dark gray fabric fall to the floor, scooping it up and placing it with the rest of his clothes on the chair near the door. There was nothing left to do but wait.

Fortunately, he didn't need to wait long.

"You may proceed."

She was perched on the edge of the exam table, gripping the sides in a way that gave proof to her nerves, even if she was attempting to hide that with her daintily crossed ankles. When his door opened, her head snapped up, her mouth dropping open at the sight of him. He was prepared for her declaration of all-consuming lust, all for him, hardly able to contain herself. Lowell felt his cock twitch again at the mere thought. She was wearing a spaghetti strapped sundress in a soft, stretchy T-shirt material that he couldn't wait to divest her of. *Definitely not a hospital gown.* Her dark red hair was pulled up in a slightly haphazard bun, and her little white hands covered her mouth as she gazed at him . . . in horror. His cock frowned.

"Lowell! Why are you *naked*?!"

His back stiffened. *See? You should have put them back on.* But he had been ex*pec*ting a hospital gown, he thought stubbornly, sputtering in outrage.

"No one told me what to wear! I thought we would be given hospital gowns!"

She had dissolved into giggles, and even though he had been feeling poorly for the past week and a half, and even though she was actively laughing at him, the sound and sight of her made his own mouth turn up in a smile of his own.

"This is the most dramatic middle child thing I've ever seen," she'd giggled against him, barely able to get the words out.

"Believe me, I spent a *lot* of time thinking about how I would wear it into the room. The way you're supposed to, back open? With my ass cheeks clapping in the breeze? Or wear it backward, cock out? That seemed like the most practical option, plus it also had the benefit of being able to pretend it was a trench coat. I was going to jump into the room, holding it open like some perv in the park. But then I got here, and there was nothing!"

She hadn't stopped laughing yet, and his gooey, gummy heart felt warmer than it had in weeks. When her hands reached out for him, grasping his shoulders and curling around his neck, pulling him into her, he went gladly, wrapping an arm around her waist as she buried her face against his neck. Her shoulders still shook in laughter, and he enfolded her in both arms, melting slightly when she nuzzled her nose against his skin.

"You're so ridiculous. You're so *fucking* ridiculous. I'm so glad you're here."

He'd heard that he was ridiculous since he was a small child, but the words never made his heart beat as wildly as it did then.

"I've been sitting here trying not to have a panic attack for the last ten minutes, and I don't think I would be able to do this if you weren't here." She snaked her arms around him, pulling herself tighter in a crushing hug, burying her face against his shoulder once more. He could feel her jackrabbit pulse against him, her slightly labored breath, and he melted further at her obvious nervous distress.

"Hey, it's fine. It's fine, right? We got all the awkwardness out of the way."

She looked up, eyes glittering. "I'm so glad we did. I don't care what anyone else says."

She pulled back slightly, and Lowell begrudgingly released her, letting her direct what happened next. "Should-should we stay here? Or do you want to go to the bed?"

Lowell looked around the room for the first time, taking everything in. There was an armless chaise, which would probably be an excellent height for humping into her from behind; the examination table upon which she currently sat, suitable for eating her out and a solid face-to-face fucking, and on the other end of the room, a small set up that looked like a hotel model. A double bed with beige bedclothes and plump pillows, the coverlet turned down as if they had just checked in, good for everything else he was planning on doing to her.

"Man, they couldn't spring for a king? They clearly don't want us getting too adventurous."

She giggled again, squeezing his arm, and he straightened up.

"I'm so glad you're here."

Her voice wavered slightly, steel solidifying in his spine. He was a child and shouldn't even be trusted with a knife to cut his own meat, but she needed him to be strong at that moment, and he would be anything she needed him to be.

"Let's stay here, just for a few minutes, okay? I want to smell you."

Moriah sucked in a sharp breath, biting her lip adorably, nodding her head with wide eyes. Lowell was relieved when she allowed herself to be pulled back into his arms, sighing softly when he tilted her head to press his lips to the side of her neck. In his peripheral vision, he caught the blinking lights of the two CCTV cameras in the corners. They were concealed by smoked glass, and he knew she'd not be able to see them, deciding not to bring it to her attention.

"Hey," he whispered, teeth nipping at her earlobe. "It's just us. Right? We've already done this before. It's just you and me."

The sound she made with something like a swallowed sob, whipping her head back around and crashing her lips into his, gripping his hair tightly. She needed him to take the lead, and that was fine. He could taste her nerves, her fear, metallic coating over her sweetness. *You just need to remind her that everything is fine. She's already done this with you before, and it's fine.* He gripped her chin, kissing her lips slowly before trailing his mouth over her jaw, inhaling deeply behind her ear, and continuing down her throat. Her head lolled. He could taste the anxiety coursing through her, but there, just underneath it, a whiff of desire. The heat caused by the hormone injections, temporarily dampened by her nerves, but still there, still hot and in need of satisfying. It was competing with her fear, but Lowell could smell nothing else once he found it.

The smell of her went straight to his cock, stiffening to steel in an instant. Hot and sweet, like cinnamon and honey, he could feel the frustration she'd gone through for the past several nights alone, desperately needing his cock to fill her. He could taste her anxiety, but he could taste how wet she was as well, and his wolf growled, wanting to wet his muzzle between her thighs.

"Fuck," he groaned against her skin, tongue darting out to taste her. "How do you smell so good already?" He was glad he was already naked, for she could reach down and grip his cock easily, running her fingertips from root to tip, before she wrapped her hand around him, pumping him slowly.

Lowell realized that nearly every woman he knew was on a heat suppressant and had been since puberty. No matter what his work schedule looked and no matter how remote the country he was in, he always ensured he was somewhere safe for the turn. Safe and as secluded as possible, especially when he was traveling.

One never knew what sort of area they might wander into in their other form, and there were many places in the world where it was unsafe to be a werewolf. He never wanted to stumble into a dangerous situation, into those who hunted his kind or other wolves, territorial over their range and their females. He never wanted his nose to catch the smell of a wolf in heat when he was traveling abroad; didn't want to risk the injury to his life and limbs by falling prey to the heat frenzy, rutting the wrong werewolf.

Nothing was stopping him now. He wasn't sure if he had ever smelled an unsuppressed heat this close before. Moriah was human, so it wasn't entirely the same, but modern medicine was working miracles every day, and the artificial cycle they had created smelled authentic to his nose, authentic and delicious. Nothing was stopping him, and she was his for the having; that was the whole point, and then he *did* growl against her skin, cock jerking in her hands. He was desperate to bury himself within her slick, tight embrace, and spend himself over and over again, wanted to feel her cunt spasming and squeezing him, wanted to empty his balls into her until his eyes were itchy . . . but he was a Hemming, and the Hemming boys had reputations to keep. He was going to fuck her until she couldn't walk, but first, he was going to lick her pussy like a five-course meal.

The rolling stool was a perfect height. The seat was encased in a plastic covering, easily disposed of, and he realized they truly thought of everything.

"My balls are going to stick to this, just FYI. I might need you to kiss them to make it better once I stand up. I'm just warning you now." She laughed again, her small fingers tightening around his shoulders as he seated himself on the bench, rolling into her. "I'm going to need you to put your feet in the stirrups, ma'am. I have an examination to do."

His wolf growled again, shifting in his bones once he had lifted her feet to the silver chrome stirrups. She was spread out before him, spread out like a feast, and he was starving. Lowell took his time, making an appetizer of her inner thighs, nipping at the sensitive skin, relishing the tiny squeaks she made every time he did so. He kissed over her mound, satisfying his wolf by letting him take a nibble of her puffy labia, earning another squeak.

"I know you want to get on with it, but my wolf wants to taste your pussy first. Can he have a little lick? Please?"

Moriah seemed beyond speech. Her head was dropped back on the raised examination table, her eyes closed as his nose bumped back and forth over her clit, whimpering when his teeth grazed its hood.

"I'm to take that as a yes," he murmured. Lowell groaned, his wolf vibrating when he slid his tongue over her, taking a long, full lick of her spread open sex. She was dripping for him already, the delicious, musky-sweet taste of her clinging to his tongue.

Don't embarrass us. Don't act like you're doing her a favor. He didn't need the so-long-ago given advice then. He truly *had* been starving for her over the past few weeks, and this was hardly a chore. He needed to get her ready for his knot, which he could already feel prickling at the base of his cock, ready to swell up and halt the party, but at least she would be aroused and lubricated by then, for he was fully intent on making her come against his tongue. Her hips were moving, little thrusts against his mouth as his tongue worked against her, flickering over her clit with the precision and speed of a hummingbird's wings, and when he slid two fingers into her, stroking against her in a come hither motion, her back arched off the table.

"You're *so* good. I love the way you lick me," she whined, head thrashing from side to side, her fingers tightening in his hair.

His Moriah —soft, sweet, chirping Moriah —was gone, supplanted by Moriah in Heat, not that he had a problem with that. Lowell could tell she wanted to buck harder against his face and come faster, and the small part of him that had been brought up on his father's disdain for humans mourned that she was one, for she would have been a beautiful wolf. The desperation of her heat rippled through her veins like liquid fire, but he pressed her hips down, the sterile paper covering bunching and wrinkling beneath her.

"I want you to lick me like this every fucking day. I want to come on your mouth. You're so, *so* good . . . please make me come." Her voice was a whine, but her words made his balls contract and his cock jump against his belly. He would be happy to lick her every day for the rest of time, particularly when she told him how good he was. Suddenly, the little stool was not enough, her spread-open legs too much of an invitation, and he was desperate to bury himself to the hilt in her heat. His tongue redoubled, his lips fastened in suction, and she moaned without restraint. Lowell felt the first ripple of her orgasm shiver up her thighs, her clit pulsing against his tongue, a gush of her sweet honey coating his mouth, and his eyes rolled back in his head.

He pushed off the stool in one fluid motion, wincing when his balls did, in fact, rip off the plastic. His cock had hardened to steel, and he was already desperate to come. He was right — the examination table was a perfect height. Moriah gazed at him through blown-out eyes, glazed with desire, gripping his cock once more and leading him to slide home.

He remembered they were being watched once he had already begun pumping into her, wondering what their watchers thought of the site of his bare ass moving like a piston, thankful the table was there to hold him up. She felt *different*, better, somehow, which seemed fucking impossible because she had felt amazing the first time they'd been together, but now everything was enhanced. The excess blood flow from her heat had swelled beneath her skin, a tighter fit around his cock, the flared edge of his head catching on every ripple and ridge within her. She was making a high-pitched little squeak every time he thrust forward, his knot pressing at her entrance, knocking on her front door and waiting to be let in.

"Come inside me, Lowell," she wheezed against his neck, still making that high little moan as he rocked against some sweet spot inside her. "Please, *please* come inside me. I want you to fill me up and give me your big knot."

He desperately needed to come, even though they had only just gotten started. The smell of her was short-circuiting something in his brain, and he needed to empty his balls to clear it out and reset his vision, and when she begged him so sweetly, he couldn't refuse. She gripped his shoulders tightly, and Lowell nodded against her, his eyes squeezed shut.

"It'll get easier. Just remember that. This is the first time, and it might hurt, but it'll get easier." His hips continued to piston, each push against her opening her a bit wider, and when he finally pushed his knot into place, the room went white. All he was cognizant of was the squeeze of her cunt around him, the pressure on his knot, and the ways she jerked as he rolled his fingers over her clit, helping her get over that final peak to join him as he erupted inside of her.

"Good boy," she keened, pulling him into her.

He was close enough that she didn't need to reach, and the examination table was, indeed, a perfect height. When her fingers closed over his scrotum, squeezing his balls rhythmically as he ejaculated, Lowell shuddered, and his wolf did as well, legs shaking, nearly able to hold him up. Her thumb pressed into that area just behind his sac where he pulsed, stimulating his prostate and giving the current orgasm a bit of extra *fuck me sideways* oomph. He didn't realize at the time that she was unlocking something in his brain that turned him to jelly, but he nearly slid to the floor.

"Good boy," she crooned against his hair. "You're cumming so much for me. Such a good boy."

This is how I want to die. It was a thought he'd had previously. Then, he'd thought the best circumstances of expiration would have been in what had been his favorite sexual position — the filling a threesome sandwich, his cock buried balls-deep in a beautiful girl, with someone else's cock kissing his prostate, everyone paying attention to *him*, the center of everything, exactly where he was *meant* to be — getting his pleasure from every side. He was forced to amend that now. He disliked words like *straight* or anything that indicated the contrary of whatever that meant; he liked feeling good, and sex felt good, regardless of with whom he had it . . . but his heart was rarely ever a factor.

You could fall in love with this girl. It was silly, foolish, completely asinine, and he needed a healthy dose of Grayson's tough-love realism, more than likely . . . but he was pretty sure it was true, and he usually wasn't pretty sure of anything.

Lowell felt dead on his feet when his cock had stopped spasming inside of her, dribbling out the last of his seed. He always came the hardest the first time. It was the most urgent, the most pressing, and the most voluminous. It also took the most out of him, and all he wanted to do now was close his eyes and drift to sleep against her until his knot softened. Not yet, he reminded himself.

The examination table had been a perfect height, but now they were tied, her feet still up in the stirrups and him unable to step back.

"Okay . . . This is what we're going to do. I'm going to pull you to the edge of the table, and you're going to lift your legs out *very* carefully, and then wrap them around my waist. I'm sorry in advance if it hurts a little."

She whimpered when his knot tugged at her, carefully pulling her legs out of the stirrups and allowing him to guide them around his narrow hips, her ankles crossing above the swell of his ass.

"Much like the hospital gown, I didn't think this through," he admitted, earning her smile against his shoulder. "I'm going to walk us to the bed. Let yourself drop down on my cock a little so it doesn't pull, okay? Then you can snuggle up until I can pull out. And *then*, I want you up on your knees, nice and deep, like you said."

Moriah gave him a huge grin, leaning in to kiss the corner of his mouth, and his gumdrop heart shivered.

"Okay, I trust you."

Lowell fought the instinct to make a rude hand gesture at the closed circuit cameras as he penguin-walked them to the bed, Moriah squeaking as he did so, whimpering when he lowered them to the mattress as carefully as he was able.

"Now what?" She questioned breathlessly, rubbing her nose against his chest.

It would be at least twenty minutes or so until he could slip free from her. He wanted to feel her contract around him again and knew that if he slid his fingers against her, rubbing circles against her delectable clit, she would. *Let her rest. You're not going anywhere any time soon.*

"Now we wait. Take a nap if you want. Play twenty questions. I'm very nosy. You can tell me all your darkest secrets. Whatever you want."

"Kiss me again," she whispered, twisting his heart like an origami crane. He was helpless to oblige. Lowell gripped her chin with a soft hand, kissing her upper lip, then her lower lip, then both together, swiping his tongue gently against the seam of them until she granted him entrance, and the kiss deepened.

"Can we have dinner this week?" Her eyes were wide, her pupils still blown out, but her voice's mindless whine was gone, and her usual chirp returned. "I know it's probably a bad idea, and that we weren't supposed to meet, but I-I don't care. Why can't we do this our way?"

Her nails skated down his chest, her palm flattening out once it reached his heartbeat, and Lowell closed his eyes before he answered.

She was going to break his heart. There was no way around it, and he knew that with absolute certainty. He was soft and weak and too fucking needy, and he should have known better than to have signed up for this program; he should've known from the start. He should've told his brothers what he was doing as they sat around their table at the Pickled Pig, should've let Gray and Trapp talk some sense into him, but he hadn't, and now it was too late. He formed attachments too easily, fell in love too quickly, and she would rip him to shreds.

But, Lowell reminded himself, it wasn't like he had anything else to do. He was lonely and depressed and worried about his future, and he would still be lonely and depressed with or without a broken heart. He was tired of being a third wheel, tired of being an addendum, tired of being utterly without purpose here. He thought what she was doing was a mistake, but it was her mistake to make. She was going to break his heart, but this pandemic wouldn't last forever. Eventually, he would be able to fly away from here and mend himself back together as best he could. And if nothing else, it would get him the fuck out of Grayson's house for a few hours.

"It's a date," he murmured against her hair, raising her chin to meet his mouth once more.

* * *

Moriah

She hadn't really known what to expect that first month.

She'd felt as if she had been sitting in the procedure room for hours before he finally entered — hours in which she had unwound her entire thought process, found it completely lacking, all of her decisions poor, determining that she ought to go home, and never leave her house again. She didn't know what she was doing. She had been so fixated on this one thing for so long, and now she felt guilty for having fixated on him. Not a fixation. You genuinely like him. And you haven't liked anyone in so long it feels weird and new and exciting. She'd wanted to get together with him again before the full moon, making the mistake of saying that to Drea and receiving her friend's judgment in return.

"I don't know if that's a good idea, babe. The whole point of picking your donor is that you feel comfortable with them, but they're not a part of this. They contribute genetic material, and that's it. You don't have to share your baby with them; you don't have to think about custody or their opinion. It just isn't the way it's done. I don't know if getting him involved is a good idea."

She had agreed with her friend's words at the time, but the more she chewed them over, the more she realized Drea was speaking of her own situation and not thinking past that. Of course, she and Elijah didn't want to spend time with their donor or have their donor be any more involved than necessary — Elijah had to come to terms with the fact that this other man was going to be fucking his wife, and while they could swallow it for the sake of their baby, they didn't want to be spending time with him over red wine and cheese fondue.

Moriah had no such constraints. She was by herself, doing this alone. *It's the dumbest fucking thing you've ever considered. What are you thinking?! You're not, that's the problem. You wanted to have a baby when you were married. Do you still want to have one now that you're alone?* She didn't know the answer, but it seemed too late to second-guess herself.

When Lowell had entered the room, at last, as naked as the day he was born, she decided it didn't matter. She'd made the right choice about him, regardless of the why behind it, and she wanted to keep spending time with him. He thrummed with energy, and she loved how ridiculous and over-the-top he was.

"You eat me out better than anyone else ever has," she'd keened against his neck, feeling him shiver at the compliment. "You make me feel *so* good."

His nearness made her twist as the heat sizzled in her veins. Her legs were ready to drop open the moment he entered the room, and when he'd groaned, his cock jerking inside her as he came, she'd gripped his testicles again. She loved the feeling of him pulsing, throbbing, emptying for her, her thumb seeking out that spasming muscle.

"Good boy. You're cumming so much for me."

His spine quivered, and his balls seemed to vibrate in her hand, and she decided she would be happy to call him her good boy forever if it made him throb in such a way.

She was ready for more when he walked them awkwardly to the bed. He had kissed as much of her body as he could while they were tied, each tug an uncomfortable stab of pain, at least, until it wasn't. He took note of the way her head dropped back in her eyes fluttered close when his knot tested the give at her opening, and his fingers had landed at her clit, rubbing her determinedly.

"I want to feel you squeeze me," he'd groaned against her hair as she began to buck up into his hand. He'd trapped her clit between two knuckles, and the pad of his thumb was working over the exposed pearl, bumping her hood and making her see stars. "Can you feel my cock getting hard again already? I want to feel your pussy squeeze it tight. Are you going to come for me, Moriah?"

Her clit felt like it was sparking, and when he had rubbed her to a fiery climax, she did exactly as he asked.

The second time he'd fucked her, he had her up on her knees, pumping his cock into her as deeply as it could go. The sound of his balls slapping into her was an obscene percussion in the room, and she wondered if they were able to hear it over the cameras.

"You feel so fucking good," he'd groaned into her neck, his hips never slowing. "Are you ready to take my knot? Because my cock is ready to explode."

When he came, the pressure of his knot pushed her over the edge, and he laced his fingers with hers, filling her with spurt after spurt of his hot, thick release until she was certain she could taste it at the back of her throat.

That time they had both dozed in the bed. She woke first, testing the give of his knot within her and finding that she was able to pull out on her own, but not wanting to. He was curled around her, an arm around her waist and his knee pushed in between her legs, his breath hot at her neck. She had only just met him, and it was beyond foolish to contemplate, but it was how she wanted to wake up in her own bed, she thought.

The third time he'd had her, she had wondered what the watchers must have been thinking, seeing them on the cameras. Lowell spent a small eternity kissing his way down her body, sucking at the hollow pulse point of her throat, sucking each of her pink nipples into his mouth, grazing his teeth over them as he pulled, kissing over her breasts and stomach and hips and mound, dipping his face between her legs once more.

"I want you inside of me," she'd whined, scratching at his neck and writhing. "I want your big cock back inside me, Lowell."

When he'd finally pressed his cock into her, she had been panting, begging for him, twisting her fingers into his hair and scoring her nails down his back, wrapping her legs around his narrow hips as he thrust into her, holding onto him as tightly as she could.

"That's my good boy," she'd keened, gripping him tighter when he moaned.

"I think my organs are starting to desiccate," he murmured into her hair after the fourth time he'd spilled into her.

She was meant to get pregnant, which would not happen unless he was buried in her deeply, his knot holding his potent seed in her body to take root, but Moriah could not stop thinking of him coming across her breasts and belly, coating her in ropes of his sticky white cream. She wanted to bring him home and let him fuck her in her own bed, wanted to get down on her knees and swallow his cock, wanted to feel him erupt in her mouth, his fat testicles pulsing and contracting in her hands as he did so.

"I think we might have to call it. You drained me dry, vixen."

She laughed against his throat, kissing the corner of his mouth. "Do-do you want to wait for me? They have to come in and fit me with some kind of plug or something, and then —"

"I can't," he'd cut in balefully. "I have to leave; they were very, very specific about that. There are security cameras everywhere 'ensuring the donors exit the premises,' before you even get back on the exam table."

He'd kissed her one last time, long and lingering, punctuating it with a soft kiss to the tip of her nose. "I hope the rest of your heat isn't too bad."

"Lowell," she called out, stopping him in his tracks when he was a few feet away from the bed. "Have a good change? Be careful, okay? Don't let anything happen to you out there."

She couldn't even begin to imagine what happened to him during his time as a wolf, how his body changed, and how it changed back, and the thought fascinated her. She wanted to know what he looked like, if he was soft and fluffy or coarse with sharp teeth and claws. She wanted to know what he looked like in his other form, how he acted, and how he changed back.

He'd grinned, giving her a wink.

"I'll make sure it doesn't. See you soon, okay?"

The plug they'd fit her with was exactly as Drea had described, the bulb firm enough to stay put but with enough squish that her muscles could contract around it, getting her through the next 24 hours of her heat. Moriah lost track of how many times she clenched around the ball, pretending it was him, deciding she needed to add a toy to her collection that approximated the girth of his knot, giving her something to focus on in the weeks between their clinic procedures.

She had called him the day after the moon, unsure of how he may be feeling. She didn't know if it was a long recovery after the change, if he snapped back like a rubber band without missing a beat or if he wound up in bed every month. *There would hardly have werewolves in positions of power all over the world if they needed to stay in bed recovering for half the week every month, don't be silly.*

I'm good. Tired, still a little sore.

Currently stuffing my face with French toast and bacon, so no real complaints.

How are you? Did you make it through the moon okay?

She had grinned down at her phone, warmth curling through her.

Drea had been right. She had been a filthy mess by the time she made it back into her driveway afterward, her cunt tightening around the bulb at every stop sign and red light the entire way home. She had pulsed her muscles, trying to re-create the sensation of him ejaculating inside her until she'd been gripping the steering wheel with white knuckles, uncertain if she would be able to make it home without pulling over to finger herself. She'd whimpered and moaned, canting her hips against the pressure of the bulb inside her, wishing it were his cock again, realizing the heat had not been fully extinguished in her veins. She'd walked up her driveway on shaking legs like a newborn fawn, already feeling the delicious mess in her panties.

You'll need to pull the plug out in the shower. It's such a mess. That's what Drea had told her. Moriah wondered, as she gripped the plug's ring, tugging it gently before pushing it back in, in a poor approximation of how he had fucked her, if her friend had done the same. She wondered if Drea had still felt the phantom presence of the stranger werewolf's knot within her, the pressure of his semen blowing her up like a balloon as her muscles tightened around him, his cock erupting.

She had gripped the shower bar, relieved there was something to hold onto because otherwise, she likely would have gone sliding to the tiles as she fucked herself with the bulb, closing her eyes and pretending it was Lowell, his thick cock dragging against her G-spot on every thrust, his heavy balls slapping into her, and his thick knot kissing the lips of her sex with every pump of his hips, demanding entrance until he pushed into place, stoppering her like a wine cask and filling her with as much cum as one.

The splash of his release against her shower tiles had left her moaning when she pulled the plug out completely, the evidence of their afternoon together washing down the drain.

I made through it okay, is what she had responded.

Maybe next month we can make plans?

She didn't know what had possessed her to ask, and her lungs had tightened as soon as she hit send, second-guessing everything she was doing.

For sure!

My parents have everyone over for brunch the day after

But if you think I'm going to say no to one on one babying, it's like you've never met me

She'd laughed aloud at his audacity, a brat to his core but an adorable one.

It was hard to feel invisible and disconnected anymore because she *existed* to someone now. He texted her throughout the days, over the next week, random little bits of humor and conversation she'd previously been lacking, and she had begun to live for the moment her phone would buzz, deflating slightly if it were Drea, or their friend Ava, a baker in town, or her mother.

He asked about her business, her family, about her travel aspirations. He told her stories from his time overseas, tales of his childhood, all involving elaborate hijinks of which he always seemed to be at the center, despite claiming no culpability in the mischief, and confessed that he didn't know what he would do next, he wasn't able to return to work in the same capacity, and that his current plan of living off his wealthy brother was being hampered by said brother's girlfriend.

The conversation came up the night they met for dinner. He suggested Greenbridge Glen, as it was mostly nonhuman, and thus its businesses were open. As she stood in front of her closet that night, contemplating what she ought to wear, Moriah couldn't help but feel as if she were suspended in some liminal space, not truly existing fully anywhere.

She felt removed from her neighbors in Cambric Creek. Sorben had been such a curmudgeonly introvert that they had never really participated in the community-wide events. They didn't attend the festivals and the street fairs, as he disliked the crowds, and she had never taken any classes at the community center. He had decided CSA farm pickup was inconvenient, and she had never wanted to attend the Saturday Maker's Mart alone. It wasn't until she met Drea that she realized she didn't have many friends in town, at least not outside their development. She'd endeavored in recent years to change that, but still — it was a delayed effort.

She didn't feel as though she belonged amongst the community in Cambric Creek, and since the pandemic had started, Moriah realized how removed she was from the human world as well. She'd not lived in a human majority town in nearly a decade. Her parents were far away, and she had no reason to venture into Bridgeton very often. The pandemic was passing her by, the entire global community of humans huddled together at this terrible time, but she was largely unaffected, content to not leave her house and to stay amongst the nonhuman population of her neighbors, amongst whom she was similarly removed.

One of the things she found so attractive about her exuberant conception partner was that he was similarly displaced and friendless, not fitting in with his family, not fitting in with his community, and not fitting in anywhere, according to him. *He fits in perfectly with you.*

"So, can I ask you a question? I apologize in advance if it's insensitive, but I just . . . I'm just having a hard time understanding why . . ."

He had been dancing around the question that he wanted to ask all night, and she knew what that was without him needing to voice it.

"Why am I doing this?"

His neck flushed, and he ducked ahead.

"It's something I wanted for so long," she murmured. "I got married too young. I know that now. I needed to live more. I needed to experience more of the world on my own. I might not have even said yes to my husband if I'd had a little bit more time to live."

The clinic would've been a goddess gift when she and Sorben were still together. A way to have the baby she wanted within her marriage, even if he would have needed to come to terms with the methodology. Now though, she wasn't quite sure. Moriah didn't know how to admit that aloud, least of all to herself. She had wanted this one thing for so long, and to *not* pursue this opportunity . . . she couldn't reconcile having changed her mind without feeling foolish for all the time wasted. The time and money at the fertility clinic in Bridgeton, the health of her marriage, all of the tears she had cried over the years. And what was worse, she didn't know if she *had* changed her mind, only that she was confused over what she was meant to want.

"I'm sorry, I don't mean to upset you; I'm probably being such a rude asshole right now," he had fretted. "I guess I'm not sure why you've chosen this method instead of . . . you know."

"Finding a partner," she supplied for him, swallowing hard. She'd been swept up in Drea's excitement, she admitted herself. She had wanted a baby for years, and so had Drea; that was the common fabric of their friendship, and now here was a method of getting one, and she didn't know how to walk away from such an opportunity.

"I mean," he laughed awkwardly, "raising a werewolf on your own is going to be a wild adventure. If-if that's what you're planning on doing. I just hope they're giving you classes or something."

She blinked at him, uncomprehending for several long moments.

"Oh, I-I won't be? That's not the way this works. I'm sorry, I guess I didn't realize that you weren't brought up to speed the same way."

Lowell's dark eyebrows drew together in confusion, and she'd haltingly explained the process. In utero suppression. It was safe to administer; she had been assured that numerous times, and she would be under the clinic's care the entire time. Once the baby was born, they would come in for monthly shots, the same as she had, no different than a typical booster.

"And that's that," Dr. Ulric had explained with a smile. "In utero suppression and then a continuation into early childhood ensures that the first change in puberty never occurs. Your child, for all intents and purposes, will be human, just like you."

It was Lowell's turn to blink, long and slow, and she'd squirmed.

"They-they won't be a werewolf? I don't think I understand. How does that work?"

The restaurant he'd suggested was quiet and dark, giving their conversation an air of private seclusion, which she appreciated.

"Well, they start administering suppressants? In utero. I'll be receiving shots directly into the umbilical cord."

Across the table, Lowell recoiled.

"That sounds really painful," he said skeptically, pulling a face.

"Yeah, I think it is. My friend, the one who's pregnant? From the clinic? She's going to be starting her first round of shots next week. It's too dangerous to start before the middle of the second trimester, but once they deem the baby is progressing well enough, they start monthly shots. Same as I get the monthly shots to stimulate the heat. And then, after the baby is born, we continue the monthly shots at the clinic until they're a few years old. And that does it."

She didn't like the look on his face. He looked vaguely horrified, whether with the procedure or with her, she wasn't sure.

"Both of your parents are werewolves?" she asked tentatively when he didn't say anything right away. "I know you said your mom, but I wasn't sure —"

"Oh yeah. My dad is most definitely a werewolf. There's no denying that." He chuckled tonelessly, his eyes suddenly a million miles away from her.

He'd still been subdued when he walked her to her car that night, and she gripped his shirtfront, preventing him from leaving.

"Tell me this is an okay thing to do," she blurted, tears suddenly too close. "I-I never considered that it wasn't? The clinic is run by werewolves, so I just thought . . . Tell me you're okay with all of this, please."

Lowell hesitated for a long, endless-seeming moment.

"I-I don't know. I'm just . . . surprised, I guess? They didn't tell us this, so . . . I'm sure it's fine. Right? They wouldn't be doing anything unethical, not out in the open that way, I'm assuming. I'm just surprised, that's all. I guess I don't know what I was expecting. Thinking things through before jumping isn't one of my strengths."

She leaned up, catching his lips with her own, gratified when his hands slid around her waist, tugging her in closer. His hands lifted her to the car, and hers dropped to his belt. Nothing about this was smart; nothing about this made sense. She understood his confusion, understood it because she felt it herself.

Her confession was made in a halting voice in therapy that week, but the sphinx, as ever, was unbothered by her words.

"And how are you feeling about it? I'm hearing a lot of concern over what he might think, but I'm not hearing you discuss your own feelings on the matter."

The sphinx's voice was casual, but she shifted uncomfortably in her chair all the same. It was not a new line of questioning.

"We talked about transference before, right? It doesn't seem like you have the same sort of personality clashes with this young man, so you don't need to carry over a fear of self-expression into this new relation-ship."

Moriah nodded, swallowing hard. She'd been given the option of a video chat, but she'd opted to go into the office. It was too easy to distract herself with her environment, too easy to slot the telehealth appointments in with her list of chores for the day, all accomplished from the comfort of her home. She felt a greater sense of responsibil-ity when she came into the office. More anxious, but the anxiousness meant she was taking it seriously, she told herself.

"I don't know how I'm feeling. I know that's not a real answer, but .. . I don't know."

"It's a perfectly fine answer. But let's dig into that a bit more. Do you not know how you're feeling? Or do you not know how you're meant to be feeling? Because what you're feeling is simply what it is. You don't need to ascribe justifications. You just need to acknowledge. So let me ask you again. How are you feeling about it?"

Her eyes welled with tears, and the frustration of the last five years crowded in her throat, choking her.

"Confused. I'm confused and frustrated with myself, and I'm mad can't just enjoy being with him. And I *really* like spending time with him."

"Why can't you enjoy spending time with him? That's not a judgment; I'm just asking. Help me understand."

"Because this isn't a real relationship. I wasn't even supposed to meet him outside the clinic. I didn't know that, though. I'm supposed to be focused on getting pregnant, that's all."

Moriah watched as the sphinx took off her glasses, smiling kindly. She had sleek black hair and a wide mouth, her broad lion paws pushing into the carpeting as she adjusted herself in her chair, her claws painted a punchy pink.

"Who made that decision?" She asked casually again. She had a way of making every question sound as innocuous as an inquiry into the weather, and Moriah didn't know why it worked as well as it did, but it uncharged the judgment she felt coming at her from all sides normally.

"That's why I'm at the clinic, it's an insemination method. The point is to get preg —"

"But who made the decision that's all you're allowed to focus on? Did the clinic make you sign a contract agreeing to not have a single other desire or emotion for the duration of your treatment there?"

"I did," Moriah answered, sniffling. "I made the decision."

"But it's a decision that seems to be making you miserable. So let me ask you this — what would happen if you allowed yourself room for other things? Would you suddenly not be able to get pregnant anymore? Because I feel the need to remind you, Moriah, there's nothing physically preventing you from conception. The issues you had in your marriage were purely based on differing biologies."

"But it's all I focused on for so long. We spent so much money at the other clinic —"

"Who cares?" the sphinx shrugged. "I'm doing a lot of interrupting today, and I apologize," she laughed, that excellent honking laugh that brought a smile to Moriah's face every time she heard it. "But I just want to keep you on track; we both know how easy it is to slide back into rehashing the same frame of mind over and over again. Who cares how much money you spent? Sorben is gone. That money that you spent is gone too. Punishing yourself for it isn't going to bring it back. The money you spent on those procedures was a choice you made in your marriage with your husband. Your marriage is over. We need to come to a point where you can stop beating yourself up for choices you did not make alone that are in the past. Who is forcing you to make this decision now?"

"No one," she murmured softly. "No one is making me. But . . ."

She trailed off, and the sphinx raised her eyebrows encouragingly, nodding.

"Go on. But what?"

Moriah closed her eyes, inhaling sharply and exhaling on a woosh.

"This is all I've been focused on for so long. What do I do next? What if Drea and I aren't friends anymore? I don't know who to be if this isn't who I am."

The sphinx smiled brilliantly. "Those are excellent questions; I'm very proud of you. Let's take them one at a time, okay?"

Moriah nodded, settling back in her seat. She needed to talk this through with someone, needed to decide what she was going to do, because like the last two years of her life, time was slipping by nearly without notice. Hours into days and days into weeks and weeks into months and months and months she could barely remember, and this month was no exception.

The full moon loomed once again, and she had no idea what to do.

* * *

Lowell

It had been a very long two weeks.

The week after their dinner outing, he'd made a good effort to have fun with his brothers. He tagged along with Grayson and Trapp every week at the Pickled Pig, a trendy gastropub in the business district, always brimming with those who came to see and be seen. Trapp and Gray seemed completely at ease, but Lowell felt the slide of eyes upon them week after week, heads coming together, whispering about the Hemmings in their midst.

He could not fathom how Grayson and Trapp had so much to talk about every single week. It seemed to him that they were on the phone with each other every waking minute of the day that they were not actively engaged at work, yet the instant they would claim their table, they would be off — gossiping and exclaiming over things and people for which Lowell had no frame of reference, making plans, and bringing each other up-to-date on the minutiae of their weeks.

It made him wonder if this was the way he and Owen were meant to act. Grayson and Trapp were very different people, but they were bonded at their cores, as close as twins, and it seemed patently unfair when Lowell and his *actual* twin had not a single thing in common. Owen was quiet, courteous, and patrician, and he always had been; the opposite of him in every way.

For as long as Lowell could remember, being in his brother's presence made him jittery. Owen was *too* quiet and still, and when they were young, it seemed to trigger something in Lowell's brain — to be louder, more rambunctious, more *more*. They never wanted to play the same games as children, and when they did, they fought. Owen would accuse Lowell of cheating, and he, in turn, would accuse Owen of dragging things out on purpose, taking too long, and forcing his hand. He'd hated being a twin when they were children. He didn't want to dress like someone else, didn't want to share his toys, share his mother's limited attention, share *any* of the crumbs he felt they got — and crumbs were all that was left after the three bickering overachievers left their parents reeling. No matter how they started playing together, it always ended the same way — Lowell was happier going off in search of Grayson and Trapp, and Owen was happiest, it always seemed to him, when Lowell was not present.

"You don't get to say no. That's the part you're not understanding. You don't get to say no to fucking *any*thing."

He didn't know the context of the conversation, but it appeared to be at Grayson's expense. Trapp seemed delighted.

"If she wants you to go diving for an oyster that has a 10-carat diamond, you damn well better make sure you have the fucking diamond in your pocket and the oyster anchored in the water beneath your hut. If she wants gold skywriting telling the whole world what an asshole you are, you need to figure out how to do it. This is an apology trip. You don't get to put a price tag on anything."

"Oysters have pearls," Lowell piped up in confusion, having just arrived. "What am I missing?"

"It doesn't matter what they have. It doesn't matter if she asks for a fucking turkey sandwich. You're going to dive down to that oyster and figure out a way to bring her sandwich up without it getting wet. You don't get to say no."

Grayson groaned. "I've already spent almost half a mil, and we haven't fucking left yet. She's going to take me for everything I have."

Instantly, Lowell understood the conversation as Trapp threw his head back and laughed. Grayson was taking his super villain girlfriend on an extravagant tropical vacation to atone for some grievous misdeed he'd committed months earlier. Lowell silently considered that he had been to French Polynesia numerous times and had barely spent a few hundred dollars — he'd met locals, ate where they ate, swam in the crystal clear water without needing an excursion, and had an excellent time every time work took him there — yet somehow his brother was managing to spend hundreds of thousands of dollars before even arriving. *That checks out.*

"You know what would cost a lot less? Couples counseling. You might learn to talk about your feelings well enough that you wouldn't be compelled to bring other women on vacation every time your girlfriend upsets you. And she might learn healthy ways of expressing her completely understandable aggression without trying to crush your scrotum. You probably wouldn't even need to pay anything out of pocket. But the fact stands — you don't get to say no to anything she wants on this trip. You did the crime, and now you have to pay for it. In blood or money, whichever she wants. And yeah, she's totally going to take you for every penny you have."

"Isn't that what prenups are for?" Lowell asked, brows drawn together in confusion. He had been away at school when Trapp had impulsively married his med school girlfriend without any sort of prenup, much to their father's consternation. When the relationship fell apart a year or two later, it had been a three-ring circus.

"She would circumcise me in my sleep if I were to try to give her a prenup," Grayson mused as Trapp nearly choked in laughter.

Lowell had drifted to the bar as the two of them continued their conversation, staring at the specialty cocktail menu at the bar's edge for far too long, his brain not deciphering a single word of it, too lost in his own thoughts.

She'd wanted to have dinner together. *It's a date*, that's what he had said. But it wasn't, not really, and in his heart, he knew that. She was trying to make herself feel better about the whole thing, make it feel like less of a transaction, and for the first time, he'd begun to wonder how he would feel if it actually worked. *What's going to happen when she's pregnant? Is she still going to want you coming around? Are you going to watch her have a baby and then . . . what? Meet someone else? When you have no legal recourses? Not that you have them now . . .*

The irony of meeting up in Greenbridge Glenn was not lost on him. The small hamlet was best known for its libidinous sex parties and a resort hotel; the things that went on there were an open secret. His brother was co-owner of a vast estate within the community, outside of the resort area, nestled in the hills on a long, winding private drive. Lowell had been there numerous times when he was home for the annual Lupercalia celebration Grayson held, in addition to other parties throughout the year, but he had never been to the resort itself. *First time for everything*, he thought to himself sardonically, leaving for the evening.

She'd seemed jittery. Jittery and nervous and unsure of herself in his presence, he knew that everything he had predicted was true. *She's the patient, and you're a donor. That's it.* Her disclosure of the true nature of the procedure and what they would do had left him feeling vaguely sick, and he disliked the feeling of being misled, which was what he was certain the clinic was doing.

He'd walked her to her car again, hand in hand, the same as they'd done that very first night, only this time she had gripped him by the shirt front, pulling him down to meet her mouth. Her nails had dragged down his neck, sighing into him when his teeth caught at her lips, and his wolf writhed in his bones. He was stupid and impulsive and always had been, and at that moment, Lowell wanted to do nothing more than sink his teeth into her shoulder and claim her for the whole world to see, to take her as a mate, and fight off anyone else that would attempt to have her, any fucking wolf stupid enough to inject her with the poison of chemical suppressants.

He wasn't sure when he'd lifted her to the car hood. He wasn't sure when her hands had moved to his belt buckle and couldn't be certain if he had helped her draw down his zipper, but they were his fingers that slipped beneath the edge of her panties, pushing into her wetness and relishing the little moan she gave when he did so.

"I like you," she'd informed him stubbornly, and he'd wondered if she was telling him or convincing herself. "I don't think there's anything wrong with that. I want you to fuck me, and I don't want either of us to feel bad about doing it."

It was fast and hard and dirty, and he couldn't help but note that this was the second time they'd been together and also the second time he'd had his cock out in public, which was surely a record, but he did exactly as she asked. He loved being independent and living by himself on the edge of the great wide unknown, but Lowell Hemming was a sucker for a woman who told him what to do.

He heard the splash of his semen hitting the ground when he slipped from her afterward, kissing her long and hard before her tail lights disappeared up the road, leaving him in the twilight once again. His feet had carried him back to the small downtown, into what looked like a dive bar, ordering a double shot of the strongest liquor they had. He had no idea how to walk away from all this, and as soon as the thought occurred to him, he was certain that was what he needed to be doing, somehow.

"You all right to drive, lad?" the bartender asked skeptically, his lilting accent softening his dubious tone as he watched Lowell staring into space as if the answers he sought might have rested at the bottom of his empty glass. "You look like you've been tossed from the boot of a truck."

"I am," Lowell assured him. "I'm fine. I'm going to be a father, maybe."

The man behind the bar smelled like something wild and dangerous, something Lowell had only smelled once before in his lifetime, in the poison market of Mardeesh. He looked like an orc or at least a halfling, but he smelled like something much, much darker, and Lowell recoiled instinctively.

The man wrinkled his nose at Lowell's announcement, pouring him another shot.

"Poor bastard. Might be needing this then."

She didn't seem to care that he was going to get his heart broken, he realized. She couldn't bring herself to do this with a stranger, and so she was going to ensure that he was not a stranger, as often as necessary, for as long as they did this.

He could back out. That was within his rights, he could call the clinic the following morning and tell them he changed his mind, for the rosy picture he'd created for himself, and whatever mad science experiment they were doing in that clinic were not one and the same, and he was a Hemming, he was a werewolf, he loved being a werewolf, had been brought up to be proud of what he was and their history, and the thought of this left him feeling sick.

. . .But he knew himself well enough for that too. He was weak, and he was soft, and he wanted to kiss her again. *Which means you need to hurry up and get her pregnant, so that you can put an end to this, and run away to nurse your wounds.*

* * *

Moriah

She still didn't know what she wanted to do, and so, rather than decide, she'd chosen an act of extreme cowardice.

She'd had a moment of ludicrous bravado shortly after the divorce was finalized. She went marching off to her gynecologist, getting a prescription for birth control, and deciding that she was going to go out and have as much wild sex as she wanted, the sort of sex her husband never wanted to have with her. She would drink and party until dawn, getting in touch with the fun girl she used to be, meeting exciting, interesting men of various species.

It had taken only one outing to remember that she wasn't a fun 19-year-old anymore, she had never been much of a drinker, and she quite liked being in bed by eleven p.m. The unused and unneeded birth control had lived at the back of her lingerie drawer since, covered up and forgotten. Until now.

She popped out one of the white pills the day before she was meant to meet Lowell at the clinic, and another the morning of. She was a coward, and she accepted that, but she still didn't know what she wanted to do. She'd talked it over with her therapist, talked it over with herself, and she wasn't any closer to an answer. The only thing she knew for certain was that she was smitten with the dark-haired werewolf with sparkling eyes, and she didn't know how to admit to him that she had possibly changed her mind.

He entered the room fully dressed. Moriah shook her head with a grin, hoping he wasn't still upset with her.

"Well?" He asked, stretching out his long, toned arms. "I'm not naked this month. Look at how much extra work you have now."

She slumped against him when he approached, wrapping her arms around his neck and inhaling a deep lungful of him. His skin was burning hot, and he breathed out raggedly.

"I need to fuck you," he murmured against her neck. "So, *so* fucking bad. I swear I've been able to smell you through the wall for the past forty minutes and . . . Well, let's just say you're back in the splash zone."

She giggled against him, dragging the T-shirt he wore over his chest, scraping her nails through the dark hair that disappeared into his jeans.

"Well, that's good because I haven't been able to think about anything else for the last three days," she told him honestly.

They spent the entire time in the bed that month, except for the point where she pushed him to his feet, demanding to suck him.

"I'm pretty sure that's kind of contrary to the spirit of knocking you up," he groaned as she licked the skin beneath his navel.

"Are they going to come in and tell us we're not having sex the right way?" she asked. "Seriously? I dare them."

He shuddered when her tongue slid over his head, circling him entirely before sucking him into her mouth, earning a throaty moan from above. His foreskin moved with her lips, pushing back until he hissed, cockhead completely exposed when she swallowed. She'd never had much of a gag reflex, a good thing, as he was far thicker than what she had grown accustomed to throughout her marriage. Lowell made a kitten-like whimper above her as she fed his cock into her throat, not stopping until her lips had reached the flare of his knot.

She exhaled on her pullback, drool connecting him to her mouth, and he groaned again.

The flared edge of his frenulum caught her lips as she began to bob her head, fluttering her tongue against his underside, sucking the meat of him on every pull back until he moaned, digging his fingers into her dark red hair.

When his hips began to cant shallowly, Moriah opened her eyes, hypnotized by the way his balls swung with the movement, until they had pulled up, tight to his body. His head was tipped back, and his eyes scrunched shut when she finally pulled back, gasping as she released him.

"Get ready for the splash zone," he choked, making her laugh again. "You won't hurt my feelings if you duck and cover."

"Finish in my mouth," she instructed resolutely. "I want to taste you."

The first burst hit her tongue a moment later, and she listened to him wheeze above her as her mouth was filled. Moriah realized he'd not been exaggerating when his release began to drip down her chin, overflowing from her mouth. He led her hand to his knot, allowing him to wrap her fingers around it with his own before squeezing. When she squeezed, he moaned, and she decided there was nothing else she wanted to do with her hands ever again. He looked vaguely horrified when he finally slipped from her lips, seeing the mess running down her chin and pooling against her breasts, hauling her up to the bed to bury his face between her legs again.

When he covered her body, her back pressed to his chest and his arms braced around her, his hips rutting into her without slowing, she wondered if this was what it would be like being taken on her hands and knees in the woods while he was a wolf.

"Come with me this week and find out," he groaned against her neck when she voiced the question, and her blood thrilled.

Moriah wasn't sure what she'd been thinking when she sat beside him in a pickup truck two days later, kayaks in the flatbed and his hand on her knee, but she couldn't find it in herself to complain. The cabin he took her to sat on a crescent corner of a giant, glittering lake, surrounded by towering pines and the Black Hills beyond, owned by one of his brothers who wasn't using it, he'd said.

She hadn't been kayaking in years and found that her arms got very tired very fast, and when he balanced her on the nose of his, she shrieked every time it rocked. They'd stripped naked and swam in the icy cold water, not that the temperature had calmed the turgidity of his erection, and when he took her on the lake's edge, balls slapping into her, grunting with every thrust, Moriah wasn't sure how she was supposed to make a decision that would include potentially not seeing him again.

She sat curled on the sofa, unsure of what she was meant to do when he left her. The moon was high in the sky, and darkness had settled around the cabin before she crept out the back door slowly, uncertain of how she would find him. The kayaks were in the same place where they had left them earlier, on the lake's edge, their wet clothes hanging out on the line. It was then that she spotted it. Him. Lowell.

She didn't know what she was supposed to be feeling, but the heat that coursed through her, the desperation for the shadow she saw at the water's edge, was not it; she was positive. He was huge. Bigger than she was anticipating, dark brown and shaggy, and fear stopped her heart when he approached her. His claws were long and his teeth were sharp, but his eyes held the impish merriment that she had quickly fallen for, and when he lowered her to the ground, she'd sunk her fingers into the thick, dark fur at his neck. *This* was what being with a werewolf was.

His cock was dark red and glistening, riddled with thick veins, rising from a short, dark-furred sheath. His balls hung heavily beneath, and when she dipped her tongue into the concave tip of his strange-looking cock, he growled, low and throaty.

He had already licked her pussy better than any man of any species ever had, and his wolf had apparently retained that skill, for the first drag of his rough, pink tongue between her thighs sent her head lolling. She was supposed to feel ashamed with herself, she was sure of it, but as his tongue scraped over her clit, back and forth, his muzzle burying into her, seeking the source of her honey, Moriah couldn't find it in herself to care. He licked her with increasing fervor until she came against him, tightening her grip in his thick fur, and she continued to moan as he lapped up her release, his thick tail swishing behind him in the most adorable, Lowell-esque display of excitement that she could have dreamed up, his hips already thrusting upwards into nothing.

Perhaps she was more accepting because she had already been in relationships with other species, for she wasn't afraid when he entered her, even if the girth of his giant cock felt as if it were cleaving her in two. Moriah had thought their couplings at the clinic had been frantic and fevered, but nothing had prepared her for the way he fucked her as a wolf. Hard and fast and deep, every hilting within her made her cry out and her eyes bulge, and she pressed a hand to her lower belly, able to feel the shape of him rearranging her insides with his thickness.

His knot threatened on every thrust, and the final pop of it within her made her scream, and the pressure of his semen filling her, rope after rope, pulse after pulse of heat made her head drop and her eyes roll back, but it was *still Lowell* she reminded herself. It didn't matter if she'd only known him for two months, for she was half in love with him already. It was probably hormones, and because they were both lonely, but that was why she saw a therapist and was the sphinx's job to sort out, Moriah decided, reaching an arm back to grip his thick fur again as he emptied into her.

"Good boy," she moaned, feeling his chest vibrate behind her, clawed hands tightening at her hips, drawing her even closer, and his cock in deeper. "That's my good boy."

When a howl came from somewhere over the tree line, he left her, streaking into the forest like the wind, and she had retreated into the cabin. She felt the bed dip sometime before dawn, pulling him to lie against her. He was weak and slightly feverish, and she stroked his hair until his body slackened, and that's where she stayed for the next several hours.

Moriah considered — as she ran her fingers repeatedly through his smooth dark hair, still overlong and curling against his neck — how she could do such a thing as what she was contemplating. How could she have a child with him and not let him know it? How could she have a child with a werewolf at all and try to make it into a human like her? How could she give up her dreams of having a child for a man that she had just met two months ago, if that was even the reason for her waffling? None of it made sense, and she still wasn't any closer to an answer.

When his thick eyelashes fluttered, his eyes opening slowly, she grinned down, leaning until she could brush her lips against his temple.

"Oh, yeah," he sighed happily. "There's that one-on-one babying I live for." Moriah laughed, tugging his hair as her fingers moved through it. "I really don't get why you want to have a baby when I'm literally *right* here. I'm a child, and I love being babied. Plus, I'm already house-broken. That's a win-win."

He pulled her to lie beside him, cracking his back and stretching until something popped in his shoulder, and he winced.

"People think the change is hard, but they're wrong. It's the putting back together that sucks."

She led his head to her breast, and he hummed happily again.

Moriah wondered as he drifted to sleep once more if he was right. *He's right here. Best of both worlds and a definite win-win.*

* * *

Lowell

He hadn't anticipated the way her heat would affect him.

He hadn't lived near other werewolves in Tokyo, there were none in his building that he was friendly with at the very least, and if they were there, they made themselves scarce the week of the moon. Nikkia was horny every day of the month, always eager to suck his cock, eager to bend over and let him stuff her full. He had other fuck buddies around town, but having a lagomorph next door had been like winning the lottery, with the excellent bonus that they had become good friends. They made dinner together, watched trashy TV together, and did their shopping together. Feelings had never been a part of it beyond friendly affection, and he had never needed to worry about sniffing out a heat from his apartment.

Now everything was different.

It was the third month since he'd started the program with Moriah. Every month since the first had been a bit worse, a bit hotter, a bit more desperate. His sense of smell had sharpened, heightened to the point that he was constantly on edge as the moon neared, and he understood fully, for the first time in his life, the concept of *breeding*. It had nothing to do with the woman. Moriah was the one being put into estrus, of course, but all that meant was a realigning of her cycle to the moon, making her horny and receptive.

It was *he* who had undergone the change. Every month he was hungrier, more desperate to rut mindlessly. Every month he came a bit harder, a bit more. He had been conflicted, and he still was, but if someone would have placed one of his brothers between him and the opportunity to have Moriah massage his balls and call him her *good boy* as he emptied into her, he'd slit their throats without a moment of compunction.

He didn't like to contemplate it, but he thought he understood how his parents had wound up with six children.

He smelled it the instant he stepped from the car three days before the full moon. Hot and swollen and dripping, the tumid, *delicious* smell of a heat. His mouth flooded and the air in his lungs seemed to hitch, nearly rocking him off his feet. He reached out for the hood of the car to steady himself as the world tipped, every drop of blood in his body racing away from his brain, being diverted to a far more pressing priority.

Closing his eyes, he forced himself to breathe. A long, slow inhalation through his mouth, sparing his nose . . . 2, 3 . . . then a hard exhalation, shaking his head, attempting to dislodge the lust-woven cobwebs. *It's fine, this is fine. She's probably on a suppressant; focus on smelling the drug.*

The smell of the heat suppressant was sharp and corrosive, like licking a battery, the opposite of alluring. Deciding his inner voice was right, Lowell sniffed the air, groaning as the smell assaulted him once more. A needy, desperate cunt, already dripping, begging to be filled, begging to be fucked, and he was equally desperate to oblige.

Moriah was doing more than triggering her own heat with the shots — she was provoking his instinct to want to protect and provide, the thought of anyone even *speaking* to her while she was in heat making him snappish and short-tempered. He wanted to do nothing other than seek out the singular, mind-erasing hit of burying his cock in a needy, receptive mate at the height of the monthly frenzy . . . and now his nose had caught one.

At that particular moment, nothing mattered at all — nothing except the lack of blood flowing to his brain, making him dizzy, and the overwhelming smell of a needy cunt, making him hard. Lowell wasn't sure his brain was even functioning, synapses misfiring in every direction as he stumbled. He couldn't remember a time when he'd gone hard that fast, his erection scraping the inside of his jeans. His cock was calling the shots now, straining to see over his waistband, to be better able to direct his movements. His balls pulsed, the dictator in his pants demanding immediate action, a slaking of his lust, and he was helpless to do whatever his smaller head commanded.

If he closed his eyes and focused, he could hear her panting — high and rapid, a slight whine on every cant of her hips. He was able to taste on the air how wet she was, her desperation a sweet-metallic tang on the back of his tongue, and he wanted to coat his mouth in her slick before he gave her what they both desperately needed.

He had taken two steps away from the car when another smell caught his nose. Another wolf, another male, already there. Cock dripping, balls full. Lowell felt his pupils blow wide like a shark, positive he could smell the wind, hear the whisper of the clouds, the entire world over-stimulating his senses. A ripple of aggression moved up his back as he crouched, completely mindless, prepared to fight for the right to fuck whoever *she* was, to calm the fire under her blood, first with his cock, then with his knot; to fuck her until he went cross-eyed and emptied himself, allowing a trickle of blood to finally return to his brain.

He was halfway up the driveway when he passed the car. It was one he recognized. Like dominos falling, once he placed the car, his nose was able to place the scent, the girl behind the instinct to breed. It was Vanessa, his brother's girlfriend, and Grayson was the other wolf. Grayson, who had been born without a moral compass and had at least sixty pounds on him, most of it muscle. He wasn't sure what sort of neurological impulse it was that prevented him from charging into the house, cock in hand, but whatever it was, he was grateful. The wind shifted, and the blades of grass in the lawn beside him scraped against each other in a way that made him whine. It was too much, too much sensation, too much sound, Moriah wasn't even here, and he was losing his mind.

His feet were frozen for several more heartbeats. He might win in a fight against Jackson, Lowell considered. His eldest brother was staid and professional. He spent his time in a lecture hall or chasing after his little boy, doing volunteer work around town, a perfect fucking Woodland Scout. He would almost certainly win in a fight against his twin. Owen hunched over a desk fifty hours a week. He and his girlfriend spent their weekends hiking and bicycling and otherwise being insufferably, grotesquely in love. Liam wasn't a consideration. Trapp and Grayson, however, were made of something different, something meaner and harder. He'd had his ass kicked by his two older brothers more times than cared to recount, and he knew that, in spite of what his drooling cockhead seemed to think, if he would ever challenge Grayson physically, he would likely have his ass handed back to him in a box, spare parts rolling around on the driveway.

His head was trying to turn him back in the direction of the pool house, his cock desperately trying to make him storm into the main house, but fortunately, wonder of wonders, the larger of the two heads prevailed. Not before he paused in front of Grayson's car, flicking on one of the interior lights before slamming the door shut, making his way around the back of the house.

He had no doubt Grayson would be well-occupied for the next day, and that he and his psycho girlfriend would not emerge from their bed until it was time to drive to the lake.

"You need to get laid," he'd regularly told Lowell in the beginning, making it sound like the easiest thing in the world, and Lowell supposed, for him, it was. Grayson was not helpless here, like a rat trapped in a rapidly shrinking cardboard box. This is where he'd chosen to stay, and he had a life here — a tawdry, gossip-spawning life filled with excess and probably too much cocaine, Lowell suspected, but a life nonetheless. Grayson had no conscience and was inured to the whispers around him, but Lowell wasn't his brother. Every time Gray had doled out the terrible opinion, Lowell had ensured he'd put the juice away with less than a swallow, had opened and left a can of tuna in his brother's closet, and had crept into the basement gym each morning to reset Grayon's weight on every machine, forcing him to maniacally increase his cardio.

He had gotten laid, and it had only made everything worse.

"I'm really sorry," she'd said mournfully, her voice through the phone thick with congestion and coming from a million miles away, or so it had seemed. "I didn't expect this cold to kick my ass. We'll have to wait until next month."

He'd wanted to bring her chicken soup and a small brick of compressed botanicals and bath salt, made by an Oni who'd hosted him earlier that year when he'd been on a shoot in Hokkaido. It was the surest way for her to gain a bit of upper respiratory relief, and the soup was from the only delicatessen he trusted, run by a shifter family who'd moved to Cambric Creek from Long Island. He would take care of her while she was sick, and once she'd recovered, he would fuck her into the following month to make up for lost time.

Visions of wrapping her in a quilt and feeding her soup were dashed when she'd refused.

"I don't want to get you sick! And I don't want you to see me like this. You're supposed to think I'm sexy. Not a snot-covered mouth breather."

"We don't get sick the same way humans do," he'd reminded her, shortly before she'd disconnected the call in the midst of a sneezing fit.

Biologically inferior in every way. He could hear the particular tone his father's voice took, the one that was specifically reserved for talking about humans, turning over and over in his mind, the thought making him slightly nauseous. What would he be contributing to this future child other than dark hair and height, if everything exceptional he brought to the table would be stripped away, diminished and erased in a flood of chemicals?

The full moon was in forty-eight hours. Two days in which to suffer through. He would leave for the lake early, he decided. He would let the ice-cold water of the Shadowbend do the hard work of cooling his blood, and failing that, he might drown.

More importantly, he thought, holding his breath as he ducked around the side of the house; he didn't intend on still being there when Grayson finally emerged, bag packed, to find his car battery dead.

It was the third month, he repeatedly thought on his drive. This was the month it was most likely to happen, or at least, the start of higher odds, most clinic patients found success between their third and fourth months, and as he seriously contemplated calling one of those back page heat helper ads, he understood why.

He wasn't sure how long he had been there when he heard the crunch of gravel, interrupting his icy cold swim. Her nose was red, her eyes were bloodshot and bleary, her hair a tangled mess, pulled up in a messy bun.

"I'm negative," she called from the side of her car once he had pulled himself from the water. "I got the call a little while after I hung up with you; I had to do one of those drive-through testing sites. But I'm negative. It really is just a cold."

"I already told you, I don't get sick, not like that! And we're not affected by the virus anyway."

She shrugged weakly, and his wolf growled, shivering up his spine. He wanted to pounce. He could smell the slightly antiseptic odor of the cold medicine she'd taken, could taste its artificial corrosiveness on his tongue, but beneath that he smelled her sweet heat, and he wanted to bury his face in it and drown.

"Can-can we go inside? I know you probably want to run and get ready for your change, but —"

"I need to have you. I *need* to have you."

They had been spending far too much time together. They texted back and forth throughout the days, got together for dinner in Green-bridge Glen at least once or twice a month, and met up at that little café again, where they had met the very first time. Lowell could be persuaded it was almost like dating, if he hadn't signed a contract, and if she weren't paying for him to impregnate her.

"Then have me. You can have me whenever you want."

"I was thinking about calling one of those heat helpers. That's how desperate you have me."

Her eyebrows drew together, and she frowned adorably. "What the fuck is a heat helper, Lowell? Is that like, a jerk-off aide or something?"

He was laughing as he crossed to her, laughed only harder as she scowled, her fists balling. "That is exactly what it is. That name is truth in advertising."

"The only one who's going to jerk you off is me, you asshole. Get your cute tush inside and let me give your balls a kiss hello. I want to see that fluffy tail wag when you turn."

He was going to wind up getting her pregnant this way, he realized, his face pressed against her shoulder, his mouth hanging open, her hand reaching back to hold onto his hair as he thrust against her rhythmically, humping away like a horny dog.

There was something about the way she tasted, something that was off. If he hadn't known better, he'd have thought it was some sort of suppressant. *It's the cold medicine, you already know that.* The thought didn't slow him, and when his hips stuttered, filling her with his knot as she whined, low in her throat, he didn't care. It was ironic he thought, as his balls spasmed, they were planning on caging the wolf in the child he was creating with her. Caging the wolf, when her heat had turned him into an animal.

* * *

Moriah

She was exiting the grocery store the first time it happened.

She didn't often come to the Food Gryphon. The supercenter off the highway had a larger selection, and more importantly, it catered to humans. Moriah felt a flicker of guilt every time she stepped into the brightly lit store with its dozens of aisles, its products all designed with her, or at least someone who looked like her, in mind. It was the same flicker of guilt she had begun to experience every time she overheard one of her neighbors or someone in line in a shop grousing over the cost of homes in town and the infrequency with which they hit the market.

It was not her fault, she reminded herself. Sorben had given up the house in the divorce and had moved away from Cambric Creek without a backward glance, and where else was she supposed to go? She'd made a life for herself here, had a few friends and a thriving business here.

You could move back home, the little unwanted voice in her head would remind her, to the town where she'd grown up, and Moriah wondered if she might change her mind and do exactly that once the baby was here. It wasn't as if she had a deep support system here, not outside her small circle of friends. *Besides,* an insidious little voice in her head hissed, *it's not as if you're planning on raising a multi-species child. You won't have any help from the father.* It was becoming harder and harder to push the intrusive thoughts at bay — she was a human, she didn't belong there. Participating in conversations about the gentrification of neighborhoods was one thing, the gentrification of her own existence was wholly different, and something Moriah was not sure she was quite ready to face.

It was on one such afternoon that she decided to do her shopping locally, stepping into the Food Gryphon and making for the section of the store that, ironically enough, catered to werewolves. Werewolves and werecats, werebears and shifters, the items on the shelf exactly the same as what she shopped for off the highway. The human-adjacent community was thriving in Cambric Creek, and she reminded herself that none of the winged or betailed shoppers would assume she was human at first glance.

There was somewhat of a bottleneck at the automatic doors as she left with her groceries a short while later, the stream of shoppers slowing as an elderly woman navigated the entryway with the aid of a mobility device.

"Tilly, you've got the whole place in gridlock. You know the chief gets real cranky if dinner is late."

The voice came from over her shoulder, and the old woman, who had the lower haunches of a goat, grinned a cheeky, toothless smile in Moriah's direction, aimed at the man who was speaking behind her.

"Oh, hush. When you get to be my age, you can take as long as you'd like, wherever you go. You tell that old crank Magruh if he's got words for my Trapp, he can take it up with me. I might set my stove on fire just so you can come 'round for a cuppa, I've got new pictures of my great-niece and you'd be a fine bit of arm candy for her." The motorized cart jerked to a start unexpectedly, and the old satyress whooped as she zipped past them.

Moriah grinned at the old woman's antics, but before she could push forward, the wheels of her own shopping cart locked into position, just as she was pushing over the doorway. The man behind her had apparently decided he was done being slowed up for the evening, moving around her and gripping the front end of her cart with a huge hand, a hand that was attached to an enormously appealing forearm, lifting her cart over the small speed bump and righting the wheels.

He was clad in navy blue — a uniform of some sort, although she wasn't quite sure what profession provided clothing that fit like a painted-on glove. Or, perhaps it was simply the way his thick thighs and round ass filled out the navy pants, his narrow waist defined by the tucked-in polo shirt he wore. She didn't need to see him naked to know that the abs the shirt concealed were undoubtedly a six pack, possibly a twelve pack, maybe even the whole damn cube. The appealing forearms extended to well muscled biceps that strained the fabric attempting to encase them, a broad back that flexed as he lifted her cart easily . . . But it wasn't until he turned, giving her a brilliant smile over his shoulder, that her heart locked in place as sharply as the cart's wheels had done.

His teeth were even and white, chocolate eyes gleaming as they crinkled with the force of his smile, his dark hair shining beneath the overhead fluorescent lights when he inclined his head. He looked like a movie star, the sort that graced the landing pages of celebrity gossip blogs; so devastatingly handsome he inspired starlets to publicly squabble over him, but he also seemed dizzyingly familiar. She *knew* that look, knew the shape of his smile and the silvery sparkle of his dark eyes . . . but his expression held no recognition for her.

"Have a good day now." He continued out the doors without another glance back, his perfect ass seeming to wave goodbye as he disappeared into the parking lot, granting her no further thought.

The second time it happened, she was at the coffee shop. A long line was the norm at the small local roaster, always busy, but she never minded, for the Black Sheep Beanery provided excellent people watching. Her eyes picked out a couple on the side of the counter waiting for their order, a tall satyr with thick dark hair, the same color as his hocked lower legs, a human-looking woman pressed his back with her arms around his waist, a billow of blonde curls behind her. And there, over at the first table on the far wall, a muscle bound human-looking man sat with a sleek woman with wings and wide lion's paws, crossed daintily at the ankle.

See? she told herself. *There are other human-looking people here, you're not the only one.* The man turned in his seat, laughing at something the woman had said and opening the newspaper on the table before them, and Moriah realized a single eye sat in the center of his broad face. The cyclops laughed again, leaning in to kiss his winged companion, and she looked away, face heating. *You've never been self-conscious in all the years you've lived here, don't start acting this way now. Look, the people right in front of you! You fit in just fine.*

The couple before her in line were indeed as human-looking as she, sporting matching tans and an exhausted air. The petite woman wore a short sundress, and the unbroken line of her bronzed skin whispered of a sun-soaked vacation as she slumped against her tall companion's mountain-like frame, her eyes closed as if she had fallen asleep standing up.

"I am *not* ready to go back to work." The man's voice was a deep, rich scrape of petulance, and Moriah watched in fascination as he ran a hand through the woman's waterfall of sable hair. They seemed to exist in their own little bubble, unaware of anyone around them, and she tried to imagine where they had been.

"What were we thinking, coming home? We should fly back tonight."

Perhaps trekking through the remains of ancient cultures on southern hemisphere beaches, the theme of several excursion moodboards she'd made for one of her fantasy trips, or maybe riding horses in the surf at some northern fishing town, the corresponding aesthetic board done up in moody marine blues and greens with pops of sun-dappled yellow and gold. Or more likely, she considered, taking in the man's expensive-looking watch and the diamonds sparkling heavily from the woman's wrist and earlobes, some private island resort, with all-inclusive everything and a swim-up bar. She was able to see the crystal blue water and pink-hued sunset in her mind's eye, having watched more travel videos than she could count for the exact type of place. *And you've still never been anywhere. This is the stuff you ought to be doing before you get pregnant.*

"Oh yeah? What are we going to do, convince the locals to sue the sharks so we each have someone to represent?"

The woman's smile warmed her voice, her eyes never opening as the man's huge hand continued down her spine, coming to rest at the small of her back before answering decisively.

"I can be a fisherman, and you can make shell art."

Moriah ducked her head to hide her smile as the woman lifted her face from the man's chest with outraged laughter, pushing against him.

"Wow, am I supposed to pay for your beachfront massages with my shell art business? You *do* understand that being a fisherman doesn't actually mean someone serves you lobster and champagne every day at 3 PM, right? Because you got pretty used to that."

"But that's what it *should* mean. We can explain that once we get there. I don't think I can ever be happy with one of your terrible blow jobs again if there's not a school of fish watching us from the floor."

Moriah knew she had turned as red as a tomato from eavesdropping on the couple's conversation, but the woman continued to laugh, scraping her nails down the front of the man's chest until he turned to acknowledge a passerby who called out to him in greeting.

He had a striking profile — a sharp, square jaw and a strong chin, straight nose, his eyes fringed in a thick fan of soot-black lashes. It was a profile she knew well, even if this stranger's was a bit more chiseled and severe. When he glanced swiftly back over his shoulder, as the other patron moved on, his eyes met hers briefly, a lightning fast up and down followed by a flare of his nostrils, before the dark-haired woman tugged his hand and the couple shuffled forward in line. He was handsome but hard, his familiar features holding an icy edge. Even still, she was unsurprised by the quicksilver gleam she saw in the dark depths of his eyes. He didn't possess the same air of energetic mischief as Lowell and he was at least a decade older, but the resemblance was uncanny.

"You know, I'm not sure they would let us stay, you would force them to overfish the reef," the woman continued, unerred by their conversation's brief disruption. "You ate an entire lobster every day for a snack."

"What exactly are you trying to say? I'm playing racquetball with my brother in forty minutes and then I'm going to the gym, so it's unclear what your point is, counselor."

"The point is we had to come home, because *I* have a trial to prepare for, Mr. Hemming."

"I can't fucking stand you," the man grumbled against the top of her head, but the woman only continued to laugh, dropping against the man's chest again as his hand settled over her hip. Moriah swallowed at the sight of his dark hair, the back of his head even seeming familiar. *That's too big of a coincidence.*

The final straw came maybe a week later, when she'd been coming out of a meeting with a client. The tiefling and her partner had recently purchased a second home on the coast, hiring Moriah to give the outdated bungalow a serene, beachy wash. She had explained that it was necessary to *feel* the difference in the several jute samples she'd picked out for the sun medallion-shaped area rug they'd chosen, and had no problem meeting the tiefling at her office.

The elevator doors were already sliding shut when a large hand cut through the narrow space, the doors reversing instantly. Moriah was glad that she had already been leaning against the railing at the back wall, as she likely would have fallen over otherwise. The young man never paused his phone conversation, reaching out a long finger to jab at the numbers. The same long fingers that had moved over her body and stroked into her heat, curling into her, his wrist thrusting until she had bucked against his hand, leaving the long digits coated in her slick, which he had sucked clean before kneeing open her thighs and settling himself between them. The same lips that had kissed her, the same tongue that had brought her so much pleasure, now engaged in a one-sided phone conversation, paying her no mind, as if she were a stranger.

It was distressing to see him there before her, to *see* him and be utterly invisible. The air in her lungs seemed to freeze and expand, pushing against her chest until she was practically left gasping as he laughed, that too feeling overly intimate in this unfamiliar space. She could still feel the silken weight of his hair between her fingers as she gripped the back of his head for support, his hand loose at her throat, his breath hot at her face as she moved against him, gaining extra bounce from where her knees pressed into the pillow-top mattress. The stretch of his thick shaft was a delicious pressure, and after every upward roll of her hips, she came down on the swollen protuberance of his knot, pressing determinedly against the mouth of her sex, begging entrance, promising a pain-pricked pleasure that would turn the world white and gold, shimmering with sparks as she lost herself against him.

To be ignored so utterly by him after they had done what they had done together, after sharing what they had shared, was not an experience by which she could abide.

The shots administered by the clinic made her irrational, made every emotion feel fraught and closer to the surface, and her face was hot when she spun towards him, fully prepared to give him a piece of her mind as quickly as she could before the tears begin to fall, but he never turned in her direction, and in facing his profile, she was able to see the subtle differences she had missed initially. This man's hair was shorter and neater, his smooth jawline absent the five o'clock shadow that had scraped against her thighs, his nose possessing a slight upturn. His voice, while similar in tone, had a different timber and flow, and his laugh wasn't as infectious. He didn't jiggle his foot impatiently as he waited for the elevator to arrive at the eighth floor, nor were his hands fidgeting at his side. He didn't sparkle, she decided, despite being equally as handsome.

The elevator bounced to a soft stop and the man exited when the doors rolled open without even glancing back to where she stood, her mouth still hanging open but her tears, thankfully, tamped down.

"Mr. Hemming, just who I wanted to speak with."

She watched as another body fell into step beside him, moving away from the elevator, and the familiar man's unfamiliar voice was the last thing she heard as the doors slid closed

"I'm on my way over to dev, so if you can walk with me, I'm all ears."

Mr. Hemming. She jolted. The couple from the coffee shop. The same name was bestowed on *that* man who also bore more than just a passing resemblance to Lowell, and she had a feeling if she'd been able to read the writing on the front of the navy blue polo shirt straining over the bulging pectorals of the gorgeous man with the brilliant smile in the grocery store, the white stitching would have spelled out the same name. As the elevator arrived at her floor, she remembered with a gasp that he had a twin, the reason why she'd almost not chosen him. *And you just rode up with him,* she realized.

Moriah wasn't sure why the name seemed as familiar as it did, as if she'd heard it before it in a completely different context, like a nondescript shadow at the back of her memory. She put the incident out of mind as she approached her client's office, deciding she would look up the name later to determine why it seemed familiar to her, but she never got that far. She had barely pulled out of the complex's parking lot before she passed the first sign, and once she passed the first, the next five and ten and twenty seemed to scream out to her — from shop windows, street corners, from her neighbor's yards as she pulled onto her street. *Hemming for Mayor.*

The very first entry of her search results told her all that she needed. Jackson Edmund Hemming the eighth, lifelong resident of Cambric Creek, grandson of the now deceased previous mayor, and current mayoral candidate. The first photograph of the man made her whimper. He had Lowell's sharp jaw and dark eyes, clearly a relation. Another link clicked showed her information about his family, his wife and young son, volunteer work in the community, and large family here in Cambric Creek.

The next link she clicked brought up an article about the man from the coffee shop, Grayson Henry Hemming the fifth, the important litigation being undertaken in the nation's capital pertaining to multi-species healthcare and the violation of fundamental medical rights, propagated by the Food and Drug Administration, according to the current allegations being made by the Werewolf Defense League. This was the brother he lived with, she realized. Imperious and haughty and expensive looking, the exact sort of person whose home would resemble a luxury hotel and who bought expensive Christmas presents for his family.

Lowell had told her that he had a large family, but he'd never mentioned he was a member of the *first* family. The middle child, a fact over which she had laughed at the time, his mother a werewolf from a pack outside their community, and his father . . .

Moriah whimpered. *His father.* She was uncertain of her place in the community, didn't know if she truly belonged and if she ought to stay. She felt removed from community events, out of sync with her neighbors, and too many years of nonparticipation with Sorben had left her feeling disconnected from the goings-on of Cambric Creek . . . But one would've needed to live under an extremely remote rock at the bottom of a particularly deep cave in the middle of the Black Hills, surrounded by nothingness for miles to have not known who Jack Hemming was. Moriah felt disconnected, but she still paid attention to gossip, and there was no one else her neighbors loved to gossip about more than Jack Hemming, his ambitions, and his sons.

He did not hold office, but everyone knew who truly ran the town. He was the most influential werewolf in the area, possibly in the entire region. His word was law, and if the powers that be did something he did not like, he simply circumvented them. Moriah remembered, shortly after she and Sorben had purchased their house, the letter that every household in Cambric Creek received from the man himself, voicing his displeasure with the current administration's refusal to grant new businesses the opportunity to expand their downtown area, forcing residents to Bridgeton and Starling Heights and beyond, forcing *pa-*

tronage of human-run industry. The line had stood out to her. As a human in the community, she hadn't known how she was meant to feel.

Included with the form letter was an application to apply for the newly-created Founder's Fund, a grant program being started by him and several members of the Slade and Applethorpe families, encouraging businesses to stay in Cambric Creek, to open doors within the community. Moriah reflected that he had gotten his wish. A decade later, the downtown area was flourishing. There were no shortages of shops and restaurants and pubs, all owned and operated by trolls and goblins, orcs and satyrs, harpys and shifters. There was very little need to go to Bridgeton at all, a prophetic blessing once the virus began ripping its way through the human community.

She felt dizzy. She felt sick. She remembered telling Lowell that he was a bit of a brat that very first afternoon they had met at the little café, and she began to laugh, and laugh, and laugh. *A brat indeed.*

The rest of the week passed in a blur, for she was busy with work, and didn't have time to dwell on the pains she had taken to keep him from meeting her in Cambric Creek, a comedy of errors if there ever was one. The full moon was approaching, and she had begun to feel the familiar prickle beneath her skin, her full moon estrus cycle beginning to warm and bubble at her core. She hadn't decided what she wanted to do. She didn't know how to tell him that she had changed her mind, and didn't want to risk not seeing him again. She could not, *would* not have a baby with the son of a prominent werewolf family and not actually *have* a werewolf.

Besides, she told herself. She had gotten used to the tail wags.

Her therapist was right — she needed to decide her priorities and the direction she wanted her future to take.

* * *

"Do you still want to have a baby right now?"

The question seemed to hang in the air. Moriah felt as if she were standing at a great precipice, with the weight of her own expectations and guilt at her back, but when she gazed down into the abyss, it was only a shallow puddle. Her reflection stared back. Her younger self, a young woman who loved color and texture and laughter, who wanted to see the world and create, who had traded all of her own ambitions for a bad marriage and a small town with interesting people that she didn't feel any connection with. She could step into the puddle with ease, she realized, without falling, changing the fate of the young woman trapped within.

"There's something I want you to consider, Moriah. I don't want you to answer right now. I just want you to think about it. We've talked a lot about transference and displacement, and I know those are big concepts. They can be scary to confront. So I just want you to think about this, and we'll talk about it when you're ready. Did you want to have a baby so desperately with your ex-husband because you wanted to create something out of your love together? Or did you want to have a baby so you wouldn't be so lonely with him?"

It had been two weeks since Despina, the sphinx, posed the question to her. Two weeks of chewing it, of folding it up like a blanket and locking it into the closet of her mind with the other things she didn't want to contemplate. Two weeks of pulling it out and wrapping it around her, feeling intense grief with its weight, not sure what she was grieving in the first place.

"I don't think I do," she murmured quietly.

Across the coffee table, Despina nodded, smiling encouragingly, and Moriah straightened in her chair, steeling her nerves.

"I don't want to have a baby right now," she said more forcefully, her conviction firmly in place. "That-that doesn't mean not ever, because I do. And I want to have one within the next three or four years. But I don't want to have one right now. I don't want to do this alone."

The sphinx's huge smile made her dark eyes narrow to obsidian slits.

"I'm very proud of you. You've worked so hard to be able to say those words."

Moriah let out the breath she had been holding, deflating like a balloon and sinking against the back of her seat. She had told her therapist that she had been taking birth control for the past several months, a little white pill at the back of her tongue every morning, and so far, they had worked.

She saw Lowell weekly now, talked to him constantly, and she knew she needed to tell him the truth. She'd been terrified when she got sick, thinking she would never leave her house again until this virus was no longer a threat, and when she'd tested negative, seeing him had been the only thing on her mind. She wouldn't be going back to the clinic. She was due for her blood work anyway, and they would undoubtedly be able to tell that she had been actively sabotaging the results. Wasting money on a dream she wasn't sure she wanted anymore seemed a fantastically foolish thing, and she was done pretending. She was done with this charade, done wasting money, done lying to herself. But she did not want to be done with him.

He had appeared on her doorstep after she confronted him about his family.

"You don't understand. You don't understand what it's like. Everywhere I go, people already know me. But they don't know *me*," he emphasized, frustration ringing in his voice. "They don't know me. They know Trapp. Or they went to school with Jackson. Or they've been to one of Grayson's parties. They think they know me because they know my father, but *everyone* knows my father. They don't know me, but they think they know everything about me. They use my name without introducing themselves, or they ask me questions about my mom, and I've never fucking seen these people before! I don't know how to make friends here or meet people because they already have a preformed opinion of my family, and I can't stand it."

She had pulled him inside. Made him dinner. Watched breathlessly as he prowled around her entire house, examining everything with a huge smile. He asked a million questions and never stopped talking, his various trains of thought intersecting and passing each other at lightning speed, tapping his fingers on the table, jiggling his toe against the chair, unable to be quiet or hold still. Her house would never be silent again, she realized. Not as long as he was in it. Pushing him down into her French café breakfast nook felt like something out of a dream, for as many times as she had fantasized about it by then.

He pulled her outside into her backyard, and they lay in the middle of the grass, head to head, staring up at the stars. She kissed the tip of his nose, and her eyes flooded with tears. *It's just the shots. It's the shots doing this, doing all of it.*

"Tell me this isn't just because of the shots they're giving me, the way I feel. Tell me this isn't some artificial hormone, that once I stopped taking them, I'm going to be horrified with all of this."

Lowell only smiled softly, bumping his forehead with hers before turning his head to look up at the sky again.

"The sky always looks the same, you know. You asked me once before about my favorite place I've been, but I don't think I can answer that. It's never about the place. I've slept on the ground in a hundred different countries, and the sky always looks the same, no matter where you are. The sunset is always a sunset. That's why I hate taking shots of landscapes and geographical things. Volcanoes in the northern seas don't look any different than volcanoes in the tropics. Mountaintops are mountaintops. If there wasn't a caption on the photo, you would have no idea where it was taken. It's people who make the difference. The mountains in one country will look exactly the same as the one in the next, but the old woman selling her hand-woven rugs at the base of it will be different. She'll have a different smile and a different story to tell. The only thing that's ever the same is they all want to bring me home and cook for me," he laughed. "And they're always excellent cooks."

"You go with them?" She asked, her question and her tears momentarily forgotten.

"Of course, I go with them!" he laughed again. "You know you're actually going to get authentic food from someone's grandma. And that's never going to be the same. The sunset will always look like a sunset, but everyone's grandmother prepares the signature regional dish a little differently. And that's why I love traveling. Seeing people. Eating their food. Hearing their stories."

"I wish I could go with you."

He turned his head, looking into her eyes again.

"Why can't you? What's keeping you here?"

Her voice stuck in her throat, uncertain of what she was supposed to answer.

"I already told you, I'm not sure why you want to have a baby so badly when I'm right here, an actual baby. I can barely tie my shoes."

She laughed in outrage, gasping softly when he caught her lips in an upside-down kiss.

"I'm not on any shots, Moriah. You *are* changing me, your cycle is changing me because now I think about you talking to some rando at the grocery store, and I want to break their fucking legs, but . . . I'm not taking any magical shots. The way I feel is just the way I feel."

When she woke with him in her bed the following morning, sprawled out with his legs hanging over the sides and his face pressed to her ribs, she knew she would not be going back to the clinic. She never thought the words would be easy to say, but she repeated them, encouraged by Despina's wide smile.

"I don't want to have a baby right now. I want to see what happens with this relationship because I really like him. And I deserve it."

* * *

Lowell

The call had come through the previous evening. Lowell wasn't even sure what he had been doing when his phone had rung — cooking her dinner, kissing her thighs, wheezing against her neck as her core clenched around him, her hand in his hair and her soft cries clouding his brain — it could have been any of the above.

The missed call was from an unfamiliar number, and premonition made his skin prickle as he tapped the icon for his voicemail .

Nonhuman airlines were resuming service, not in all countries but in most. He would need to show up for health screening and take new photographs and fingerprints, but he could get back to work as soon as the following month if he returned their call that day.

He didn't know what to do. Lowell hated making decisions, particularly for anything important, and this was perhaps the biggest decision he'd ever had to make in his life. He didn't know what the right thing to do was, didn't know how to say goodbye to Moriah, if he even could, and found the thought of saying goodbye to his family harder than he had anticipated.

She was gone when he woke, checking his phone as he rolled over. Once he had, all thoughts of going back to sleep were done. Lowell was pulling himself out of bed, too anxious to even pretend to sleep. He didn't know what to do, didn't know what to decide, and at length, realizing he was not going to come any closer to an answer by fidgeting his way through his brother's house, he decided to seek the counsel of the one man who dispensed advice to the entire town.

Jack Hemming's office was on the top floor of a building that had housed Cambric Creek's theater house at the turn of the last century. The building's facade had undergone significant modifications since its construction more than one hundred and fifty years earlier, but the golden cupola at the roof's peak had remained an unchanged part of the town's skyline since those early days. The crystal chandelier, visible from the street where it hung suspended over the stately building's foyer, was similarly a part of the original interior. Lowell had marveled over the chandelier as a child, gripping his mother's or elder brother's hand as they made the trip to visit his father in the middle of the afternoon, staring slack-jawed up at the massive, glittering light fixture, mesmerized by the rainbow prisms it cast upon the walls.

His eyes raised instinctively as he crossed the street now, taking in the chandelier and feeling himself shrink, a clumsy, tongue-tied child once more, seeking his father's counsel.

Dedication of the Cambric Creek Public Theatre

August 11, 1878

Commissioned by and gifted to the town

by J. Edmund Hemming III

He'd passed the plaque at the building's front doors a hundred thousand times in his lifetime, giddy at the sight of his own surname when he'd been very small, needing to stop and point, announcing to anyone within earshot that it was *his* name on the wall.

He hadn't realized then that it wasn't; that it was someone else's legacy and burden to shoulder. It was exciting to him when he was very young before he truly understood. It was far from the only plaque in town, the Hemming name inescapable as he would pass the bank and town hall, dodging around corners and up back alleys in an effort to avoid his father's office as he cut class as if his mere presence on the sidewalk would be enough for his father to choose that moment to look out the window.

There were no other Lowell Hemmings, his mother had explained when he'd been in grade school, throwing tantrums every time he sat on a bench with Grayson's name upon it, or entered a building bearing a plaque bearing Jackson's. It was *unfair*. *He* should have a building or a bank or a bench, why wasn't he special enough?

"Because you're one of a kind, sweetheart. You're the only one who gets to say you're *the* Lowell Hemming. But if you want, you can make a plaque and we'll hang it on daddy's door at the office. How does that sound?"

Owen had been holding her other hand at the time, as they crossed the busy intersection, and had been unbothered at the lack of benches and plaques bearing his name.

He'd been embarrassed by the excess of his family's generational largesse as a moody adolescent, and increasingly chafed by the Hemming name as he grew older. The sight of his family name on the walls had made him desperate — desperate to escape the plaques and inscriptions and oil paintings all over town; the expectation that he would be *somebody*, somebody of worth, of importance, for the town to hold up as another shining, golden example of the Hemming family, and not an impulsive, needy screw-up who couldn't even decide if he wanted to go back to work or not.

The sight of the plaque now, as he entered the heavy, gilded doors made his stomach bunch and twist, the ghosts of his forebears crowding into the marble-floored foyer, aghast at every decision he'd made thus far.

"To what do I owe the pleasure of this unexpected hour? We didn't push breakfast up, did we? Don't tell me you're ready to take up your mother's offer and move back home."

He wasn't sure what expression his face had pulled automatically, but his father's deep laughter set his clenching guts at ease, at least somewhat. Lowell dropped into the armchair in front of the mahogany desk, the anxiety of the previous months leaving him exhausted.

That he and his brothers all had the Hemming look was not news to him — his mother had often joked about merely being a conduit for a superior bloodline, and the cluster of family photos atop the piano in the front room of his childhood home showed the six of them looking like clones of varying ages and hair lengths — but it wasn't until he'd been forced home this past year, the fatigue of the road and his lifestyle and the stress over being sidelined showing on his face, that Lowell appreciated just how much he resembled his father.

He and his brothers shared the same dark eyes and dark hair, and Lowell had noticed with startling clarity how their eyes crinkled identically, smile lines creasing his forehead and around his mouth in just the same way, and had found a handful of silver hairs at his temples, in the same pattern as Jackson and Grayson, exactly the same as their father.

He wondered if his own son or daughter would bear the Hemming look, and tried to imagine a little girl with Moriah's sparkling green eyes, her dark hair pulled into a ribbon. *Why does it matter? You won't be around to see it, you won't have anything to do with it. They'll probably figure a way to make her blonde.*

"I need your advice," he blurted before he could second guess his reason for coming in early, before their breakfast date, hands tightening over his knees. "I'm–I'm trying to help a friend, and I don't want to tell them the wrong thing. It's. . . important."

His father cocked his head, holding Lowell's eye for an interminable moment, just enough time for him to shrink, before gesturing for him to continue.

"So . . . I have this friend. She wants . . ." He sucked in a deep breath, forcing himself to get it over with. "She wants to have a baby. With a werewolf. But not to co-parent or anything, just a baby. She's had trouble conceiving before and I guess she's, um, read that her chances at conception are higher or something."

Another dark chuckle came across the desk, and Lowell took a moment to swallow hard.

"Yes, I know all about that. Believe me, six of you eating me out of house and home was never the plan. So what sort of advice are you trying to give this friend?"

Heat burned up his neck at his father's cocked eyebrow, and he steeled his nerves before continuing.

"She doesn't want to raise the baby as a wolf. You know they have all those suppression drugs now, and she said her doctors told her it's completely safe. She's pretty sold on the idea, but I just . . ." his hands raised in a gesture of helplessness, voice breaking off, feeling his composure fishtail, "I'm just not sure it's right. She wants me to tell her she's doing the right thing, wants me to reassure her, but I just don't know that it *is* the right thing."

Across the table, Jack steepled his fingers, pressing them to his mouth. His forehead had creased as he listened, the same way his own did, Lowell thought. An image of Jackson's little boy passed through his mind, sharp dark eyes and messy dark hair; ice cream-smeared face and gap-toothed smile, and he knew his nephew would one day feel the freedom of packed earth beneath his feet and the wind rushing in his ears, freedom that came with the monthly turn. It was a preposterous, unthinkable thing in a family of werewolves. *But this child won't be family. They won't have anything to do with you or this community.*

"You already know my feelings on artificial suppression," Jack began slowly, and Lowell nodded, knowing well. "So I'll spare you the lecture. I'm assuming this friend of yours is—"

"Human," Lowell supplied, wincing when his father grunted.

"I suspected as much, that's typical. Well . . . I would caution her that raising a werewolf is no easy feat, whether she's medically suppressing the turn or not. Trapp and his temper nearly broke me. When you and Owen came along, if it hadn't been for your mother, I would have left you in a box next to the river."

Lowell huffed in outrage, but his father only shrugged unapologetically.

"You were monsters. All of you. Always getting up to something, breaking something, jumping out of trees, burying each other. Jackson pushed you off the roof when you were five, do you even remember that?"

Lowell laughed, thinking of the text received on their group chat just a few days earlier from Jackson.

On this day in history, I pushed Lowell off the roof and he broke his leg.

If I hadn't, you'd probably be a gym teacher.

You're welcome

Jack scowled at his laughter.

"Trapp convinced Owen he could grow a money tree in his stomach if he swallowed a fistful of dimes. Grayson fucked the *entire* town when he was in high school. And you? *You* are the reason I drink. And this isn't even getting into the pranks. The five of you have collectively broken nearly every bone a single body contains. The full moon was the only time I *didn't* worry. Your friend might have the best doctors, and it's true that suppression technology has come a long way . . . but you can't harness the wind. If she's not ready to raise a werewolf, she shouldn't be having one, because she's going to have her hands full, with or without chemical intervention. This isn't some nebulous thing that exists on a spectrum. The wolf will always be there, just under the skin, only now it doesn't have an outlet."

Lowell let out a shuddering breath at his father's words, nodding. It was what he already knew, but it was good to hear the reinforcement of what he suspected.

"What else?" A note of familiar impatience crept into his father's voice, and Lowell felt his fists bunch, felt himself shrinking to that frustrated 10-year-old all over again. "You didn't come here for me to tell you what you already know, Lowell."

"How do you know?" He demanded, feeling his hackles raise in aggravation. "Maybe that's all I came for. You don't know."

"I know, because I know you. I know you because you are as transparent and predictable as all of your brothers, and just as big of a pain in my ass, if I'm being honest. Do you know what your problem is, Lowell? You think you're special. You think you're different. You think you're the only person in this family who has wanted to get away from this name, you think you're the only one who feels crushed under it. Do you think I don't understand the impulse to run? Do you think I wanted to stay in this town? That I wanted to raise my boys here, under this microscope for these jackals?"

Lowell felt pressed back into his chair, unable to move. He had never really been on the receiving end of his father's attention, and he had been a fool to seek it out now, he realized. For there was a reason all of his older brothers were so tense.

"Jackson thinks he has something to prove, thinks he needs to rewrite history because he's been breathing his own oxygen for too damn long. Grayson thinks he's the smartest person in existence, and while he's busy congratulating himself on being so brilliant, he lets himself be manipulated. By you. By Trapp. By his girlfriend. Take your pick. Trapp can't abide any storyline where he is not the hero. He dropped out of medical school, wasted a fantastic amount of my money and broke your mother's heart. So what did he do? He comes back here and becomes a fireman. Because who the fuck can get mad at someone who's saving kittens and running into burning buildings? *You* think you're the only Hemming in existence who's wanted out, who wants to see the world, who can't be happy with just this name. And your brother thinks if he's quiet enough he can skate through life without ever having to make a hard decision on his own. Do you know he's been carrying around an engagement ring for almost a year? He can't pop the question because *he* would have to do it, and it's so much easier to just let Gray and Jackson bicker over bullshit and let you throw your tantrums and he can just exist in the background. He's probably hoping one of you steals it from his pocket and does it for him. You're all equal amounts of predictable. And you, my dear boy, are just as annoying to me as all of your brothers. No more, and no less. So if you have something else to say, Lowell, let's get the fuck on with it, so we can get breakfast ordered."

"My office called. They're reopening flights for nonhumans. I can go back to work. I have paperwork to process and a new visa to get but, yeah. I can be back to work by next month."

Jack steepled his fingers, and Lowell swallowed hard.

"That's all you've been champing at the bit for, and yet you sound so conflicted."

"I don't know what to do," he choked out. "I hated being home, and I think I probably still hate it. I don't like the person I am here. But — I'm going to miss everyone. It wasn't as bad as I thought, and it's been nice just..."

He sucked in a shuddering breath, suddenly feeling as though he were about to cry, proving his father right. He was still a child that threw temper tantrums.

"I think I love this girl, but I don't want her to do this. I'm not ready to be a father, I'm not. I'm a fucking idiot, I can barely function like an adult. I can't afford to live here even if I wanted to, I'm burning through my savings right now. She wants this, but I don't want to know that I have a kid out there somewhere and I'm not part of . . . I just don't think I can do it, but I don't want to leave her, and I don't know what to *do*."

His father said nothing for a long moment. Lowell was used to that. Grayson was the same way. They let silences stretch, and waited for the other person to get uncomfortable and fill them, giving them more time to gather information and plan their attack.

"Do you know why I have this piece of yours?"

His eyes raised to the photograph on the wall, one of his, professionally framed and matted. It was a group of Komodo dragon children, with wide, toothy grins, holding pieces of melon that only grew on the island where they lived. They had spent the last two hours teaching him how to shimmy up the trees to pick them without slicing his legs on the treacherous trunks, the particular way they had to be cut, to get through their tough outer shell without damaging sweet juicy flesh inside. Behind them, in the middle distance, was the crater of a recent volcanic eruption, still belching black smoke. He had been there to cover the volcano, and had played Ketterling with the kids while he waited for the boat that would bring him closer to the caldera.

There had been several dozen other photographers there, all jockeying for tenders to get closer to the crater, documenting what was left of another cluster of islands in the archipelago, decimated by the resulting tsunami. He had been the only fool on the island snapping pictures of children, but this one had won an award. Civilian life continuing against tragedy, which had become his signature, the bulk of his body of work, at least what he'd been acknowledged for.

He donated the piece and several others to an auction, a fundraiser gala for the Werewolf Defense League, the organization Grayson now worked for. It had been a moment of hubris and pride, quickly extinguished the next time he came home, several months later to surprise his mother for Christmas. Two of the pieces he had donated had been hanging in Grayson's home, an indication to him that they'd either not sold or had been bid on for so little that his brother had felt sorry for him.

"Because it was what was left at the end of the auction, with the other raffle baskets no one wanted?" He asked tonelessly, not really wanting to hear the answer.

His father scowled at him, a familiar look that he himself made often.

"Did I mention that you are also disgustingly self-pitying? Please add that to the list, I apologize for the exclusion. I have this piece, because your brother outbid me and everyone else on the other two. At first, I thought he was just driving up the price. I was a little annoyed, because he knew I wanted them. Then I realized he was bidding to win. He wound up being outbid on the piece from the orphanage, one of the foundation executives got that one, I believe, and he was so mad, I thought he was going to flip his table. I used his distraction to get this one. And I think he was shitty with me about that too."

Lowell felt as if his lungs had been injected with the paralyzing agent, leaving him unable to draw breath, huffing through his nose as much as he was able.

"I didn't raise fools, Lowell. I didn't raise any of you to be less than your worth. Everyone misses you, and everyone wishes you lived a little closer to home, and it would be nice if you picked up the phone for someone other than Grayson once in a while, but you're very, very good at what you do, and we're all so proud of you. You are living completely on your own, on the other side of the world from your family, in, according to Gray, occasionally terrible, dangerous circumstances and situations. The last explorer I can think of off the top of my head was Balthazar Hemming, he was the third younger brother of Jackson the . . . third or fourth, I can't think of which. His brother Grayson is the one who died in the fire. The blue apatite monument in Hostun Park is his, the inscription is on the back side, on a bronze plaque, facing southeast."

Lowell blinked. Hostun Park was the one behind the cafe, where he'd sat with Moriah, that first afternoon.

"So, who knows, Lowell. You may get your monument and plaque after all. On the day you decide you want to come home, there will be a place for you. No one is pushing you out, no one forgets you exist, or all the other nonsense you moan on and on about. Your brothers have lives, just like you do, and you're all completely self-absorbed."

"I can't imagine where we got that from."

His father smiled, spreading his hands in an expansive gesture.

"At least you come by it honestly. That does not mean I'm willing to let you come home to live, because I would sooner burn down the house with myself in it. This is one instance when I don't care what your mother wants. You're a monster, and if this human girl, whoever she is, can put up with your insatiable need to be the center of attention and moping and resulting tantrums, I wouldn't be so quick to let her get away. I do agree that you're not ready to be a father, but I can speak from experience and say, that you never really are. Not until it happens."

He was finally able to breathe again, and he sucked in a huge, shuddering breath. His brothers would be there soon, he realized, as his father hit the intercom on his phone.

"Rhonda, let's get breakfast ordered if we haven't already, please make sure you get yourself something. And if we could cut my son a check from his account, please. One hundred thousand. Thank you."

Lowell gaped. He was a pauper compared to his brothers, and he had accepted that he traded a lucrative career for his freedom, and he prided himself on the fact that he lived completely on his own money. He forgot, sometimes, that he had a trust fund and money in the bank. It was Grayson who had dragged him by the scruff of the neck to their father when he turned 18, demanding that he turn over trust he'd been left by their grandfather.

"You're irresponsible and you're going to piss it away on something stupid."

"I have equipment to buy!" he'd argued vehemently, earning Grayson's eye roll.

"Like I said. Something stupid. Let dad invest part of it. Let the rest collect interest. Then it won't matter if you get a degree in fingerpainting, you'll at least have money to live and retire on."

Lowell knew he was kissed with the golden seal of privilege, for he had grown up in affluent, comfortable surroundings, told he could be whatever he wanted to be, and given the education and opportunity to do so. He had been told his entire life what life was like on the fringes, but he never experienced it. He'd seen it, and documented it, had been personally touched by it, thinking of his own mother and the other young she wolves out there like her, but when he packed his camera gear up, he got to go away from it, leave it behind and go back to a world where he had nothing more pressing to worry over than what movie he would stream and what he would order for dinner. Not living off his trust fund was a point of pride. He had called it his something stupid money ever since, and most of the time, he forgot it existed.

"Grayson does the same thing, you know. Lives on what he makes, keeps everything else in the bank. It's the only way he can justify marble and gold fountains with inlaid pictures of Jackson's face for him to piss on."

"His girlfriend is going to take him for everything," Lowell shared gleefully, gratified by his father's laughter. He was the fourth son, the middle son, lost in the crowd, and he had very rarely ever received one-on-one time with his father, but Lowell thought he understood why the entire town sought him out.

"She is an excellent asset and he needs to hold onto her with both hands. And if he's stupid enough not to, then he deserves to be taken for all he's worth. Why is it that you need to live on the other side of the moon, exactly? I never really understood that."

Lowell sputtered, not expecting to be challenged.

"Because of the airports! And work! I'm not covering potato festivals in Idaho, I'm flying into different parts of Asia and Oceana, Europe."

His father held up his hand.

"I'm not arguing with you, I am just asking the question. Hypothetically speaking. If you're in a relationship with someone here and they are not willing or able to move overseas long-term, are you willing to negotiate and be flexible. That's a simple yes or no, I don't know the specifics of your job, because you don't share them with anyone, Lowell. But it's something to consider. You're the only one who can decide the rest. The only one who can decide what you want to do, where you want to go, who you want to be. I have wanted to leave you in the woods, drop you off at the bus station, put you on a boat and push it out to sea. But if there is one benefit to having a family like ours, it's that you're never alone, no matter what stupid choices you make. You can rest assured that your brothers have made their fair share."

Liam arrived shortly thereafter. Lowell realized, listening to his inane high school chatter, he had been so preoccupied with being someone else's little brother, that he had forgotten he was someone's big brother. *And you've done a piss-poor job of filling the role all these years.* Trapp breezed through the door shortly thereafter, carrying their breakfast order, and Lowell was surprised by the addition of Jackson and Grayson a short while later.

Jackson had been at the house almost every night for the past two weeks, strategizing with Grayson, working on tells and beginning debate preparation. Lowell had initially panicked, wondering if his brother was going to hold his shifting allegiance against him, but he merely clapped him on the back, took his chair, and stole his beer.

"Rhonda, love of my life, please tell me you have my messages."

Grayson sauntered to their father's long-time assistant's desk, and Jackson took advantage of his absence to swap seats. Some things would never, ever change, and Lowell realized how much he was going to miss all this. *You can come back more often. You can visit in between jobs, instead of goofing off at home and doing nothing. You can text more, tell them what you're doing and where you are.*

"We have some excellent news to share this morning," Jack announced, pulling Lowell's attention for the moment. "And yes, mom already knows, so we're not keeping her out of the loop." He inclined a hand towards Liam, who was already beaming. Trapp raised his fists in triumph, already anticipating what their youngest sibling was about to announce.

"I got into my first choice," Liam admitted, ears reddening as Trapp whooped. "I'll be starting pre-med at Mercy in the fall."

"I knew it! I knew you were going to make it. Just think, dad. Two Hemmings from the same generation doing med school at Mercy. One of us might actually wind up as a doctor!"

Lowell joined the laughter around the table, always relieved when he was not the butt of the joke, and Trapp had no problem being self-deprecating.

"Liam, I know you have years to work on this, and we will do our due diligence to ensure it doesn't happen, but don't be the gunner. Don't be the fucking gunner. Write that down. Put it under your pillow. That's the only thing I'm asking of you."

Trapp laughed at Grayson's words, nodding his head in agreement.

"We will kick your ass if you're the gunner. Don't worry, kid. We won't let it happen."

"If we're sharing news, I have some as well." Jackson cleared his throat and glanced around the table with a smile. "Mom doesn't know yet, but we have a cake and a bracelet waiting for her at home when she and Jack come home from swimming today. But since we're all here now . . . we're expecting. Victoria is due at the beginning of summer, so congrats. You're all going to be uncles. Again."

Lowell felt his insides twist and bunch as the noise level in the room rose to what would be considered unacceptable if they were anywhere else. He hoped she would change her mind. He had a flash of himself making the same sort of announcement to his family, flush with the expectation that he too would be raising the next generation of Hemming werewolves, Moriah blushing prettily at his side, her hair burning like the sunset beneath the overhead lights at his parents' house. He hoped she would change her mind about what she was doing, but he hoped she wouldn't change her mind about him.

"Can you *please* have a girl?" Trapp asked. "There is too much testosterone in this family. Is it too late to put in a request?"

"Liam," Grayson began, over Jackson and their father, "let this be a lesson to you. It's one some of us have already taken to heart. Clearly, it's a lesson others have missed. Don't ever take pull-out advice from a man with six kids." Jack nodded grimly at Gray's words, raising his Bloody Mary to clink against Grayson's as the rest of the table laughed raucously once more.

"If we're sharing news, I have some too," Lowell blurted. There was no sense in pretending he didn't know exactly what he needed to do.

He would miss them, but he was going to leave. He had known from the moment he'd listened to the message from his office, he realized. *You already signed up for a broken heart, and now the universe is collecting.* He couldn't tell Moriah what to do, only what he hoped she would do. *It's up to her whether or not that's going to happen.*

"I, um, I got a call from my office. From the publishing group. Travel is starting to open up for nonhumans, and the airlines are all scheduling flights. I'll be back to work in a few weeks."

He wasn't sure if he expected his brothers to cheer the news that he would be leaving again. Several beats of stunned silence met his announcement.

"Wow," Trapp murmured. "I was *not* expecting that."

"Congrats, Lowell," Jackson said seriously, eyebrows drawing together. "I know you've been eager to get back at it. Jack is going to miss you for sure."

"We're all going to miss you, Lowell. It's been really nice having you home for a while."

His throat closed at Trapp's words, and the reminder of his nephew.

"I'm-I'm going to try to come home a bit more often. I don't want the kid to forget me. And I have to be here for the new mayor's inauguration next year, and to meet my new niece, Lowellina."

They all laughed again, and as the conversation turned, his heart felt lighter than it had since he'd arrived in Cambric Creek, which felt like a hundred years ago.

"You know my door is always open for you, kiddo."

Grayson's words, as he collected himself to leave, were low, just for him.

"I know. I won't forget that again," he laughed, leaning into the huge hand his brother placed on the back of his head, wincing when Grayson's fingers pulled through his hair, tugging.

"You need a haircut before you leave. You look like a fucking hobo. It would be nice not to be embarrassed internationally by my kid brother."

"Yeah, I know, Gray. I'm going to miss you too."

"Wait a minute," Trapp called out suddenly, freezing them as they collected their things. "Where's Owen?"

"Oh, shit. We did it again."

"How the fuck do we keep doing this?" Grayson groaned, laughter ringing through the room once more, the hallmark of his big, ridiculous family. Imperfect and in desperate need of therapy, probably, he thought, not for the first time, but his. And his father was right. It didn't matter how much he screwed up, nor how invisible he felt — he would never be completely alone.

* * *

Moriah

He had told her, that very first afternoon, nearly four months ago, with his customary giddy enthusiasm, that his brother's house was like a hotel. She realized the truth of his words the previous evening as he swung the door open, extending his arm for her to step inside first.

She recognized the colorscape immediately. Baltic Sea Blues, a color palette designed by an exclusive pigment house, distributed almost exclusively through elite design firms. He'd obviously hired an interior designer for the home and had probably spent a pretty penny on their services. *You clearly don't rate high enough to be on **this** radar.* The moody color palette was offset with subtle silver and gold accents that warmed the space, lending itself to an atmosphere of quiet, cool luxury, and she understood why Lowell had likened it to a boutique hotel.

He made her dinner, karaage chicken that she ate with her hands, her lips and fingers glistening with grease, sliding against his as she leaned over the marble countertop to kiss him. He told her stories about his brothers and the mischief he caused as a child, and she laughed delightedly, sure he had been an absolute terror.

"I was always trying to do everything my older brothers did. I was probably a huge pain in their asses," he laughed. "No, I *know* I was a huge pain in their asses. They told me frequently," he corrected as she giggled, sucking her fingers.

"But you're all close today?"

He hesitated a moment before answering.

"I'm closest with the two of them," he said slowly after a moment. "The oldest, Jackson—"

"He's the one running for mayor?"

"Yes. Jackson Hemming the eighth. He was nine, almost ten when Owen and I were born. Gray was eight. Trapp was six. And the two of them did everything together, still do. They're the ones I trailed after all the time. I was a pain in their ass, but I guess it stuck because they're the ones who put up with me today."

"What about your twin? Owen?"

His eyes didn't leave the wok as he turned up the heat, and she squealed at the flash of fire moving up the sides of it as he expertly flipped the vegetables within.

"We don't have a single thing in common. I need people and crowds and attention; he's an introvert that used to stay in from recess to read in the library when we were kids. And not much has changed since then. I love him, we text all the time, but when we're together, we have nothing to talk about." He looked up, the sparkling smile she'd chosen more than four months ago replacing the pensive wistfulness that had lived on his face in the moment before. "It's fine, though. We're all different."

She told him about summers spent with her cousins in the seaside town where they lived year-round, riding her bike to the boardwalk and the small amusement park, pretending she, too, was a townie, attempting to act tougher than she was amidst all the tourists. She picked up the julienned peppers he'd sautéed, crunching into them, ignoring both the fork and chopsticks on the countertop. He told her about shoots in Paris, and Nepal, in the middle of the desert and in the heart of the jungle, and she told him about her meticulously curated travel boards, color palettes and accessories, and photographs of the scenery of places she had never been but always wanted to see.

"We should. Go someplace, I mean. We could be on the redeye as soon as the borders reopen. I can show you everything there is to see in Tokyo, and then we'll go to Amsterdam. We'll ride bikes, get completely shitfaced on the Leidseplein, and watch the sunrise over the canals. We can visit the oni I know in Hokkaido, and the wolfpack I stayed with in the dolomites. There's no reason you can't see everything you want to see, plus all the places you're not even thinking of."

"I don't see borders reopening for humans anytime soon."

At that, he laughed.

"Ah, but you see, I'm an over-privileged punk. You wouldn't be just a human; you'd be the human traveling with Jack Hemming's son."

She thought she would never get tired of the way he smelled, inhaling against his neck once the dishes were cleared away. Her heart had buzzed around her chest like a hummingbird, desperately wanting to follow the promise of his words and follow him into an irresponsible, uncertain future.

"I'm going to get greasy fingerprints all over your brother's expensive house, and he's gonna kick your ass," she giggled as he scooped her up, carrying her down several dark hallways until they reached a large bedroom with an attached en suite.

"Then we'd better clean you up."

She'd never been much of a fan of shower sex, always finding it too hard to maneuver, too nervous about falling, her ex too impatient to help her find a position she could both sustain and take him comfortably. She needn't have worried. Lowell was more intent on covering her in a thick, rich lather, exclaiming gleefully when she was coated in white like a snowman.

He toweled her curls until they were free of excess water before laying her out in the center of the giant bed, the lattice panes of the windows behind them giving the room an exotic, cathedral-like feel, ornate and beautiful, and as his mouth moved down her body, she understood why he'd chosen this room. They were due back at the clinic in two days, and she'd not be keeping the appointment. She didn't want to tell him now, though; she wanted to have an honest conversation when they were both vertical.

She felt as though she were buzzing. A low-frequency vibration tickled beneath her skin, and as his mouth traveled down her neck and over her clavicle, the hum followed the trail of his lips. She bit her lip, stifling her moan when his teeth nipped at her nipple, his lips sucking the bud into his mouth a moment later. The hand he pressed against her front drifted down her stomach, fingers tickling over her mound but going no further. She could not hold back a breathy sigh when his mouth released her swollen nipple; the tip hardened as his tongue stroked it.

"We're alone," he reminded her. "You can be as loud as you want. Frankly, if the neighbors aren't calling to complain, I'm going to be offended." She laughed, cutting off on a gasp when one of his long fingers pressed between her legs, stroking in the slickness it found there.

Moriah sighed again as he gently pushed her to lay back against the pillows, another finger joining the first.

"I want to hear you sing," he whispered against her lips before kissing his way down her throat again, his fingers rubbing slow, sloppy circles against her clit.

He worked his tongue against her as if he'd been doing it for years, not just a handful of months, unwinding her like a clock. She ought to have been used to the sensation of falling by now, she thought. Coming against his mouth like dropping off the edge of a building — a breathless rush as she plummeted, liquefying on her landing as she shook against him.

It was the difference of a partner who paid attention to her, her reactions and her pleasure, she thought, and not just the finish line.

Despina was right, and she knew it in her heart, even if she'd not had the courage to say it aloud quite yet. She'd wanted a baby desperately but had never been able to picture anything more than the idea. She, who was able to imagine *everything* — the Azul blue and bright pea-cock green of the tiles in a hallowed eastern temple, the crimson scrape of the sunset sinking between mountains, and the soft golden curl of the dawn over hillsides of olive trees. She had never visited any of those places, but she could see it all clearly in her head, created her designs around them . . . but she'd never been able to picture the child she so desperately wanted. *A mitigation of the sorrow.* It had been a blessing, perhaps, that things had ended as they had.

He had moved her to her knees, each thrust within her dragging over her G-spot and making her gasp, the slap of skin-on-skin overtaking the sound of her heartbeat.

She could picture her hypothetical child now, though. A little boy who would be a clone of his daddy, with a sharp jaw and a sparkling smile, or a bright-eyed little girl, with a spray of freckles over a nose like hers, with her father's dark hair and a bevy of uncles to spoil her. They would leave her each month, once they were old enough, disap-pearing with their father to run against the wind, connected to a world of non-humans despite having her as a mother, and she would learn *everything* about that world. How to ease their sore muscles and aching bones and navigate the wolf that lived beneath their skin. She could see it clearly for the first time . . . but not yet. Not now, not for several years, perhaps. For now, though, he was right — he was right there, happy to be babied if she wanted a baby that badly.

He had shifted her again, upright, splayed over his hips, impaled on his cock, and she could tell from how his thighs tensed and shook beneath her that he was close. Every upward thrust brought her down firmly against his knot, kissing the mouth of her sex a bit more insistently with each roll of her hips. She was gasping, desperately trying to maintain her composure and keep him going for as long as possible, even though she wanted to do nothing more than sink down upon him and feel the tight, white burn of his knot stretching her wide. The heavy-lidded, blissed-out expression on his face told her he was ready for the same.

Not yet. The longer she kept him going, the harder he came. She had already learned that lesson and intended to put her newfound knowledge into practice. She wanted him to fill her to the brim, make her belly bulge with the pressure of his release, seal her with his knot and keep every creamy drop stoppered into place. She'd never had a fluid kink before, the thought of a man coming in her face or getting it in her hair making her sick, but now all she wanted was to drip with him. His fingers tightened on her hip, and she dug her nails into his neck, determined to keep him going for a bit longer.

"Don't stop," she breathed against his lips, the thumb at her throat trailing until it gently pressed into her pulse point. "Not yet, Lowell, please. Just a little bit more. I want you to make me come again." In response, he bucked up into her, harder and deeper than before, and

Moriah moaned as he hit a spot within her that made the world go white and sparks flare at the corners of her vision.

"Just like that. Good boy. I love the way you fuck me." He shivered against her, and she gripped him tighter in response. "That's what you are," she keened against his jaw, pressing herself against him. "My good boy, my big wolf. You always make me feel so good."

The hand that had been at her throat dropped to where they were joined, rolling against her clit, forcing her to catch up with him, and she wheezed at the sensation, bucking her hips against him. Every time she came down on his knot, he rolled over her clit, making her jolt, her lungs seize, and too soon, she begged him to finish her off.

"Come inside me, baby. Fill me up."

She hadn't paid attention to how close the neighbors actually were to his brother's giant, luxury hotel of a house, but if their windows were open, they would surely hear the way she moaned when he pulled her down completely, stretching her wide, the pressure of his knot and the eruption of his cock within her enough to push her over the edge. He groaned as she clenched around him, the roll of his fingers over her clit making her shake as if she were being electrocuted. He choked out another grunt when her hand dropped, squeezing his balls as he emptied in one throbbing pulse after the next.

"I have an early meeting, so I'm going to need to slip out of here at the crack of dawn," she murmured as she laid across his chest after the evidence of their activities was cleaned up in the shower. "I'll try not to wake you up."

Lowell had rolled his eyes, tucking her securely under his arm.

"Or you can wake me up so I can kiss you goodbye. That would work too."

But the next morning, he'd looked so soft and peaceful, his baby face entirely at rest, slack in sleep, she'd not had the heart to do so. A gentle kiss to the tip of his nose and at the corner of his wide mouth, slipping out of bed silently, finding her clothes on the floor.

She heard a man's deep voice coming from the kitchen when she was still in the hallway, and she paused, wondering if she ought to attempt to find her way to the front door instead. *There's probably an alarm set, and you'll wake up the whole neighborhood when the police arrive. Don't be a baby. Besides, your shoes are at the side door kitchen.*

"Yeah, I got in last night; it was a late flight. I know. I'm meeting Jackson this morning, and then we're having breakfast with my dad and the boys, but I can pick you up after, if you want. Do you want to drive up to the lake this afternoon? Well, make up your mind. We should be done by nine or ten . . . okay, faster conversations. It's a yes or no. I don't need to hear the schedule of every person in the building." He laughed as she edged into the room, a rough scrape of a sound. "Mhm, whatever. Love you too."

He was like a mountain. Tall, much taller than Lowell, with wide-set shoulders and a broad back that rippled with muscle. It was the man from the coffee shop, as she had suspected, his vacation tan still holding strong, glowing against the bright white of his open dress shirt. *The lawyer. Spending money is his love language.* He was dropping a scoop of protein powder into a handheld blender as she entered the room, and if he was surprised to see her, he didn't let on.

Maybe he heard you last night. Or maybe he got in after you were both asleep. Or perhaps he simply has an excellent poker face.

"Good morning."

His voice was mild, and he never looked up from what he was doing once his phone call had ended, allowing her to look him over quickly. Very handsome, but very hard, just as she had thought that day at the Black Sheep Beanery. *But he's the one Lowell likes best. Him and the one with the weird name.*

"Good morning. I-I'm so sorry; I hope my car wasn't in your way. You have a stunning home. Is there a code I need, or . . ."

He glanced up then, meeting her eye with a cool smile. He had a dimple in his cheek, the only softness in the chiseled planes of his face. *Very* handsome, but she much preferred the sparkling smile and baby face of the wolf asleep down the hall.

"Not at all, plenty of room. I've already been out, so there's no code necessary. If you're coming back tonight, park on the left behind my truck. The birds love sitting in the tree on the right side. Your windshield probably paid the price."

Her cheeks flushed as she moved past him, slipping her feet into her flats at the door.

"Um, nice meeting you? Have a good day," she called out before opening the door, letting herself out of the house. *He's the one who will buy your daughter one of those over-the-top Victorian doll houses.*

The teifling and her wife were thrilled with everything Moriah had chosen for their beach house, the meeting being a green light on everything she proposed. She felt clear-headed for the first time in she couldn't remember how long, with a bounce in her step and an unconscious smile on her face. Her mind was made up, and she would tell him that day. They would not be going to the clinic that week, but she would like to see him again that night, the next night, and the next. It was going to take at least a month for the drugs to completely work out of her system, and she would still need him for the heat that was only just beginning to prickle beneath her skin, and once they were . . . she still wanted him in her bed, in her breakfast nook, in her life.

Happiness begets happiness. Joy brings more joy. She only had to let joy find her, she remembered, her stomach flip-flopping in remembrance of those cards. She had picked joy out of a catalog, as easy as buying a pair of shoes. She was finally thinking clearly, seeing clearly, and nothing, she thought with a smile, could ruin this day.

When her doorbell rang a few hours later, she was surprised to find Lowell on the other side. Surprised and happy, for there was no time like the present to set the record straight.

* * *

Lowell

His resolve lasted all the way to her house. It was comical now, how close she had been all this time. She lived just a few blocks away from Owen and his girlfriend, Creek Rock Estates, one of the newer developments. *We could have been together all this time.* It was too late for regrets, Lowell reminded himself. Too late to think about what may have been, only what lay ahead.

The sparkle in her eye and the wideness of her smile nearly killed him when she answered the door, squealing in excitement to see him.

"Oh my goodness, a gentleman caller in the middle of the afternoon, how thrilling! To what do I owe this very welcome visit?"

He was a child. He was three five-year-olds in a trench coat, immature and still prone to tantrums, and the tears he had been biting back in his father's office now rose to the surface in a mortifying rush of heat.

"I'm leaving." Her smile slid sideways off her face, the dawning realization of what his words meant coming a beat later, and the tears that flooded her eyes pushed his to the surface at last. "They're opening borders up again for nonhumans. I need to process the paperwork and get my new visa, but I can be back to work by next month. I'm probably going to leave in the next two weeks."

Lowell was uncertain of how he managed to get out so much without his voice breaking, but the sight of her tears ripped his heart in two. She nodded, her lips pressed firmly together, nodding with a tight smile.

"I understand. It's okay. Thank you for telling me." Her voice came out as a sob, cracking as she finished.

"It's *not* okay. Fucking stars, Moriah, it's not okay! But I have to get back to my life, I can't just stay here and be a third wheel forever."

"You've been my second wheel," she choked out. "I know that doesn't matter, and I know you have to get back to your career. I know it's stupid because we've only known each other for a few months, but-but for what it's worth, you haven't been the third wheel for me. You've been it."

Lowell dragged a hand across his face, wiping away the tears blurring his vision. *You can't make her decision for her, you can only give her an option.*

"I know, it *is* stupid. We've known each other for like five minutes, and it's been a heightened situation and probably really unhealthy, and I am a fucking baby and according to my family I'm, like, really terrible and selfish, but most of them are too, so I don't know if I can really believe them." She choked out a laugh, her tears not subsiding. "But I don't like the person I am here. I can't get out from under my name here. I'm always going to be one of my older brothers' little brother here, that's all people see me as. I have a life and I have a career, and I'm really, really good at what I do. And I need to get back to it."

Lowell could tell that every word he forced out was a knife thrust into her, and she jolted with each one as he paused to rake a hand over his face

"I'm getting on that plane in a week or two, Moriah. And it's too soon and a stupid idea, but I want you to be on it with me."

Her mouth dropped open, but she said nothing.

"I don't want you to stay here and have a baby with some fucking double-dicked asshole, I don't want you picking some random werewolf out of a catalog. I want you to come with *me*. I'm selfish and self-absorbed, and I'm not willing to share you. I want to travel with you, I want to show you the world. And who knows what will happen? Maybe we'll come back in a few years and have kids. Maybe we'll have kids on the road like wandering minstrels. Or maybe you'll spend a week with me and decide I'm just as fucking terrible as my family claims and you'll come running back here, and you can start this all over again with someone new. But I know what I want. And I want you. But I want my career too, and I can't give one up for the other. And I know that's selfish, I know I'm asking you to give up what you want. I know you want a baby . . . but I want *you*. I want you to come with me."

"I don't want a baby," she whispered, tears still coursing over her cheeks. "I *do*, I mean, I definitely do . . . but I don't want one right now. At least, not until we have a chance to really decide that together. I meant to tell you, I've been *wanting* to tell you . . ."

It was his turn to gape.

"What the fuck are you talking about? What have we been doing? What is going on?!"

"Happiness and joy," she croaked, her eyes shining, still with tears, but something else as well. "That's what's going on. I had to let them find me. You. It's you, you're the stupid fucking cup, aren't you?"

Lowell floundered.

"I-I don't know what that means. Sure, yeah, I'm a cup. If that's what I need to be to make you come with me, I can be whatever fucking cup you need."

Her face crumpled, and launched herself into his arms with a speed he'd not been anticipating, nearly knocking him to his feet.

"Yes. I want to see Paris and Vienna and Marrakech and everything. This is so stupid. Like, *so* stupid. But I want to be stupid with you. Yes. Let's do it."

It was stupid and impulsive and probably a mistake.

But as he caught her lips with his own, Lowell couldn't remember a time in his life, save for the moment he'd decided he was going to leave home in the first place, that he'd ever been more sure of anything in his existence.

"I'm going to be the *best* cup. A plaque worthy cup. Just you wait and see."

* * *

A Most Auspicious Beginning

The Mr. Toasty Stand was open. It was the best sign he could have hoped for.

"The forecast in Denver is clouds and a low chance of precipitation. The local time is 11:14 a.m."

"Wow, it is *always* fucking raining in Denver."

"Hmm?" she asked, pulling her attention away from her tablet. The Tokyo moodboard was full of punchy colors, grounded in grey and black, and he heartily approved.

It had taken some maneuvering. His father had made a few calls, tried to pull a few strings. In the end, though, it was Gray who had the right contact to make it happen. A friend from his frat days, who now worked in the State Department.

"She might not be able to make it over every border. You have to have common sense. Some places aren't going to give a shit what her visa says. She might need to hang tight in Tokyo."

"Yes, of course. We'll be careful. And thank you."

When his brother pulled him into a hug at the curb, Lowell felt his heart trip. He wasn't going to stay away so long this time. He wasn't going to let himself feel excluded and forgotten. He would make his presence known in every conversation, every time they tried to make plans, every time they did anything. After all, he was very good at being more *more*.

He had already said his goodbyes to the rest of the family, and Grayson had driven him back to the airport, as he had done countless times before.

"Be careful out there, kiddo. Call me when you get in. Don't lose your human."

"I will. And I won't. I'll call you once we get into town, we're staying with a friend until my apartment is ready. Don't let your dragonlady pop your balls."

Now they were waiting, counting down the minutes before it was time to board.

"I'm pretty sure I'm in love with you, you know."

Moriah squinted.

"What does that have to do with Denver?" She resumed stroking her fingers through his hair, her attention returning to her work. "I'm pretty sure I love you too, but I sure as fuck don't want to go to Denver, so get that right out of your pretty little head."

Lowell grinned, shoving the rest of his Mr. Toasty churro into his mouth, settling his back against her. Nikkia was moving in with

Daiyuu, and Lowell would be taking up her apartment, a serendipitous arrangement. Moriah had put her house on the rental market, and it had been snapped almost immediately by a dragonborn who would be relocating to Cambric Creek for a new job. He had no idea what his work situation would look like once he'd arrived, but for the first time in months, he didn't feel stressed over it. The whole world seemed possible.

"What do you want to see first?"

Moriah looked down as his upside-down face, craning back to interrupt her again. She leaned down, kissing the tip of his nose.

"I want to see everything."

* * *

Lowell & Moriah
& the rest of the Hemming Wolfpack will return

Welcome to Azathé – Coming 2023

She'd discovered Azathé completely by accident, but the odd little tea room had quickly become her favorite place to be: it was quiet and quirky, full of interesting books and a vast tea selection, and best of all, there had never been a single moment when she felt as though she didn't belong. Towers of precariously stacked books dotted the space, in between small tables that were hardly large enough for two people to squeeze around.

The interior was a curious mix of English garden and a witch's fever dream, with little needle-point chairs and chintz poufs nestled in amongst the grimoires and artful piles of animal skulls. Her social anxiety seemed to melt away in the shop's dark corners, and she never worried about being the odd goth out.

The table top was, she saw at once, a spirit board. Some of the tables featured scrolls where she would write in what teas she were contemplating, a recommendation bleeding up from the scroll a moment later, as if written by an invisible hand; while still others held decks of elaborately drawn tarot cards, the order determined by a simple three card spread.

Harper took her time settling in at the table before taking up the planchette. The shelf above she held a line of books, a small bowl of incense, a glowing red candle, and what appeared to be a monkey's paw. There was always something new to discover that she'd not previously noticed, regardless of how much time she spent prowling around the hidden nooks of the shop.

The planchette began moving the instant she laid light fingertips to the smooth edge. H...O...W...D...I...D...Y...O

"I think I did well," she cut in, saving them the trouble. "I packed each answer with every single fact I could remember, so there's not much I'll be marked off on."

They had a particular interest in how she performed in her Uni classes, as though unfavorable marks would reflect poorly on the tea house. Her heart tripped when the dark corner on the other side of the alcove seemed to shift and solidify briefly, giving her hope that this might be the moment she'd been waiting for, before the corner was just a corner once more, but the moment passed.

"That's good."

Her fingers curled around the edge of her chair as she fought the instinct to arch like a cat, tingles moving down her spine at the unexpected voice from the corner. The voice — their voice — was a sinuous whisper, like a silky slide of black satin, tickling up the back of her neck, as dense and dark as the shadows where it resided. She couldn't be disappointed that they hadn't taken shape before, not when they gifted her with their voice.

"What are you reading today?"

Azathé was the only tea shop she'd ever been in where "what are you reading today" was a preferred method of deciding one's tea order. She normally drank green teas and fruity blends when left to her own devices, but her shadowy host had deemed that personal preference was an inferior way to pair literature and tea. The cover of the book she pulled from her bag depicted a stormy sky and roiling sea, an eldritch mass of tentacles and eyes looming in the surf and a little girl, standing at the water's edge.

The shadows purred thoughtfully in contemplation.

"Which part?"

"The girl just came back to the house at the shore as an adult."

"Hmmm...wistful nostalgia. The bittersweet certainty that things can never be as they once were...I know just the tea."

She felt the precise moment when they left her table, the little nook seeming somewhat brighter, even as the air took on a flat quality, the absence of its crackling energy being nearly tangible. The toneless groan of the shop's bell sounded just then, a couple stepping through the doorway. She watched the little cat leap from its cushion, hurriedly greeting the newcomers before attempting to shepherd them down the aisle to one of the tables with the scrolls.

"Look, it wants us to follow it, how cute!"

She hid her laughter in her napkin when the cat yowled in frustration, glaring at the befuddled couple as they continued to loiter about the entrance, before turning to where she sat with an exasperated shake of its whiskers.

She'd be forced to share today, Harper conceded with a sigh, once the couple finally got the idea that they were, in fact, meant to follow the impatient cat. She could see them puzzling over the scroll at the small table, and knew that her shadowy host would have their hands full placating the newcomers. She tried not to let her disappointment show when the little nook where she sat remained devoid of whispers, the corner remaining a corner when a little gong sounded, alerting her that her tea was up.

Vanilla pear was not what she was expecting. For starters, she didn't especially like white teas, and she had been preparing herself for something darker, heavier in flavor, and not a delicate fruit. *Maybe they're losing their touch...*

She should have known not to doubt the shadows.

The first sip tasted oddly old-fashioned, making her nostalgic for drawing rooms and doily-covered furniture and creaking old floors, a childhood she'd never even known. The second sip had a tinge of melancholy, and on the third, she reopened her book.

As the girl in the pages moved through the rooms of the home she'd known as a child, tears pricked the back of her eyes. The girl had lived through something fantastical and traumatic, something that had shaped the woman she became, yet the house was just a house, despite all of the things that had happened there in the preceding chapters, the rooms just empty wooden boxes, the time spent playing there lost to the wind, and with each sip of the tea, she felt she heart grow heavier.

"What do you think?"

She jumped when the voice sounded from the shadows just behind her head, curling around her ear like a whorl of smoke. She didn't like to admit that the reason she came to the tea house so often was the reliability of *feeling*.

She sometimes felt like an empty vessel, the cavernous hole in her chest a great, echoing void, but here . . . here it was filled. Filled with the emotions the shadowy host imbued in their tea selections, filled with the pairings it suggested, stories and emotions that filled her completely and made her feel whole, for the brief time she spent at one of the little tables. Filled, she thought, with the shadows themselves.

As usual, ther had exceeded her expectations.

"Perfect," she admitted, quickly wiping away any evidence of tears with a blush. "I would never have tried that one on my own."

Their pleased hum was like a burst of static against her skin, making her stomach tighten as she shivered again. It felt silly to admit, but she had a mad crush on the unseen proprietor of her favorite tea house, a fact that seemed even more preposterous when she was forced to admit she didn't even know what they were.

PRE-ORDER NOW https://amzn.to/3KpDexi

ABOUT THE AUTHOR

C.M. Nascosta is a USA TODAY bestselling author of high heat small town monster romance and professional procrastinator from Cleveland, Ohio. As a child, she thought that living on Lake Erie meant one was eerie by nature, and her corresponding love of all things strange and unusual started young. She's always preferred beasts to boys, the macabre to the milquetoast, the unknown darkness in the shadows to the Chad next door. She lives in a crumbling old Victorian with a scaredy-cat dachshund, where she writes nontraditional romances featuring beastly boys with equal parts heart and heat, and is waiting for the Hallmark Channel to get with the program and start a paranormal lovers series.

Do you love exclusive short stories and character art? Early release ebooks and mailers of stickers, art prints, and more? Want access to an exclusive reader group? Join the Monster Bait community on Patreon!

https://www.patreon.com/Monster_Bait

Printed in Great Britain
by Amazon

40558005R00189